Schlock!

Editor: Gav

This month's cover image is [Strike Suit Zero](#) by [Born Ready Games](#), licensed under http://creativecommons.org/licenses/by/3.0/. *Graphic design © by [Gavin Chappell](#), logo design © by C Priest Brumley.*

EDITORIAL..3
DARK LEGACIES: HEART OF STEEL #1 by Chris McAuley and Claudia Christian................5
PUBLISHING NEWS by Mickey Mikkelson...............17
THE WHISPERING CAMPAIGN by EW Farnsworth..21
ILLEGAL ALIEN by DJ Tyrer...................................34
THE SCOURING OF SILVER COAST Part Two by Jesse Zimmerman....................................43
THE DRAGONS' PLAYBOOK by Carlton Herzog.......56
KASSI AND THE DESERTED ISLAND by Ste Whitehouse...72
THE BARGIS by Shreyas Adhikari..........................99
CHORDS by Lamont Turner..................................138
THE LUCK OF IT by Joseph Farley.......................141
RARE by Toban Barnes...148
THE DEVIL'S DOWNFALL by Andrew Bell.............159
CREMATE YOUR DEAD by Carl Bluesy................180
EMPIRE OF THE MOON AND STARS by Simon Bleaken..191
THE TESTIMONY OF JESTER THOTH by Scott J Couturier...208
OCCUPATION by Michael W Clark Ph.D.................226
WHAT MARNIE TOOK WITH HER by William Couper...252
DIABOLUS ET PROPHETIIS by David Philips.........273
CAITLYN'S KITTY by Stephen Faulkner.................288
THE BELIEVERS by Christopher T Dabrowski.......315

SCHLOCK! WEBZINE

Welcome to Schlock! The webzine for science fiction, fantasy, and horror.

*Vol. 16, Issue 24
January 2022*

Schlock! is a monthly webzine dedicated to short stories, flash fiction, serialised novels, and novellas, within the genres of science fiction, fantasy, and horror. We publish new and old works of pulp sword and sorcery, urban fantasy, dark fantasy, and gothic horror. If you want to read quality works of new pulp fantasy, science fiction or horror, Schlock! Is the webzine for you!

*For details of previous editions, please go to
www.schlock.co.uk*

*Schlock! Webzine is always willing to consider new science fiction, fantasy and horror short stories, serials, graphic novels and comic strips, reviews and art. Submit fiction, articles, art, or links to your own site to
editor@schlock.co.uk*

*We no longer review published and self-published novels directly, although we are willing to accept reviews from other writers. Any other enquiries also to
editor@schlock.co.uk*

The stories, articles and illustrations contained in this webzine are copyright © to the respective authors and illustrators, unless in the public domain.

Schlock! Webzine and its editor accept no liability for views expressed or statements made by contributors to the magazine.

ISBN: 9798791314253

EDITORIAL

In this New Year's edition, Commander Ivanova takes the helm. In the first of six episodes from their new Dark Legacies universe, Chris 'StokerVerse' McAuley and Claudia Christian of *Babylon 5* fame, introduce us to mech combat and social unrest on the planet Mars. We follow with more news from the publishing world. A whispering campaign is under way on Picklock Lane, while the Bassetshire police force have their hands full coping with illegal aliens. Flora and Fauna investigate the strange and inexplicable troubles that have beset their hometown while they were away adventuring with the Challenger. Dragons cause trouble in Carlton Herzog's new story, while Kassi finds herself washed up on the shores of a deserted island.

We meet monsters and mayhem in medieval India. A guitarist's pact with the supernatural leads to unfortunate and gory consequences. Panglot ventures outside to learn that it is a very different place from what he expects. Harvey undergoes the process of memory transfer. Detective Corbin employs a demon in the pursuit of his investigations. Lem gradually comes to terms with his new situation. Three survivors of the apocalypse wage war against the leeches. Jester Thoth tells a tale of long ago. The Pe-li-tooians rise up against the human invaders. Marnie takes a keepsake from her dead parents. A dedicated killer tenders his resignation. Caitlyn struggles to escape her destiny. And the believers worship their god in ignorance of their own identity.

—*Gavin Chappell*

DARK LEGACIES: HEART OF STEEL #1

by Chris McAuley and Claudia Christian

Blood covered Williams' cockpit readouts, his mech's chassis was rocking from the metal fists pounding on it. His opponent had blindsided him and was now unleashing an unrelenting attack. Wiping the blood from his mouth, Williams examined his options. Making a decision, he moved his arms upward, his muscles feeling the strain of the hydraulic limbs. Pistons hissed and gears whined as Osgood continued to batter the midsection of Williams' mech. Beads of sweat broke on Williams' brow but he refused to allow himself to acknowledge the fatigue of the long battle. He was a seasoned Mech-Brawler and his determination to win took over. As a two-time circuit champ on the off-world colony arenas, he refused to give in to the newcomer. He managed to successfully block Osgood's incoming attacks with his left arm and slam his mech's right fist into the head of his opponent's mech.

Williams' vox-box sputtered into life and he heard the voice of the other brawler taunting him. The vox unit emitted a low hum which kept pace with Osgood's words. It hurt Williams' head but it was the cocky nature of the young competitor which truly pissed him off.

"Hey, old man, you starting to feel the heat in there?"

Who the hell did this youngblood think he was? Sure, he was riding a shinier mech, bought for by a recent sponsorship from a cybersecurity corporation. As he gritted his teeth, Williams was determined that he would soon teach him that the latest tech was no match for experience.

Engaging the last of his energy cells, Williams gambled on finishing this match with a powerful offensive. The booster units glowed blue against the older mech's yellow paint as Williams slammed into Osgood. Williams' mech design was heavier, a relic from the days when the first Mech-Brawler units were converted power loaders. A wolfish smile passed Williams' lips as he used the weight to his advantage. He mercilessly punched and kicked the plating of the younger man's unit. Even with the in-built noise dampeners housed in the cockpit, Williams could hear the crash of each impact.

Osgood attempted to defend himself but it was no good, the vicious assault of the older unit had damaged the servos in his left arm. He was wide open to the aggressive ministrations of his enraged opponent. With his proximity to the rival mech, Williams could see inside his opponent's cockpit. Osgood's face was bathed in a red glow, a sure sign that his readout was registering serious damage. A lucky hit from Williams' right arm had damaged Osgood's internal coolant systems. It would be moments before the newer mech unit would shut down and Osgood would be ejected due to overheating.

With no other choice, Osgood swallowed hard and reactivated his vox-unit.

"Hey, Williams! I give, you win, man. What does that make it? Three to nothing?"

Williams smiled and stopped his attack; he took a few steps backwards and responded.

"You are getting better, Osgood, but you're still too cock-sure. Confidence can be advantageous in a brawl but beware arrogance. If this hadn't been a training session, you would have been splattered like jam by my mech's fists."

Unable to filter the thermal pressure, Osgood's mech unit kneeled and ejected its pilot. Osgood performed an exaggerated gesture of disappointment towards Williams' mech then moved towards the changing rooms. Williams laughed, the tension in his body and mind eased after the victory. The kid had done well, he had been worried that he would have lost the bout. If he could teach Osgood to temper the enthusiasm and become more aware of the tactical situation, the kid could go far. Maybe even as far as becoming a two-time colony champion.

Piloting his mech to the engineering bay for repairs, Williams steeled himself for another conflict to come. Eddie, the tech on duty, would be ready to berate him for taking the training too far. Analysing his read outs, Williams felt a degree of guilt. There was probably a whole night's work ahead for the beleaguered tech and that was just to replace the damaged plating. The aging champion knew that it was important for his team to get used to the pressure of combat before a big match. On Sunday they were facing off against the Detroit Maulers, who had a vicious reputation.

Eddie was already waiting for Williams as he powered off the mech and exited the frame. Williams braced himself for the anticipated barrage of abuse from the sandy haired tech. It didn't come, instead they shot the shit about how far the sport had come. Reminiscing about the matches they had both been involved in and how the newer mechs no longer resembled anything space port dockers would use.

Starting as a way for dockers to cool off some steam after a busy series of shifts, Mech-Brawling had evolved to become the most popular sport on Mars. The governor had realized its potential to take citizens' minds off recent political events and the increase in reported mutations in infants. The pay for the mech pilots was pretty good as well and could increase with corporate sponsorship.

As the week progressed, Williams pushed his team harder every day. When Sunday came, he wanted them suitably aggressive and aware of their opponents' weaknesses. As captain of the team, he had to ensure that each of them, from greenhorn to veteran, was ready to face anything Detroit could throw at them. When match day came, Williams looked over his team as he gave the customary pep-talk. Passing his eyes over the determined faces, he was certain that the Mars Crusaders would be up to the challenge.

The arena was packed with Mars citizens who wanted some violent escapism. Weighed down by recent news reports concerning increased civil unrest and supply shortages, the atmosphere in the space domes was grim. The ruling government of the Sol system, Con-Fed, had sanctioned additional Mech-Brawl tournaments. They even made stars from some of the pilots by featuring them in propaganda videos to curb rising tensions. It had been an idea of a Con-Fed think tank to introduce new game modes this year. Capture the Flag had proved to be the most popular of these, each team having to defend their own flags and make it back to base with the flag of their opponent. The announcement of the chosen game mode hadn't shocked Williams, he had anticipated it and trained his team mates accordingly.

The Detroit Maulers got off to a great start, they proved themselves to be every bit as vicious as their reputation had suggested. The Maulers' focused aggression surprised the Mars team and they had lost one of their five flags by the end of the first quarter of the match. Detroit had long been known for its manufacturing capability and this had extended to the mech units. Featuring a streamlined design which gave them an edge with regards to speed and manoeuvrability, they darted through the Mars team's defence with ease.

Williams' team's mechs had resilience on their side, they could take more of a beating. Focusing the Mars team on their offensive capabilities proved to be an effective counter to The Maulers' speed. By the half time buzzer, both teams were even.

"Frack you!" Osgood spat as his head rebounded off the inside of his suit. The strength of the impact made him see double and caused his ears to ring for a moment. As his mech slammed to the ground he could hear Williams scream at him through the vox-box unit.

"Get up, get up—get up!"

"I am!" Osgood grunted with exertion as he pushed himself up with both hands. Each arm was enclosed in a framework of metal plates with servo-mechanisms that added many pounds of pressure to his normal physical strength. He flipped on one leg and pushed his unit into a bounding leap after his attacker.

>*Suit warning! Back-Plate—5%...*

Osgood attempted to flank his opponent as his suit's cockpit flashed the unwelcome incessant warning. He intended to smash into the side of the rival mech, taking the pilot by surprise. He came close to the enemy when without warning an excited voice broke through on his voice unit.

"We have their Flag!"

It was Adams, a junior member of the team. His lack of experience was balanced by his tenacity; in the last few games he had surprised Osgood by his initiative and grit.

"Engage boosters, Adams, get back to base as quickly as possible, we will cover your ass," Williams' authoritative voice rang through each of the squads' vox units.

If they could obtain the advantage now, it would give them the psychological edge that they needed. Osgood watched as Adams raced past him, travelling in the opposite direction towards base. His peripheral vision caught sight of a streak of blue as Adams engaged his booster rockets.

It was then that everything changed.

Williams felt it first, a deep rumbling under his feet. He had been preparing to tackle one of the Maulers who had been chasing Adams. Along with the trembling ground, Williams could hear the sound of several explosions booming through his audio circuitry. Flashes of light and clouds of fire erupted across the steel pit of the stadium. Spectators flew across the arena like ragdolls as the explosive charges ignited. Human bodies shattering onto the concrete surface of the combat zone and internal fluids spread across the steel walls.

Before the ground collapsed beneath him, Williams could have sworn that a severed head bounced across his vidscreen. A middle-aged woman with platinum blonde hair wearing a shocked expression on her face. Williams hoped that her death had been quick. With that thought, the concrete cracked under his mech and he fell into the darkness below.

14 Days Later

Everything ached, from his head to his ass. Williams issued a low groan of agony which brought a nearby medic to his bed.

"Can you open your eyes, Mr. Williams? I know that you feel like hell but it's important that we assess any ocular damage now."

The matter-of-fact tone of the physician appealed to the pragmatist in Williams and he slowly opened his eyes. The overhead florescent lighting caused searing pain to erupt in his head. Encouraged by the medic, he took several slow blinks and his vision began to clear. The attending doctor looked younger than Osgood, Williams hoped that was a sign of eminence in his field.

"Where am I?"

Setting his chart to the side, the doctor began to recount the events after the explosions. As he did so, Williams couldn't help but feel a sense of dread.

"The stadium was attacked by the 'Free Mars' movement. It seems that they take umbrage at the 'bread and circus' policies of our current administration. Several high-powered explosions were placed around the arena and thousands of spectators were killed. After a few hours of sifting through the rubble, you were found, your mech suit crushed under the weight of heavy debris. Medical teams extracted you and we have been treating your injuries as best as we can. I must warn you that they are severe, however."

Williams tried to process this information as best he could. There was another important question and when he gave voice to it the medic looked downwards and adjusted his glasses awkwardly.

"I'm afraid you are the only surviving member of your team, Mr. Williams. A few of the Detroit brawlers were found. They were in considerably better condition than you. I feel I must impress upon you how lucky you are to be alive."

The doctor continued to explain the extent of Williams' injuries. He wasn't listening, however, the faces of his dead team members flashed across his mind. He felt hollow and unable to process the loss and guilt which overwhelmed him. His attention returned to the physician as the condition of his legs was being discussed.

"I'm afraid the unit couldn't quite protect your legs, Mr. Williams; the considerable damage could mean that you may never walk again without robotic assistance."

'Robotic assistance' was a way of saying that his legs would be amputated and bionic limbs grafted into place. A neural chip would be inserted so that he could control their movement. He would be transformed from a recognized star in the city dome and darling of the Con-Fed to the status of a cyborg. He would be considered as part of the underclass along with the mutants in the population.

On the third day of his convalescence and thinking over his options, Williams received an unexpected visitor. The man was dressed in Mars marine fatigues and sported more medals than Williams had ever seen. As he spoke, the gravelly voice outlined a proposition.

"Son, I used to watch you in those brawling games with my buddies over a few brews. You were the best I have ever seen. It's rare that a brawler continues in his career after the age of thirty and you're now, what? Thirty six? You've got the fortitude and guts that I need for my new unit."

Williams sat up a little straighter in the bed. Was this guy offering him a job?

"I see you don't quite understand, Mr. Williams. You see, I'm putting together a new team. It's the first of its kind. We think that it would be effective in certain... urban pacification situations. Maybe it could help stop a lot of these terrorist bastards from pulling any more of their shit. Hell, I don't know and quite frankly, son, I'm out of my depth."

The aged soldier moved closer to Williams; sincerity blazed from the old man's eyes.

"We call it A.I.M. The higher-ups say it means 'Armoured Infantry Mech Division', some shit like that. To me is sounds like good old-fashioned ass-kickery. I think it could give us an advantage to fight back."

Williams shook his head; he was still unsure as to what all of this meant. Seeing his continuing confusion, the general placed a hand on the Mech-Brawler's shoulders. Speaking slowly, he outlined the deal once more, in terms that Williams could understand.

"Son. I'm offering you a chance at some God-damn revenge."

A moment passed; Williams once again saw the faces of his dead team mates flash before his eyes. He grasped the general's outstretched hand.

"Why the frack not... sir."

TO BE CONTINUED

Watch out for the up and coming Dark Legacies *series, co-authored by* **Chris 'Stokerverse' McAuley** *and* **Claudia 'Commander Ivanova' Christian**.

PUBLISHING NEWS

by Mickey Mikkelson

SUNSET DISTORTION
The Pyramid at The End of The World

The Mind-bending New Novel by Paul Bahou!

Lazer is an almost made it, middle-aged guitarist who plays in an 80's hard rock cover band at a Sunset Strip dive bar. While not quite a rock star, he plays to a packed house nightly. His blissful inertia is disrupted one night, however, when he is abducted by aliens and given a strange imprint on his hand: a key which will send him on an intergalactic journey in search of an artifact that gives its possessor "infinite life." With the help of his new friend Streek, a timid floating octopus-creature with an English accent, Lazer will have to survive encounters with monsters, robots, alien pirates, inter-dimensional brain leeches and much more. Will Lazer get back home? What does 'infinite life' actually mean? And why does everybody in space speak English? All answers await at the pyramid at the end of the world.

Amazon.com: Sunset Distortion: The Pyramid at the End of the World: Bahou, Paul: 9780578804187: Amazon.com: Books

Barnes & Noble: Sunset Distortion: The Pyramid at the End of the World by Paul Bahou, Paperback | Barnes & Noble® (barnesandnoble.com)

About Paul Bahou

PAUL BAHOU is the author of Sunset Distortion: The Pyramid at the End of the World. He holds a B.A. in Political Science from Cal State University Long Beach with a minor in music. He began his career writing grants while playing in his rock band, eventually moving out of music and into the sustainability sector. He lives in Southern California with his wife Melissa, daughter Sophie and son Harrison. He writes fiction, music and the occasional dad joke in his spare time.

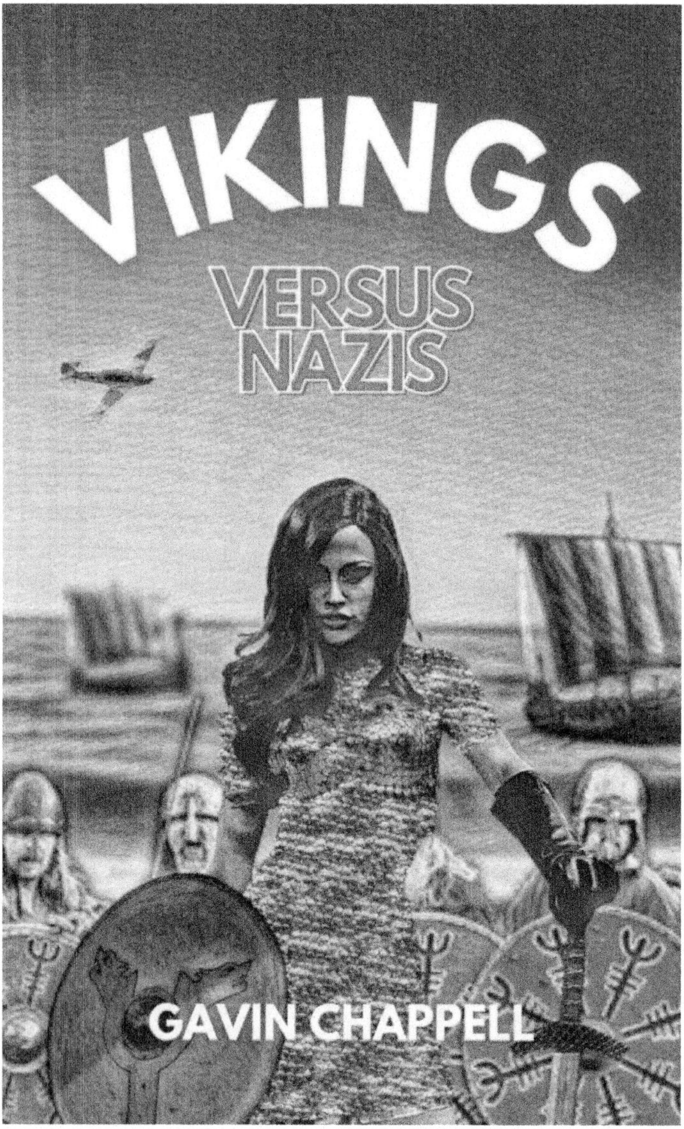
VIKINGS
VERSUS
NAZIS
GAVIN CHAPPELL

THE WHISPERING CAMPAIGN
by EW Farnsworth

The enormous woman pressed straight through the throng of customers at the Cracked Bell pub to find Sheriff Fatty Millstone deep in contemplation in front of his second pint with bitters at his special table in the rear.

"Sheriff Millstone, something must be done about the whispering campaign." He turned to see the woman changing colour from red to livid, so he gestured for her to take a seat and raised his hand to get the attention of the waitress.

"Bring this lady a pint right away," he ordered. Then he sat up in his chair and gave the woman his entire attention. "Madam, please tell me what is on your mind."

The woman appeared to gather her thoughts till her pint arrived. She opened the floodgates of her mouth and issued an incredible conspiracy theory which caught the attention of everyone in the range of hearing her. The gist was a person or persons unknown were stirring up anti-alien sentiment and inciting violence among the populace.

Fatty waited through her heated exposition largely because he could not get a word in edge-wise, but the more he listened, the more he was convinced the woman had a point. His eyes narrowed in a way suggesting he was being affected by the woman's argument. So she stopped talking and hunkered over her drink to let her message sink in.

The sheriff touched his glass to hers and quaffed his drink. "Madam, I also have sensed a growing sentiment against aliens lately. Like you, I am outraged, as we are supposed to be a civilized nation. We are, of course, also a nation of laws protecting the rights and dignity of aliens. So I must have proofs as well as reliable and willing witnesses to raise the matter to the proper levels of the magistrate and courts. Can you please provide what we need to proceed?"

The woman, seeing the sympathy in the sheriff's eyes, adjusted her body in her seat and took a breath and another sip of her brew. "That is precisely the problem, Sheriff. You see, I hear the whispers but when I turn to locate the source, no one is there."

"Are you absolutely sure you heard a voice or voices?"

"I know what I heard. And my ears are fine. I have heard the whispering on the underground, in shops, walking the streets, morning, noon and night for the last three weeks."

"I want to believe you, Madam. One recourse is to make a statement giving all details of every instance you can recall—the time, place and exact words you heard. Perhaps if you kept a diary it would help you remember."

"I do not regularly keep a diary, but I am willing to do so to record these abusive whispers—if you think it would help us."

"Madam, I urge you to take that initial step. Meanwhile, mind your surroundings to identify suspects. I shall be seated where you found me today during the pub's open hours. Today, let's finish our drinks and look forward to our future review of your new evidence. One more thing: during the last few weeks, did you mention your whispers to anyone in the press?"

"In fact, I was interviewed by a man from the tabloid Quotidian Scourge. He suggested I come directly to you with my complaint."

"Was the reporter, by chance, named Crenshaw?"

"That was his name. He was so good about listening, and he knew exactly what I should do. He did not violate my privacy when he published his article about the matter."

"So you were the source for that front page article in Friday's Quotidian, the one with the headline, 'Whispers?'"

"I assume the reporter had many other similar reports or he would not have made such an assertion."

"I will talk with Mr. Crenshaw about the matter for clarity's sake. Meanwhile, please keep your diary and stop by when you have the evidence we need."

After the woman departed, the sheriff brooded. By writing a piece about whispering, the yellow-rag reporter had created the very hubbub he claimed to be uncovering. Susceptible citizens, like the enormous woman, were bound to "hear" whispers, not all of them from external sources. Consulting the tabloid in question, Fatty read the article carefully three times. Crenshaw's insidious insinuations were mischievously wrought. The sheriff wondered whether the article satisfied the requirements of the "incitation to riot" laws.

The sheriff looked up to find Crenshaw in the chair the woman had formerly occupied. The man was smiling maliciously, flattered the sheriff was reading his latest scribble.

"Sheriff Millstone, I had no idea you were one of my fans. What do you think of my latest creation?"

"Crenshaw, I think the magistrate would be amenable to discussing a prison sentence for you and your publisher for incitation to riot."

The reporter got a moue for an expression and shook his head. "Come now, Sheriff, reporting the views of the people is no crime. Besides, I sent my last interviewee to you to be sure the authorities were aware of the issue."

"And you knew your action would imply good faith. How many others did you interview for your article?"

"Why, it's synecdoche, the part standing for the whole!"

"A literary trope that would not hold up in court as justification for a scurrilous article meant to swell subscriptions and start a thousand hares of rumours and innuendoes."

The waitress brought Crenshaw a pint. She saw the front page of the Quotidian lying on the table. "I have heard the whispers too, Mr. Crenshaw."

Crenshaw gave the sheriff a knowing look and sipped his drink.

"This will be the reporter's last drink before he goes back to his newsroom to pen his retraction."

"That's unfair, Sheriff. Everyone is talking about the whispers."

"Thanks to your article, they will not have to consider what they are sensing. They will make two assumptions: the whispers are general, and they carry grains of truth."

"News organs sharpen what the people vaguely understand. Who cares if the whispers come from within the nation's psyche or from within the individuals' minds? The important thing is the truth getting out for public interest and open debate."

"Unfortunately, you cannot un-sing your song. The damage has been done. I give you fair warning: stop writing drivel that unsettles the citizens, or consequences will follow."

"Sheriff, are you threatening me?"

"I never threaten people like you, Mr. Crenshaw."

The newshound finished his pint and raced to the door. Fatty thought the man had just enough time to write a follow-on piece about police brutality before the next issue of his paper went to press.

The next day's Quotidian carried the banner headline, "Authorities Try to Squelch Whispers Story." Crenshaw and his editor evidently had fun at the sheriff's expense. Having anticipated this course of action by the tabloid, the magistrate appeared at the Quotidian offices with a summons.

The sheriff's friend the MP raised the issue of anti-alien sentiment in Parliament, saying, "Subversive elements are stoking the embers of sedition in the yellow press. This body will not stand for such blatant incitation. Any further evidence of such foul rabble-rousing will meet with condign measures." The speech was lauded in OpEd pieces in the respectable press, and the Quotidian muzzled itself for fear of government censorship, or worse.

Crenshaw looked contrite when next he visited the sheriff at the Cracked Bell pub.

"Well, Sheriff, you got what you aimed at this time. My publisher has spiked my latest articles on whispering, so I am considering a book. To my credit, the mainstream press has taken up the issue through covering the MP's speech. Still, the anti-alien prejudice seethes beneath the placid surface, and the public knows it. You will rue the day you shut down my reporting on this matter."

"Crenshaw, I understand how your devious brain thinks. Your book idea is DOA. My resources will be watching you carefully for any other attempts by you or your friends to stoke protests or revolution."

The reporter left the table in a huff without finishing his pint. As he exited, he passed the enormous woman, armed with her new diary. She sat next to the sheriff, her back stiff like a ramrod. As she drank her pint, she read her diary entries one-by-one.

When she had finished, Fatty asked her whether she wished to write a deposition, but she shook her head. "I know the way the wind blows. My intent was to raise the public's consciousness by crying out in the wilderness."

"Do you think you have raised enough commotion now?"

"Yes. On the issue of whisperings. But now I have a new cause: Global Warming. Have you heard of that?"

"Yes, Ma'am. Do you have a civil or criminal complaint to raise with me?"

"Not yet, Sheriff, but I have only just begun my investigation."

"Out of curiosity, how were you inspired to think of Global Warming?"

"I heard a whisper saying, 'Think of Global Warming!'"

"And where and when did you hear this whisper?"

"It's right in my diary—last Tuesday at six o'clock in the morning. I read that entry to you. As I recall, the fog was just beginning to burn off in the park."

"Did you hear sounds of footfall or see anyone within whispering range?"

"I did say hello to old Mrs. Fanfare, the bandmaster's deranged widow, bless her soul."

"Do you often bid her a good morning as you walk through the park?"

"Yes I do, always as I pass her park bench. I mean to be civil, especially to the less fortunate."

The sheriff continued their chitchat till the woman departed. He resolved to walk through the park the following morning on his way to the Cracked Bell.

In the pea-soup morning fog, Fatty heard Mrs. Fanfare's imprecations before he made her out on the bench. She was wheezing and muttering in a constant torrent of abuse on all topics, the chief of which was the "alien invasion."

The sheriff stood in front of the old woman for almost half an hour till she sensed his presence.

"Who may you be?"

"Good morning, Mrs. Fanfare. I am Sheriff Fatty Millstone. I trust you are well today."

She squinted at him a moment before she nodded and continued inveighing.

"Aliens are everywhere. They are going to outnumber us someday soon."

The sheriff listened to her daft rambling. She was beyond consolation from rational conversation. Evidently, she did not need an audience's response. She was fuming about disappointments of a lifetime, but her main theme was the alien invasion. The sheriff realized hers was the whispering campaign.

At his table at the Cracked Bell with a pint with bitters before him, the sheriff was approached by a beaming Mr. Crenshaw. "I will only take a moment of your time, Sheriff."

Fatty gestured for the newshound to sit. He waved for the waitress to bring the man a pint. Crenshaw's jaw dropped at the princely treatment.

"I am suspicious, Sheriff."

"Why are you here, Crenshaw?"

"I wanted to thank you for being kind to my mother in the park this morning."

Fatty's jaw now dropped. "Mrs. Fanfare is your mother?"

"Indeed, she is."

"Then you knew she was the source of the whispering campaign?"

"Yes, but what could I do?"

"You could have written the truth. Instead, you seized upon an impressionable, uninformed young woman to write your poppycock theories about a mania against aliens in this nation. Disgraceful!"

"Maybe so, but I have been interdicted, by you and the others. So my tune has changed."

"To Global Warming?"

"Why not? It's certainly an issue that sells newspapers."

"Are you following Greta Thunberg then?"

"Was Walpole an Englishman? Of course, I follow Thunberg and the other Global Warming tribes. Are you going to indict me and my publisher for that?"

"Of course not. And I might not have been as harsh on you if I had known your poor, old, raving mother was the genesis of your whispering pieces."

The two men drank in silence ruminating separately. When Crenshaw departed, the enormous woman arrived with her latest report.

"I walked through the park this morning as I always do, but Mrs. Fanfare was silent. I had no idea what happened to stop her whispering. When I bade her good morning and asked why she was not gabbling as usual, she held her finger to her lips for silence and shook her head. I pressed her to tell me what was wrong. She just shook her head. I worried she may have reached a new stage of dementia when I saw a twinkle in her eyes. I asked why she was happy. She smiled but did not answer me."

"What do you deduce from the old woman's behaviour?"

"I think someone she respects spoke to her, and it changed her disposition entirely. Who that person could be, I cannot guess."

"So you are continuing your Global Warming campaign?"

"Yes. In fact, I am scheduled to meet the tabloid photographer before noon in the park. I have never had my picture appear in the newspaper before. I hope I have dressed well enough for a good appearance."

"My dear, you look splendid. And if you smile, your face will sell a thousand tabloids. Don't forget to spell out your terms before they publish."

"Terms?"

"I certainly hope you realize how much money you will be making for the tabloid that publishes your image."

"I never thought of that."

"It's your image. You are entitled to use it however you like."

"I should be going now. Thank you for your advice, Sheriff. Now that Mrs. Fanfare is smiling, a whole new day has dawned for me as well. Ta ta!"

Alone again, Sheriff Millstone sat musing on the whispering business. He was of two minds about reporting what happened to his political friends. On the one hand, the truth deserved telling. On the other hand, he was wary of the whispering idea affecting political strategy at the coming elections. Disembodied whispering voices was all the parties needed to complicate their campaigns.

Looking back on the events of the last few weeks, Fatty was glad Parliament had reaffirmed their stance against anti-alien rhetoric. He was gratified the main line press was still respected enough to refocus public opinion from rumours engendered by the yellow press. He was also delighted the root of the whispering matter was a poor, old woman muttering in a public park bench on foggy mornings. It almost troubled him that he might have been the cause of Mrs. Fanfare's sudden change of heart.

Fatty was resilient. He raised his hand for a refill, and he tried to recall what he was doing before the enormous woman stepped into his life.

Two days later, that enormous woman's picture appeared on the cover of the Quotidian, under the unfortunate headline, "Gargantuan Forces of Nature: It May Be Too Late!" The Sheriff could not help laughing through the rest of the morning.

EW Farnsworth's Picklock Lane stories are available now in book form from Amazon.

LOVECRAFTIANA
THE MAGAZINE OF ELDRITCH HORROR
INSIDE THE LABYRINTH
David A Riley
PLUS
CTHULHUVIAN
POETRY AND
ART
NIGHT
MUSIC
Connor Oricco
VOLUME SIX, ISSUE TWO
LAMMAS EVE 2021

ILLEGAL ALIEN
by DJ Tyrer

Inspector Lender was regarded as something of a hero by the bobbies of the Bassetshire Police Service, being well known for the stiffness of his upper lip. Now, in modern policing, a stiff upper lip wasn't regarded that favourably, being a relic from an earlier age when the baton was preferred to the diversity monitoring form, which may explain why his advancement had stalled at the rank of Inspector rather than speeding towards that of Chief Constable. Still, to the rank and file, his ability to maintain a stiff upper lip in the face of violent thugs, hordes of rowdy drunks, and mountains of paperwork, was a wonder to behold and truly something to admire.

"He's amazing," PC Won exclaimed, watching Lender head for his patrol car.

"Quite," agreed PC Constable. "You know, I've never seen his lip tremble, not even once. Not even when he got the memo about the new suspect shoe-size diversity monitoring form. DCI Armand burst into tears when he saw that one."

"Yeah," Won agreed. "Who cares what size shoe a suspect wears? Are they worried we're persecuting Bigfoot?"

"Nah," Constable replied with a shake of his head, "they're just worried we might have a spare five minutes for a tea break."

"Hmm," Won hummed, "his lip didn't even seem to wobble when the vending machine ran out of tea; not even when they restocked it."

"An amazing guy," Constable concluded, as Lender drove out of the station yard and into the Bassetshire night.

Inspector Lender always made a point of getting out and about in order to keep a personal eye on his division whenever he had time free from paperwork and from filling. It was interesting to see how much things had changed in the last six months.

Bassetshire was a largely rural police service and the Inspector's division covered several villages, a market town full of drunks, and lots and lots of fields, mostly full of cows and the occasional wreck left behind by a drunk driver. If you ignored the flytipped rubbish blowing along its lanes like England's answer to the tumbleweed, the county could appear quite idyllic, yet Lender knew it held a seedy underbelly of crisp snatchers, Special K addicts, and petty vandals. With so many lanes and so few police, it was impossible to deal with more than a tiny fraction of the reported crimes; currently, they were concentrating on thefts from sheds. The Inspector's lip had been completely untroubled by the thought of missing lawnmowers.

As he negotiated a particularly difficult series of bends, Lender heard a report of a strange light in the sky over the area he was in.

"It is suspected it may be a Chinese lantern," the voice said, "a severe waste disposal violation."

He managed to keep his lip under control as he listened and considered the many potential disasters the lantern could cause: littering was merely the one most likely to tick a box on their crime sheets.

"Show me as dealing," he radioed back. He flicked on his lights and picked up a little speed. It felt good to be back on the mean streets, even if said street was a quiet country lane.

Lender craned his neck, looking up at the night sky, trying to spot the lantern. In theory, without too much light pollution, the sky was clear, but the stars were obscured by the number of planes flying overhead. Still, a glowing light shouldn't be too difficult to spot.

Then, he saw it.

Lender didn't think it was a lantern. It was bright like one, but was moving swiftly. As far as he knew, lanterns floated along sedately and didn't whizz about like that. He wondered what it could be. Perhaps a light aircraft?

Whatever it was, it appeared to be descending. If deliberate, that could mean drug smugglers and he might score some arrests. If it was in trouble, well, he was the perfect man to take charge of a disaster; he might even earn himself another commendation.

He flicked on the siren and slammed his foot down, speeding towards it.

There it was! Whatever it was, it seemed to be ablaze. Clearly it was coming in to crash. Too late, he realised it was coming straight for him.

Lender slammed on the brakes and yanked the gearstick into reverse, but before the car began moving, the ball of fire had smashed into the bonnet, pulverizing the entire front of the car. The sound of the siren died.

The Inspector tried to stare at the wreckage in shock, but the thing that had crashed into his car was glowing white hot, and he couldn't bear to look at it, the brightness burning his eyes. The heat was too much to take and he had to bail out of the car.

Lender reached for his radio and reported what had happened and asked for backup.

He shook his head. This wouldn't look good on his report. Still, such unexpected reversals of fortune were only to be expected. He remembered having wrapped a panda car around a lamppost early in his policing career.

He had to shuffle back as the heat of the object began to melt it, metal and plastic pooling about it.

As the object slowly cooled and he could look at it, Lender saw it was a globe or egg-shape.

"It must be a meteorite," he said to himself. Then, as he looked more closely, he thought maybe it was made of metal. "Or, maybe a satellite."

As he looked at it, he became aware of a soft grinding sound and realised that a section was rising up from it like some sort of hatch. For many officers, that might have been cause for fear, or, at least, a case of nerves. A few might even have been excited, but Lender just watched impassively, stoic to the core.

After several more turns, the hatch popped free and fell to the tarmac where it spun a few times on its side like a coin.

Lender watched and waited. Internally, he was a storm of emotion as he waited to see what might emerge, but on the surface, his features remained still as if the scene were barely of even mildest interest.

His lip didn't even tremble as the inhabitant of the vessel slowly slid out through the narrow hatchway and unfolded itself. The creature could be described as humanoid, but was over twice as tall as Lender with limbs and a body so thick that they made the Inspector think of matchsticks. It was a pallid, sickly-seeming grey in colour and had large, black, multifaceted eyes. But, it was its mouth that most caught his attention, being large and filled with what appeared to be hundreds of sharp fangs.

Still, as horrible as it seemed, Lender reasoned it had to be intelligent if it had flown across space to visit earth, and, surely, his line of thought continued, intelligent creatures weren't monsters that would kill you out of hand upon first meeting you.

"Welcome to Earth," Lender said, trying and failing to emulate the Vulcan salute, whilst wondering if he should arrest it. "I come in peace. If you would like," he added, "I can take you to my leader."

He would love to see how the Chief Constable would deal with it.

The alien being leaned towards him, looked closely at him, as if examining him, and drooled a little.

Inspector Lender didn't flinch. In fact, his lip didn't even flinch when the alien lunged for him, bowled him over and began to devour him feet first. Even as he fought back, punching wildly, he never lost his composure and showed no sign of terror that surely must have engulfed him just as surely as the creature's gullet.

It had munched its way up to his chest by the time backup arrived.

Two cars pulled up, lights flashing and sirens whooping, and disgorged their contents. Unlike their Inspector, the PCs were quite clearly terrified as they saw the being turn to face them, belly distended and the remains of Lender dangling from its jaws.

Slowly, unwillingly, they advanced on it, tasers in hand. One fired, then another and another. The last wet himself and forgot to press his trigger. Electricity coursed through the wires to the darts that had struck the creature, but it seemed utterly unaffected and just continued munching on Inspector Lender.

The four officers hung back, unwilling to engage it with batons, unwilling to get too close.

It swallowed the last of their superior down and advanced a few steps towards them. Then, it stopped suddenly and began to convulse. It shook and hacked as if choking and the PCs looked at one another, uncertain how to behave. There was a sudden pop, like the sound of a cork shooting free, and it vomited out a ream of forms and a small piece of flesh.

They stared at it in shock. The being was even paler now and looked distinctly queasy. Shakily, it turned and returned to the object from which it had come, folded itself back up, climbed back in and sealed the hatch behind it before the metallic globe shot up into the sky and vanished from sight.

The bemused police officers looked down at the pads the creature had vomited up. It had managed to swallow flesh, bone, uniform fabric and even an anti-stab vest, but it seemed the alien couldn't swallow the rules, regulations and paperwork inflicted upon the Bassetshire Police Service

"Isn't that...?" Won asked.

Constable nodded, grimly.

Gummed to a form with viscous alien saliva was the Inspector's upper lip. Stiff until the bitter end, it seemed the alien had been unable to swallow it, either.

GAVIN CHAPPELL

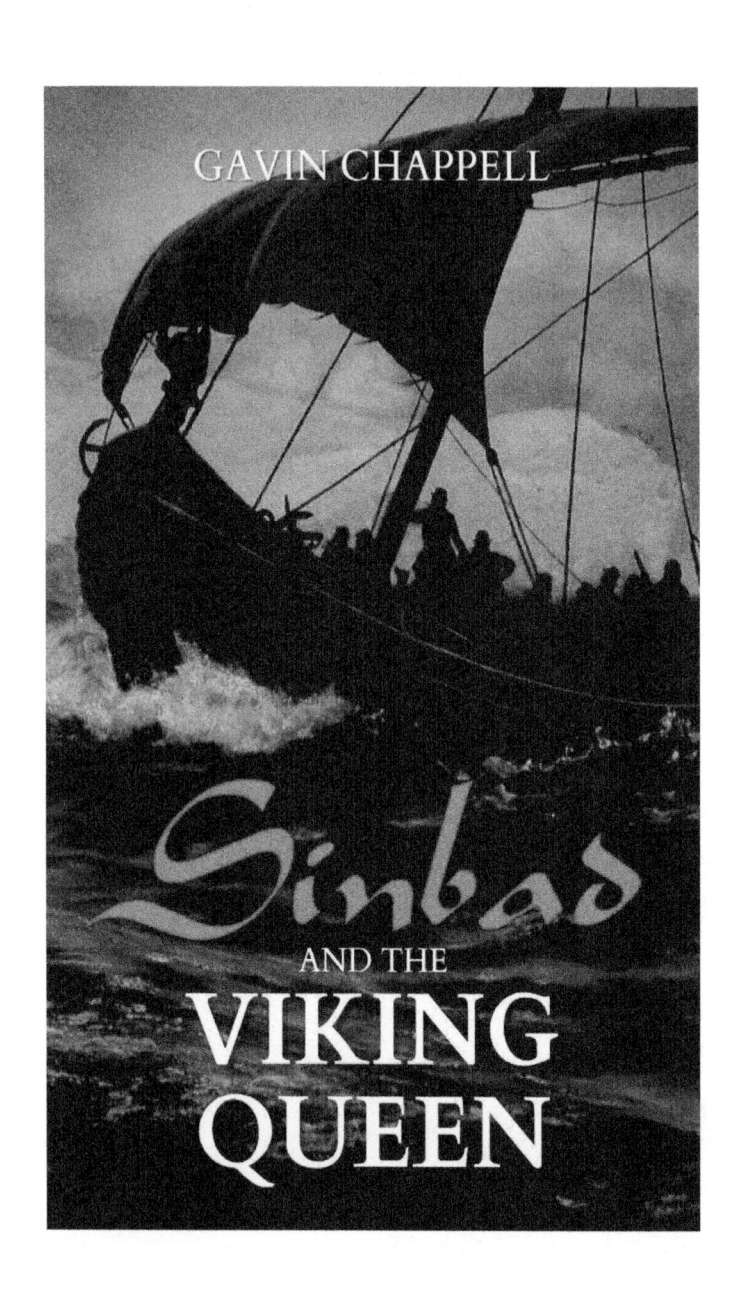

Sinbad

AND THE
VIKING
QUEEN

THE SCOURING OF SILVER COAST
by Jesse Zimmerman

Part Two

"Welcome home," we sisters say to one another as we step out of the archway.

I immediately recognize the scape, the slug in my brain, the one that grants me instant recollection of everything I ever learned, reminds me. We are inside the walls of Silver Coast. The splashing of fountains is the first thing I hear and the second thing I see after the immense cobbled square, the entrance of the city, as it was when we left though maybe only a third of its usual crowd. It must be because the city is cut off from itself; the four canals, as we learned before entering, are seemingly on fire, magic fire. The whole city is cordoned off into its four major quadrants; we are in the Southeast, our home is in the Northwest.

As we walk from the walls things become busier. A few crowds of pedestrians pass through markets, and I've counted at least a dozen carriages drawn by burdensome beasts, many belonging to merchants either heading towards or leaving these busy markets. We consider buying some food as we look upon sultry flat-breads, fruity pastes, and honeyed syrups, along with steaming pies and buttery biscuits, but we opt to instead eat the leftovers the villagers gave us back at the mountainside hamlet. As I bite into the stale-ish bread I think of the contrast between that place and here, even if the crowds are not as large as usual. As we munch Sister leads, taking a turn down a narrower way. On our left side stretches a row of two-storey buildings, and at our right side there are numerous houses, many stacked together, some four or five stories.

I can see a few of the tallest spires in the distance to the North and West-ish, beyond this quadrant. Ever since I was really little those sky-piercing towers gave me a sense of lofty majesty, especially on a clear day or at night when the lights from within make them appear as star-filled themselves. Mother's library is among some of those towers, further to the Northwest, the campus district. I feel annoyed that I cannot now waltz in, step on through the great sunny atrium and find a desk to get lost in a tome or two, or at the very least take a long nap in my old room. Sadly, we might not even be able to see Mother for some time still. We have left the corridors between structures and are in another square. Here there are two fountains, one at either end of the wide space, each with a bronze fish-shaped spout.

"The most crowded place I've seen in weeks, yet I've never seen the place so uncrowded!" Fauna says as we move along between more market stalls. These are largely small wooden desks or portable carts that folks have set up. I see some with jewellery, others with tools, and more than a few with glass bottles, some with water, milks, and a few of bright colours, potions, all beautiful and some obviously magical.

I remember this place, recalling having come here more than once with Sister or friends, usually after classes were done. We were younger and interested in buying shiny stuff with whatever coinage we had, and then we'd go northward to a place called The Slope for some entertainment. The Slope is at the edge of this Southeast Quadrant, right where the four canals meet. There is an X shaped series of bridges that connect them all.

"Where are we going to stay for the night if we can't get home?" I ask Fauna once we've reached the middle of the square. Looming over us is a silver statue of a tall javelin that rises thirty feet in the air. I recall the history, but am too preoccupied. By now the light of the sun has faded and the lights of the city are taking over.

"Have you ever slept on the street?" she asks playfully as we come to one of the many benches sprawled out around the spear statue. I place my backpack on it and Fauna does the same with hers.

"Before meeting the Challenger I wouldn't have considered it," I say of our ranger friend. "We've toughed it in the bush and mountains, but for the last few days and nights all I've thought about is sleeping somewhere cushy!"

"Me too! Maybe an inn?" says Sister, unfastening the strings on her pack and rummaging through coins and mushrooms. A crowd passes by, some stragglers at the back decked out fully in dark red robes. Small children play in the nearby pools, some of their nearby mothers calling them out as it is getting darker.

"Shell house?" I ask her, suddenly recalling the strange term.

"Huh?" asks Fauna, raising an eyebrow into her cap.

"Remember? The guard at the front? 'You're not with one of those shell houses, are you?' she asked us? What did that mean?"

"Oh," says Fauna, closing up her bag and placing it onto her back again. "Well, you have the slug in your head, what does it tell you?"

"Nothing," I answer, shrugging. "I never heard of 'shell houses' before. They must be new, something that happened since we left."

"Well, Qilla also told you there is another brain slug somewhere in the city, so lots of weird things going on?" Sister says. "We have some coins, maybe an eccentric innkeeper will take some glow mushrooms?

Best brassy inns are in the Entertainment District, centre of town near the Slope."

I catch the glint of emergent moonlight in the surface of the silvery javelin monument and I ask her: "Do you have any friends in the area?"

"We don't talk anymore, she knows why. An inn looks like our best wager," she says, flicking a curl of red hair from her face. "Unless we can figure a way over the fire."

"If no one else has figured a way I doubt we can," I say.

She smiles. I can read her expression: she thinks after all we've lived through that we can find a way and I wonder if she may be right, but I'm doubtful. I know already that magic fire that burns on a body of water cannot be doused by water, so my water rod is useless here. Maybe I can use the Mighty Magnet to bring down a massive building and squelch... no, I won't be doing that.

"Well," Sister says, glancing about the semi-crowded square. "To the Slope. From there we'll figure out what to do." With these words she mimics pulling out her sword from her belt, though not really, because it's an unwise move in a crowded urban space. She points her arm instead to what she thinks is North.

I curtly nod, noticing, as a procession of red robes moves from my sight, a single horsed cart that is idle against a lamppost. Its conductor is slowly crawling up the side, lifting their small body shawled in black. There is a snug-looking bench positioned in the back. I look to my sister and she immediately knows what I'm thinking.

"We have coin and mushrooms, take your pick or both!" she calls as we make our way through the shifting crowd.

The cart-driver looks down, having just set down upon the front perch. This is an older one, one I cannot tell is man or woman, not that it matters. The cart-driver's eyes are piercing and they have a withered long face that looks to be partly scowling.

"Where to?" they grumble, nodding toward the backseats.

Fauna places a handful of coins and glowing fungi aside the conductor, cautioning to eat neither as she reaches for the side rail and pulls herself into the back. I follow nearly as gingerly, ourselves and our belongings soon nestled nicely.

"To the Slope please," says my sister.

"Why the red?" the cart-driver asks her as the horse begins to trot.

"My favourite!" she answers.

The driver conducts the horse to start galloping once we're clear and I feel a breeze as the heads of the crowd float by like ice floes on a frozen river. We move from the square down a wide alleyway between squat buildings. There are fences in front of many of them, these open shops and lavish homes. The cart turns into another aisle, this one more cobbled than the last, sending the cart into a frenzy of tittering movements, prompting me to reach for the rail. There are stone balconies a few feet overhead, whole rows of them zipping by, dangling flowery vines smacking against our faces. Next we are moving uphill on a more even street. Overhead at the summit is a stout chocolate brown-bricked structure. The cart-driver takes us along its side for a while before scurrying around another corner.

Sister gasps. Beyond her side of the cart stands a blackened structure. We can see that the bricks are bright red where they are not charred with soot. A single crumpled chimney sits atop a collapsed roof and one wall has fallen over, revealing a smashed interior as we whiz past it.

"Shell house," utters the cart-driver with a dry laugh.

"And what was a shell house?" asks Fauna, taking off her cap, placing it on her lap. I lower mine too.

"You two not from around here?" comes the response.

"Underground," my sister quickly quips.

"Not been around lately," I say. "The shell houses, there were none when we left?"

The cart driver tells us: "The shell houses have been popping up since as long as the canal fires burned. There was a bloke by the name of Sharkoo. He came when the fires burned, told the young ones not to be afraid. Some listened. Sharkoo told them the magic fire cannot hurt them, was only an illusion."

"Sharkoo?" I echo. "Such strange named beings we've met already!"

"Slug-Lord, Lobster-Man, the Straw Man, Gemmok, Bub!" Sister lists some of our previous rogues' gallery with a giggle.

"Yeah," I agree. "So Sharkoo started these shell houses?"

The cart driver nods. "They began popping up here and there, small at first. So many were confused, angry about the fires."

"The fires, what caused them?" Fauna asks the driver.

"Ah, you really have been gone a while!" the driver says while extending a hand to their front. We see the semi-distant wall of reddish fire. The cart turns onto a large wide road. There are some people walking along the sides here. The buildings here are larger, five storeys mostly.

"It's said that they leaked from the Zoma warehouses," says the driver solemnly, a hint of anger in their voice.

"Zoma?" asks Sister.

"I remember them," I say, recalling with the help of the slug. "They were starting up when we left, delivering letters and goods throughout Silver Coast. Named after the Zoma Rainwood in the South."

The cart-driver nods and grunts. "They are destitute after this. Everyone knows it was their mistake caused this. We traded safety for convenience, aye? You girls wanted to be dropped at the Slope?"

Fauna gets out first, thanking them for the ride and information. Here we stand in a semi-crowded square as the cart drives off. A thickly set inn is near, just across the small way. My sister tells me that she will grab us a room and negotiate a good price. I give her my belongings, save my magnet and water rod, telling her to store them beneath a bed and to meet me at the Slope. It's nearby, across the way.

The crowd becomes a little thicker near the canal. The Slope is built on an old hill, its surface covered in flat stone. It juts upward, this large semi-circular shape that seats around thirty, into the nearby canal, the X-shaped bridges just beyond it, accessible from the sides of the Slope. It is like a raised amphitheatre, a stage. I can see the flames licking the air a fair twenty feet or so above the waters beyond. I move to stand at the edge of the canal where only a brass rail separates me from the burning waters. I've never seen anything like this. The flames burn high, as tall as five of me, everywhere the water flows. Beyond I can see spires and stouter structures. To my left the bridges start, and I can see the canal meeting another channel, not far from here the four of them criss-cross and that's where the bridges also cross over. The fires, I can see, have overwhelmed the stone bridges. We cannot cross over there, no way.

"This must be some twisted magic experiment gone seriously wrong!" says someone nearby. I see there are two young boys looking to be near my age standing further along the rail. The one who just spoke has short dirty blondish hair, not unlike the Challenger. At his belt is a small bug catcher net, must be a collector. The other is a bit taller with darker hair that runs to his shoulders. Both are wearing plain brownish clothes, tunics and breeches.

"Well, I heard it was Zoma's excess fuel," says the lanky one, shaking his head. I look away when the first one who spoke glances over at me. I see now that there is a small crowd filling up the little stools on the wide end of the semi-circle that is the Slope.

"Come on," he says to the other. "Carma's show starts!"

"Flora!" my sister calls. She bears a great smile. "We got a giant-sized room! They took the rest of the mushrooms, except this one," she says, holding a big blue one in her hand. "Also, left the weapons, can't be out in the street with weapons, they said. Fair! At least we get a nice cushy sleep tonight!"

I feel a bit of joy erupt inside me as I thank her.

"Whoa," she says, gazing upon the flames.

I nod in answer, and then I look over at the Slope to my right. I see there, standing with her back to the fiery river, a young woman who looks to be maybe a bit older than us. She is decked out in a short purple robe, and has bright red pants, her hair black with silver and pink strands. Like me she wears spectacles, only not as big as mine. She is speaking loudly into a broad horn that expands her voice. Fauna is looking curiously over at her as she hands me a small vial of water while holding one in her other hand, telling me that they are complimentary. We sisters walk over, finding a small set of stools in front of a little round wooden table that resembles a tree stump. The rest of the seats and tables are occupied with folks, many of them young, the two boys I saw earlier at the next table over.

"Welcome, welcome, welcome! I'm Carma!" calls the apparent host, the strangely decked out young woman, a great smile upon her roundish face. The fire burns directly behind her. None of the audience seems fazed by it, likely adjusted to it by now.

Fauna takes a drink of the water. "Ah!" she says in refreshment. "I miss this city."

"Okay, so we've got some jokes, some stories, and a special guest tonight!" cries Carma, raising her free hand in a friendly wave.

"Who's the guest?" calls the dirty blonde-haired boy from the table over from us. Some snickers rise up among the assembled.

"You came here to find out! Our guest tonight, even though he's been called 'the enemy of the people of Silver Coast', and is said to be very dangerous, I thought it would be good to extend a peace token and bring him over here! Please welcome Sharkoo!"

We sisters both gasp, others in the assembled crowd following.

"Wait? What?" someone shouts from a few tables over, and then a silence overwhelms the space as I take notice of a group of red cloaked figures approaching from behind the seats—a small crowd of these along with a taller figure: this being is easily the height of three of me, he too decked in a long red cloak, towering over his underlings. He throws back his hood and I see a big crimson head, the head of a shark, its jaws set open in a frozen shriek. Between rows of knife-like teeth I see two red eyes and I realize this is only a costume.

"You know he is dangerous yet you bring him here?" my sister suddenly shouts to the one called Carma at the front of the little stage.

"Well!" she laughs in reply, speaking into the horn. "My plan is to mock him while he's here! Hey Sharkoo! Made anyone leap into fire lately? Ha ha!"

The one called Sharkoo seems to peer beyond the fake jaws at us sisters for a moment before patting one of the shorter robed figures on the back. I just know something bad is on the verge of happening.

TO BE CONTINUED
same shark zine, same shark website...

HYPERBOREAN BOOKS

WITCH-QUEEN OF THE LOST RACE

by Rex Mundy

THE DRAGONS' PLAYBOOK
by Carlton Herzog

I was not your typical knight. For one thing, I was a broad, and a good looking one at that, both in and out of my armour. For another, my boyfriend was Gorn the dragon. Together we were quite the pair.

Gorn wasn't always a dragon. He had been a reasonably handsome mook that I presented to my mother as a prospective marriage candidate. My mother, who coincidentally was a witch, wanted me to follow in her footsteps. She objected to the marriage and promptly turned Gorn into the fire-breathing scourge of Vandis you see today.

Now, my mother as you may have guessed was not tightly wrapped. Nor was she a saint by any stretch of the imagination. Her head had been on more inn pillows than a chocolate mint. If her vagina had been a video game, it would have been rated E for everybody. And when I informed her that I didn't want to join the coven she said, "You must have been switched at birth with another baby because there is no way I could have given birth to such a hateful child."

I got into the knight business to make enough money. I needed fast cash to make Gorn human again. So, the two of us concocted a scheme where he would fly into a town and terrorize its inhabitants. I would come along and promise to drive him away for a fee.

We would milk it for all its worth. He would be setting wagons on fire and stomping his feet. I would ride in on my faithful white steed Tuggy. Whereupon Gorn and I would engage in some canned banter. Something like:

"What-ho fiend, doth thou terrorize yon peasants on no good account? Forsooth I say."

As a human, Gorn was not the brightest monkey in the meadow. When he turned full-on dragon, he got a bit dimmer.

"What's that mean?"

"It means scaly hellhound, your days upon God's good earth are numbered. I am here to slay thee and carve thee up like a bit of mutton."

"Since we're doing Shakespeare in the park, how about I breaketh my giant foot off in yon metal ass? And maybe roast you alive for good measure."

"Do your worst, monster. I have bested many bigger than you."

We would then run around one another. He would blow fire and miss, and I would swing wide and miss. Eventually, Gorn would pretend to turn tail and fly away. We would meet up later, have a good laugh, count our shekels and consider our next mark.

I guess you're wondering how it is a planet inhabited by humans in the 28th century would be a throwback world to earth's medieval era. Simple: the planet was colonized by Luddites, namely, those who eschew technology and favour a simple life. And simple they got. This burg is like Earth's Dark Ages. Right down to all the wacky magic.

Vandis has it all: witches, wizards, warlocks, werewolves, vampires, and demons. It's one big supernatural stew. The only things missing are the Winchesters and Castiel.

As the daughter of a witch, I had more access than most to books. I read up on the history of Vandis. It didn't take long for me to get that it was a planet of superstitious slack-jawed yokels. Because of the inbreeding, many of them thar' goobers lacked thumbs, sported unibrows, and ate paste. In this kingdom of the blind, I, a fallen woman of sorts, had the one eye that made her, if not queen, a reasonably successful grifter.

Things were going well. We were on our way to coming up with the coin for Carnacki the necromancer to bing bang boop Gorn into a man again. But Gorn got cold feet. He said he liked being a dragon. As I said, not smart.

"I'm going to live for hundreds of years. I can fly. Nobody can hurt me, and everybody thinks twice about messing with me. I love you but I don't want to give that up. Have you considered using the money we have to change me to change you instead? Think about it. We could spawn a race of dragons and run the show here. Enslave all the humans. Make them feed, wash and worship us."

"I need to think about that. Have you included our inability to use toilet paper in your lifestyle calculation?"

"Toilet paper! We don't need no stinking toilet paper! But if you need to think about things then go ahead. In the meantime, I'm going to Wessex and feast on Goodman Brown's heifers. If you want to follow, we can still do "White Knight to the Rescue". But wait until I've had time to swallow a few jerseys before you show."

"Like I said, I'll think about it. So, feel free to start without me."

"Suit yourself."

With that Gorn took flight. I pondered his words then chose a course of action. I would visit my mother and ask her to make Gorn human again.

I found the monster who bore me stirring a steaming cauldron. She had become less than human, a half-barracuda, half woman abomination, with scaly female breasts that glistened in the colours of the rainbow.

A torrent of words issued from her fishy throat.

"Let us look into the Garden of Time and see what weeds may grow. Look there: the mare doth eat her foal. And over there: the graves yawn and yield up gliding ghosts. See here: the heavens rain blood on the worlds below."

Then she shrieked with glee.

"Look! Babies born without heads. These signs bode well for our rebellious enterprise. Soon will we gather in great numbers and retake Heaven. I must tell the King of Hell these glad tidings."

I had come to make amends, but after seeing what she had become, I couldn't resist taking a swipe at the old she-devil what bore me.

"Hello mother. What is it today you are working on so industriously? An alternative fuel source made from puppies, perhaps."

"Greetings, hatchling. Where's your dragon lover? Has he run off with another serpent? They're like that, you know. Can't hold a steady job. Can't stay faithful."

"We're still together. I want you to change him back. Make him human again."

"And why would I do that?"

"I'm your daughter."

"So, I've been told. Did you know that you were so ugly as a child I had to tie a porkchop around your neck so the dog would play with you?"

"Yes, I was no beauty then. But I'm a hottie now. Will you help me or not?"

"That boyfriend of yours is as dumb as a bag of hammers. If I decide to make him human again, you'll need to invest in a unicycle and juggling pins because he's too dull-witted to be anything but a burden on society."

"You haven't changed. You're still the same hateful, hatchet-faced narcissistic bloodsucker who drove my father to an early grave. And made me endure a cold, loveless lonely childhood."

"If you can't abuse your family, then whom can you abuse?"

"Poor Satan, someday he'll come for your soul, and have to leave empty-handed because you don't have one. Do me a favour: make sure your funeral is an open coffin affair, so I'll have a place to spit."

"My, aren't we the damaged little climber? Well, that's a hard no on changing your lover back. If you come around here again, I'll shrink you down to the size of a roach and have you fight spiders for my amusement."

I left empty-handed but full of bile and rage. The Hag had gotten to me again. I had met a lot of despicable, malignant people in my day. So, my bar for scumbags was high. But my mother cleared it easily in street shoes. If evil ever becomes an Olympic event, she'll get the first two lanes in the relay.

I went looking for Gorn. When I got to Wessex, he had already come and gone. Apparently, some of my mother had rubbed off on him because several cottages were burning. The charred remains of villagers littered the streets. Unusual circumstances, since Gorn made it a point to minimize property damage and avoid harming people at all costs.

I didn't know whether my mother had made him mean-spirited following our last encounter or the power at his disposal was slowly corrupting his heart, from that of a gentle giant of a man to a winged fire-breathing fiend. I needed to find him—fast.

I rode through town after town following trails of black smoke. As I did, the destruction and mayhem he had caused grew progressively worse. In Sweet Briar, he had swallowed the constable. In Sylvan Glen, he had devoured a small mob of defenders carrying pitchforks and torches, then ate the town's prize pig, Goliath. It was looking more and more like Mad Dragon Disease with each new atrocity.

I kept riding. But Tuggy was getting tired. So, I stopped in Ligos. Oddly, Gorn had bypassed the town. When I inquired at the Dragon's Head Inn if anyone had seen Gorn, the barkeep, a Mr. Mulroney, said, "He stopped here and visited with some friends then flew away."

"I didn't know Gorn knew anybody this far south."

"Apparently, he's good friends with Grim Fire and Black Wing. They're our protectors. We feed them pigs and cattle, and they make sure nobody—be they human or otherwise—gives us trouble. Gorn wasn't here long. He flew in, they all had a meal, and he left."

"Where can I find these dragons?"

"At the edge of town. The giant red barn is where they live. We stock the field behind it with animals for them to eat. As long as you're respectful, they'll speak with you. But if you give them lip, you'll be the main course at their barbecue."

"I understand."

I let Tuggy rest while I walked down to the Dragon Barn. Grim Fire and Black Wing were out front taking a sunbath.

"Excuse me, honourable guardians, might this humble knight have a word with you?"

Grim Fire chuckled.

"You're a woman. Imagine that. A woman knight. That would blow the patriarchy's mind if it found that out. You go, girl."

"How do you know that?"

"Human females have a distinct odour that we dragons can detect. Musky with a hint of hyacinth and orange."

"I did not know that. Perhaps you can help me."

Black Wing asked.

"What made you become a knight? Was it to slay dragons?"

"No—it was to con gullible humans out of their coin. The reason I'm here is that I'm trying to find my boyfriend Gorn. He's a dragon."

Grim Fire gave me the 411 on Gorn's visit.

"So, you're Billy. Pleased to meet you. Gorn came and left. Said he wanted to fully explore the dragon experience before he decided whether to stay a dragon or go back to being human. He asked for our advice."

"What did you tell him?"

Grim Fire said, "We didn't advise him one way or the other. Instead, we said it was his decision alone to make. I suppose if he had more on the ball, we might have provided a more definitive answer. But truth be told that boy is not the sharpest tool in the shed."

Black Wing laughed.

"That's putting it mildly. If there's a zombie apocalypse, he's got nothing to worry about. Cause zombies eat brains, and he ain't got any. He's been torching villages left and right. That makes the whole dragon community look bad. Admittedly, your little dragon versus knight theatre isn't the greatest publicity, but it makes folks believe that while we might be a threat, humans will always win over us. Gorn's reign of terror is having the opposite effect. If it keeps up, we might have to pool our resources with the other local dragons and take Gorn down—permanently. And I for one do not favour dragon on dragon crime. It makes us look stupid and backwards. Like humans. So, if you have any pull with him, then you need to get him under control before things run any further off the rails. Get me, sister?"

"Oh, I get you, Big Daddy. It's time to put the horse back in the barn. Tell me where he was headed next?"

"He didn't say. But he took off in the direction of Black Moor."

I thanked them for the information and set out for Black Moor. Coincidentally, Black Moor was the home of Carnacki the necromancer. I rode all day and all night.

When I reached the town of Black Moor, I found dust and ash. People were lying in the street, many of whom were dead, many more scorched. Gorn had laid waste to the town. I headed to Carnacki Castle. It was intact.

Carnacki met me at the drawbridge.

"Come no further. Your lover must be stopped. I got close to him and tried to undo your mother's spell before he could hurt anyone else. But it was too complicated even for me. And her magics are far too powerful for me to kill her. The only way Gorn can be stopped is if you convince him to stop this madness or kill him yourself."

"I'm not sure he'll listen to me. And I can't kill him. He's too powerful."

"Only if you remain human. If you were a dragon, you could enlist the help of others like Grim Fire and Black Wing."

"I've been down this road before. I don't want to be a dragon."

"Then your only other option is to kill your mother. That will undo her spell."

"I would be as unsuccessful as you would be. She's protected by all manner of enchantments and warding. It would take dragon fire to penetrate them."

"Then you have answered your own question. Become a dragon and stop Gorn yourself with the help of others, or kill your mother. If you agree to become a dragon, then I can always change you back."

"Fine, do it."

Carnacki waved his hands. A moment later, a slip of parchment and a necklace appeared in the air before me.

"Put on that charm. Then repeat the words written on the parchment."

I did as he asked.

"Spirits of the North, South, East, and West,
Mother of Beasts and all living things,
Turn me into a dragon,
With scales, clawed feet, wings, tail, and crimson hide.
Give me control of fire
And the power of flight.
Let me join the ranks of the Dragon Borne,
If only for a time."

No sooner had I uttered those words than I felt myself being stretched in all directions. When I expanded, my armour burst from me. My pale skin went from pale white to red, my flesh to scales, my fingers to claws, my toes to talons. I could feel my head growing and sprouting bony protrusions.

When the metamorphosis was complete, Carnacki materialized a large mirror before me that I might gaze upon what I had become. As I did, Carnacki remarked, in a smug self-satisfied way, that I was his "...greatest creation yet, a most magnificent creature, godlike and magical."

"Now what, wizard?"

"Now you live your life as a dragon. Go find Gorn. Get him to stop his madness. If he refuses, then you have two options: kill him or kill your mother."

"So be it."

Although I had not been a dragon for very long, I had an intuitive grasp of how to move, and more importantly how to fly. My main concern was, could I kill and eat a cow or pig while it was still alive? The thought seemed repugnant in the abstract, but as my belly growled more and more, the idea seemed less unappealing.

I flew south until I came to a pillar of smoke. I descended into a town, at the centre of which was Gorn. He was making a meal of the courageous townsfolk that had dared to oppose him.

"Hold it right there, big boy. Play time is over."

"Billy! Is that you?"

"You're damn right it's me. What's with all the carnage? Are you auditioning for The Crazy Dragon Gazette?"

"I'm living the life. And now you can live it with me."

"No—you're being a douchebag. The people in those towns you destroyed never did anything to you. So where do you come off burning the towns and eating the people?"

"It's in the Dragon Playbook."

"What playbook is that?"

"This one sent to me by your mother, Medea."

Gorn pulled a large musty tome from underneath his wing pouch. Then he popped it open and with a foreclaw gently turned the pages. "See, it's right here on page fifteen:

When humans say they want peaceful co-existence with dragons, the humans are lying. They are constantly conspiring to enslave and kill the dragon kind. It is therefore incumbent on all dragons to keep the human population off balance through terroristic acts. To burn their cities, towns, and villages. To eat their livestock and poultry, and to eat them. We cannot give them any opportunity to consolidate their forces and move against us.

It didn't take a master alchemist to know my mother was gaslighting Gorn. For what nefarious purpose, I couldn't say. But she was clearly up to no good.

"That's not true. If it were, your friends Black Wing and Grim Fire would be here doing the nasty with you. This is just another one of Medea's tricks to drag you down. For both our sakes, please stop being an asshole to the humans. We have our entire lives ahead of us. We can live them as dragons or as humans as long as you give over this insanity."

"So, you would stay a dragon?"

"If that's what it takes for you to stop, then yes. I will gladly do the whole fire-breathing wing flapping bit with you right down to swallowing cows whole."

"What about your mother?"

"We need to kill her before she can do any more mischief. We're the only ones who can do it since dragon fire is the only thing that her magics can't affect."

"Okay—I'm in. Let's go kill the bitch."

We took wing. After a few refuelling stops at dragon friendly communities, we winged to my mother's ginger-bread hut. When we got there, we called her out. But she didn't show.

"Maybe she's not here."

"Or she's hanging upside down like a bat wrapped in dalmatian fur. Then again, she could be in the cornfield scaring away the crows."

"You really don't like your mother."

"Did you forget she turned you into a dragon?"

"No, but you seem consumed with hate."

"My mother is ugly inside and out. The only reason she never became a coke addict is that she can't stand to look at herself in a mirror. And she would be only too happy to join Hitler's Nazi party, but he stopped taking applications."

At that moment Medea materialized before us. She smirked as she pointed to Gorn with her gnarled, time worn finger.

"He's a sweet kid. Too bad he won't be anything more than a burden on society. After all, he has the attention span of a monkey chewing on a flyswatter."

"We're here to kill you."

"You're certainly welcome to try. Because frankly I would rather get a maple syrup enema and sit on an anthill than listen to your insufferable whining. Or did you think the threat of incineration by dragon fire would make me grovel like a leper at a kissing booth?"

"I've had enough of you. Gorn, let her have it."

Gorn and I lit her up. In an instant, Medea and her ginger-bread house were nothing but ash. I congratulated myself for finally having rid myself of that evil millstone around my neck. Then I heard her cackling the stereotypical laugh of the broom-stick riding witch of old.

I looked around. The only thing I could see was the black smoke spiralling up above us. It seemed to be alive, and it was. My mother's hideous harpy face formed itself from the smoke particles, and clear as a bell I heard her say,

"Silly dragons. You have fried an old, withered body that had outlived its purpose. Now, thanks to you both, and the mystical energy in your dragon breath, I live on as a spirit, one capable of finding a new host. I could not be happier. Trust me, we'll meet again."

The smoke drifted away and with it, Medea, to parts unknown. Gorn and I stared at each other. Any doubts I had about remaining a dragon were dispelled after I learned that Medea was still in the picture. I might not be able to kill her, but as I was ensconced in a dragon body, she would have a hard time killing me. Now the only thing left was to figure out where Gorn and I would live and raise a family of little fire-breathers. In my spare time, I would write a Dragon's Play Book of my own. One where people and dragons for the most part get along, and cooperate for a better life. Sappily sentimental stuff from a mother to be. Did you expect anything less?

KASSI AND THE DESERTED ISLAND
by Ste Whitehouse

'The Pipe-world, Ah'kis, is five thousand miles long and just over ten miles in diameter. It was one of a dozen Arks sent out from Earth to populate distant planets; each meant to journey a mere 200 years at one third light speed. But some accident knocked Ark Six from its course and now 10, 000 years have passed. Kassi seeks her brother who has been kidnapped by 'demons' and now travels north to the end of the world. She is accompanied by Sebastian, a sentient bot of dubious origins with whom she can communicate telepathically. That ability seems to set her apart from the rest of the world's population. This story is set just after she left the City of B'jing.'

The sea lapped against the red sands as gulls wheeled overhead, calling to one another. The sunline held steady in the air above them as the small boat gently cut its way through the water. The four men sat, two alert with swords ready and the other two rowing. In the stern sat Kassi, naked but for cotton shorts. Her skin darkening under the ever watchful line of light far above. The men scowled at her, partly in hope that she would do something stupid so that they had a reason to hit her again. Kassi smiled sweetly, listening not to the sounds around her but to Sebastian's last set of instructions.

To be fair she had made life difficult for the pirates and their captain ever since they had killed most of the crew and passengers from the *Sant Maria del Costa*. They had not actually set weapons upon them but had instead taken only those they deemed 'worthy' and allowed the rest to drift in a damaged and, frankly, leaking boat [1]. Undoubtably none had survived. So Kassi had set herself against the captain and his crew. Become a thorn in his side. Until he'd had enough and had sent her to this island as punishment. The only surprise was that he had lasted twenty three whole days. Twenty three days of taunts and disobedience by the warrior.

The captain's plan, as Sebastian understood it, was to leave her alone for a few weeks. Soften her up so that when they returned she would be much more amenable. There was water and food to be had on the island but nothing else. The four men were to leave her on the beach, hands still tied, and when they returned in a week or two *if* she was alive then so be it. Kassi could still sense Sebastian from the ship as he stood alongside the captain in 'obedience'. The only thing either feared was that loss between them. The telepathic link they had shared for over ten years. What if

---

[1] See Kassi and the Pirates.

it was lost forever? What if the pirates never returned? There were many variables to Kassi's insane plan (Sebastian's words) but what choice did they have? If she stayed, eventually the toil would wear her down.

The small boat slid up onto the beach and the four men exited swiftly. The two oarsmen dropping their oars into the boat and unsheathing long thin rapiers. All four looked at Kassi with a nervous glance. She stood, causing three of the men to step back, before languidly stepping out onto the hot sand. She felt the warmth seep into her toes and couldn't help twist a foot so that gloriously hot sand covered it. She had spent almost seven weeks afloat and this was her first time on dry land (even though Sebastian insisted that each island actually floated around the Circle Sea.)

The one man who had not stepped back, the first mate, a man named Jaqu, indicated that she was to step away from them and the boat. She acquiesced. He indicated further and again she silently walked up the beach until she stood near the deep green fronds of grass and small trees. Birds called overhead and she was sure she heard the chatter of other animals. Sebastian had mentioned monkeys and pigs. Perhaps cats. All feral. Warily the four men pushed the boat back into the surf and jumped in. She blew them all a kiss as best she could with hands still tied firmly. Ten minutes later the narrow pirate ship had hoisted its sails and was already picking up speed, travelling clockwise in a corkscrew around the ocean and away. Eventually Kassi could no longer 'hear' Sebastian's words. For an hour there was a slight 'buzz' and then silence. All around her the island sang and squawked and called and caroused.

She was alone.

Kassi hunted for a rocky outcrop, finding one close to the beach. She then sawed at the ropes that tied her hands together until they split. Already the sunline was beginning to dim, so she quickly found some dry grasses and small twigs before using the small fragment of flint that Sebastian had smuggled to her to light a fire. As the darkness spread she tried a few of the fruit she had collected along with the firewood. The sounds of day faded as the creatures of the night awoke. Insects chirped and the shadows loomed over her. A flickering dance trying hard to escape from the camp fire. Wearily she lay down and slept.

Her first full day was taken up with finding water and gathering more fruit. She found shelter at the foot of a large rock where she could rebuild her fire and sleep better with her back to the rock. She found a number of flattish stones and began to 'knap' them as Sebastian had 'shown her' telepathically. A large stream flowed down from the steep mountain, running crystal clear. Sebastian had said it would be fine to drink, and it was, but she still worried about the fish she saw darting away from her shadow. After all, fish had to pee so even though this was eminently pleasant water to drink, wasn't it also full of fish pee? And poo? Kassi decided to ask Sebastian the next time she saw him. If she saw him again.

The second day she took a curving path up the central mountain, watching the island below just in case she actually was not alone. She saw no signs of human life but from her vantage high up she could see flocks of gaily coloured birds rise as one from the tree tops and heard the odd growl of bigger animals. It was unlikely, or so Sebastian had said, that the island held anything really large; say a tiger or elephant. Even the likelihood of Trolls or other machines was remote. The islands had been playthings, holiday resorts, for the rich thousands of years ago. Places to explore the 'wild' as it were. A wilderness unfettered by machines. There was not even depth enough for a single dwarf. So she felt safe, at least.

During her journey she found a number of bamboo clumps and used the sharpened edge of one of the stones to cut a number down. On the higher slopes she found some firs and brought back a handful of long, straight branches. Back at her camp she found the remains of the fire had been disturbed but she was not concerned. The few paw prints in sight indicated an animal no bigger than a cat. Instead she spent the dying ebb of the day sharpening four of the bamboo shoots and whittling one of the longer firs. She gouged a notch at one end ready to take a long, sharpened stone.

By the fifth day she had found vines to make twine and bound two short spears and sharpened all of the bamboo poles. She had cleared the high ground around her camp and set a small stone wall barely a foot high. Some of the bamboo she used to create a lean-too bound with broad leaves to keep off the occasional splash of rain. Then she went hunting.

By the end of her first week Kassi settled into a routine. She kept at her collection of stone implements and gathered more bamboo and fir branches in the mornings. Using the time to exercise and build her muscles. At noon, when the sunline was hottest, she hunted, catching mostly rabbit but the occasional wild pig. There was a pack of wild dogs but they kept well clear of her, preferring to hunt on the far side of the island.

The afternoons she spent on digging up the small pathway she had created and building what she needed. All the time her mind emptying of the clutter she had carried around with her. She was surprised to find that she enjoyed the solitude. It had been over ten years since she and Sebastian had become linked telepathically and the quietness was... refreshing. She sewed rabbit skins as best she could, recalling tricks her mother had tried patiently to teach her years ago. She took to standing in the stream, spear in hand, ready to catch fish. Enjoying the sublime movement of the cold water around her legs. The smooth touch of the rounded pebbles beneath her feet.

By week four she was fully clothed and meditating. Freeing her mind and losing herself all at once. Taking in the smells and the sights of the world. Relishing the smallness of her boundaries. Happily reciting each tree in her mind as a mantra. In truth she had never been so happy despite the grimness of her daily tasks. The trenches were dug. Not deep. They did not need to be. Just deep enough for men to stumble. Finding the sharpened bamboo ready to receive them.

She carefully created large nets and then wove leaves and small twigs into them. Spreading them over the trenches and covering them with dirt. She steadied the springs and hid the cages of spikes. She practised with a sling using the smooth pebbles from the stream. At night she ate and pondered her existence. If she had remained on board the pirate ship she would have become exhausted. Worn from rowing. Stiff from been chained in place. The burns and scars down her back were worth the effort she had put into annoying the captain. In truth really she hadn't needed to annoy him much.

Now she was free to exercise; to practice with stone knives. To build herself up again.

For ten weeks Kassi worked her body and the island. She felt a peace descend. A loosening of her mind. If the pirates never returned she was good. Great in fact. Happy in herself for the first time in years. Complete in and with herself.

Then one morning she sensed the buzz at the back of her mind.

From the higher slope Kassi could see the narrow pirate vessel approach the island and then wait. She had lit the fires, wet leaves and kindling which created a pleasing smoky finger that literally pointed to where her 'camp' was. She had walked the path from the beach and back two or three times every day until even the most stupidest person could follow. As a long narrow boat was lowered into the water she hurried back down the hillside. Spears and pebbles at her side.

Eventually the narrow skiff was pulled up onto the beach and twelve men stood around waiting. Kassi watched from a tall tree to their left. Hidden in the fronds, her skin muddied and smeared over a deep golden tone. She waited calmly, her mind blank.

Eventually the most heavily armed man muttered a few words and the rest split up. Three men followed him along the well-advertised pathway whilst two groups of four scurried either side. A flanking movement. So they weren't *that* stupid. She swung on vines silently. (Why Sebastian insisted she made a sort of *Aaahuuaa Uaaa Uaaaaaaaa* whenever she swung was beyond her.)

To the right, one of the men was slow and had become separated from his group. She waited. Spun her sling and sent a pebble accurately into the side of his head. He fell with a soft thud. She dropped down. Tied hands and feet and stuffed some leaves into his mouth. Softly she followed the men.

The heavily armed man, she recognised him as Jaqu the First Mate, held a hand up, stopping his group just before the trail of pits and traps. He stepped gingerly forward and pushed his sword down on one of the tight leather springs. Four arrows shot across the clearing. There were a number of grunts, some of appreciation, and then they spread out to avoid the obviously placed traps. The man on the far left never felt the less obvious trap. All he saw was a movement either side and then the cage of spikes was tight around his body. Not even a scream, although the remaining men cried out. One stepped forward, his foot finding not solid ground but netting. He tumbled with a scream that ended with his body impaled on long bamboo spikes. The group of men to their right rushed at the sound and found their own pit of spikes.

Kassi spun her sling and shot a pebble at the third man whilst the First Mate ducked away. The pebble smashed through his skull, splattering the broad leaves with fine red blood and brain matter. The lone remaining survivor of the righthand group staggered into the clearing only to come face to face with a pebble travelling at close to one hundred miles an hour. His face collapsed in on itself. His nose, eyes, vanishing into a dark pit that oozed blood.

An arrow shot over her head as the third group of men entered from the left. Two were archers but neither had any idea where she was exactly. She tugged the vine close by her and something vaguely human swung across the clearing. Both archers fired, hitting the collection of vines and leaves dead centre. If it had been human it would be dead. As it was Kassi was halfway to them before they even noticed. Righthanded she threw a short spear catching one of the archers in the side and throwing him off balance. The second archer dropped his bow and started to draw a short sword. Kassi caught him mid-draw with a second spear in the throat.

As he stumbled to the ground, dying, she took his sword and finally felt complete. Stone was well and good against defenceless pigs and fish but these bastards deserved cold steel. She stepped over to the second archer and tried out her new toy. It cut through the leather jerkin with ease. She was a hoppy bunny as Sebastian said (although as all bunnies hopped she was unsure what it meant). The remaining two men ran at her, each with a curved simitar gleaming in the sunlight.

She danced elegantly to one side. Pirouetted and cartwheeled, just for effect to be honest. The men were used to the feel of wood beneath their feet and cramped decks. The wide open spaces, albeit confined by large acres of trees and vines, confused them. They actually stood still. Looking around and waiting. Like shooting fish in a barrel, as Sebastian would say. (Again this confused her as she had tried it once and the little buggers were hard to hit! Had no one ever seen how *fast* a fish can dart?) With a sigh she danced across the clearing, parried their desultory swings and rearranged the musculature on their arms for them. One screamed and ran away, the second fell in a heap unconscious. The running man found another of her spiked cages. He stopped screaming, (and running, obviously.)

She turned towards the First Mate.

He sneered. "You think you have won? All I have to do is signal and the captain will send the experienced men over. You did well against this swill but once he sends our best you'll die."

She bared her teeth in vague resemblance of a smile. "You forget. I spent a good few weeks aboard. Seven of these were your best." She swung her sword in complex patterns, rolling her shoulders in preparation. "The rest were your most trusted crew members. Good with a sword but not great. Okay at snarling at terrified passengers and concerned crew but pretty hopeless at actually killing someone. It's an art."

"Then I am an artist." He leapt forward, scimitar cutting through the air where Kassi had been seconds before.

She danced again. A delicate mixture of ballet and fighting stances while the first mate stood still.

"You have this whole area trapped, I bargain," he said witheringly.

"In truth you've found all traps. I did not wish to skewer you all. There are things to put in place."

"Like my sword in your gut," he said.

"You took the words right out of my mouth."

He leapt at her, a strong sweep of his blade forcing her backwards. Still it was easily parried. She stepped back and he lunged forward again; and again. Each time she expertly parried. Deftly sidestepping. Shifting weight. Countering the man's every move. Kassi again felt that love of battle bubble up. The sheer joy of pitting yourself in a life or death situation. Unsure how it would be resolved. Aware that at any moment some stray filigree of fate could upend all of your plans and lay you on your back, helpless before your opponent. Some egregious circumstance could cause utter chaos.

Kassi smiled. The sheer exhilaration of combat filled her with glee. She nicked the man's upper arms, each precisely; an inch from the elbow on either side. This really was showing off and Sebastian would be appalled but she could not help herself. When you are at the peak of your abilities you wish people to see; and the man saw. He understood that he was outclassed. Raiding ships at sea. Boarding vessels and cowing merchants was one thing. Taming this wild warrior was something else entirely. He glanced back to the beach, trying to figure out if he could make it back to the boat. If not, could he swim? Could she swim?

"Sorry. My plans entail a certain amount of discretion," she said before forcing him to turn back into the jungle. He began to tire. Made stupid errors but still she did not finish him. Not until they came to a sled resting on a series of rollers. Kassi grinned mischievously. "My apologies. I really did not want to make too much of an effort."

She moved forward. Two thrusts almost blindingly swift. A jab. He parried as best he could, set his feet to carry as much of his weight on the next swing, then found that somehow his body was not responding to his commands. He tried to move but his legs went from under him. A warmth spread across his abdomen. Warm and sticky. Wetness. He could smell blood. Smell his death.

It came quickly. The woman moved into his line of sight. Then shadows engulfed her and all was black. Kassi waited a heartbeat or four then rolled the First Mate onto the sled. This was so much easier than hefting them on her shoulder. At the forest edge she knelt and waited. Waited for the sunline above to fade.

The moonline was a faint smear, high above in the darkened sky. Above that it caught the Circled Sea and reflections glimmered briefly. It seemed to Kassi to be much like stars, as Sebastian had explained them. Dots of light far away. Usually on Ah'kis you can see the light from distant towns or dwellings. Looking up or down the pipe one could see for hundreds of miles and clockwise was always a mere ten or so miles away. That always gave one the sensation that one was enclosed. You could feel the world rise up around you and meet above your head. But here, on the vast ocean, the water appeared as black as a dungeon. Only the odd wave caught the distant moonline. The odd glint of starlight.

She had spent the early part of the darkness dragging those dead onto the small skiff now bobbing gently on the waves. Arranging them so that they 'sat' slumped in the boat. A more motley collection of men she had never seen. Eight of them sat. Dead and bled out. The stench already starting in the humid heat of the night. Kassi untied the rope, pushed the skiff into the waiting ocean, nimbly leaping aboard. She took two of the oars and began to row towards the dark ominous shape of the pirate ship anchored a way off-shore. This was going to take time and effort.

The captain stood on the forward deck viewing the island with unease. Jaqu and the others had set out late morning and despite the dark plume of smoke drifting skywards they all understood that finding the barbarian would prove difficult. Ever since they had boarded that merchant ship she had proven difficult. Most of the men were wary of her and those that weren't had soon found reason to be. Despite the lashings. The withheld food. The brutality. She had proven too hard. He knew that eventually she would break, everyone did. It was just that having such a fierce symbol of resistance on board could be disruptive.

The idea of the island seemed a good one. They had used it once or twice, and once they had found only a few bones and once a deranged slave now more than willing to work for them. Fifty-fifty. Not the worst odds. Still he wondered. The woman was unlike any he had met before. Even her companions from the merchant ship had been an unusually eclectic group. And the merchantmen! They had admitted to murder yet still held the woman in high regard. It was as though she inspired confidence. Such a dangerous trait to have in a slave.

So he waited for his men. Pensive. He had not thought they would discover the woman immediately but Jaqu was supposed to indicate before night fell. It did not bode well. As the captain waited he felt the curve of water around him press in on him. Oppressive and heavy. He caught himself drumming the rail nervously. He'd had the lights above deck dimmed, better to observe the island, and he was pretty sure that the skiff was returning but could not be certain. Damn that bloody machine, he thought. Earlier that evening the thing had brushed accidentally against his desk and somehow dislodged the spyglass he used. He brought it to his eye in any case but all he could see was fractured shadows twisted in the cracks of the lens. When the woman was back in her place he would ask her how better to control the machine. Until then he had locked it away in his cabin. If she could not tame it there was always The Circle of Sighs in B'Jing. He was not quite a Sigh himself but had accrued many of their instruments including a wonderfully ornate short wand which he patted absentmindedly.

'There!' Movement to port. He squinted in the darkness. Shadow on shadow appeared to shift and move. He heard the splash of an oar.

"Ahoy, Mr Jaqu!" he called out, indicating to his crew to stand ready on the port bow.

There was no reply.

He called again. Still nothing. Except the steady splash of oars. 'Why were they not answering?'

"Torches," he whispered, drawing his wand. The crew had thick 'wands' from the Sighs that threw out the sun on command.

Lights splayed the ridged surface of the water, catching spray in brief rainbows. The men waved the torches, indiscriminately zipping back and forth until suddenly one caught the edge of the skiff.

"There! THERE!"

All the lights focused on the lone boat. Long shadows draped from the huddled men on board.

"Jaqu? Drew? Handstadd?" the captain called, but still no one answered. The boat continued to ply its way towards them. He felt, no, knew, that something was wrong. Then it hit him as the splash of oars ceased. Not one of the men he could see was rowing. They merely huddled like waxworks in the bow of the boat. A single man stood. One torch managed to catch them. He saw the woman. Just briefly. Even as he fired his wand she was moving, diving off the skiff and into the black ocean.

The water was cold but Kassi did not mind. She had learnt to swim in the lakes close to her home, way up south where snow lay on the taller hills all year round and people were used to the freezing cold. Bullets hit the water where she had been. Someone, most likely the captain, had a gun; or wand as they called it. She could 'hear' Sebastian muttering but shut him out. After months of solitude she was used to her own thoughts. She pushed on further below the surface, propelling herself forward and under the low sitting vessel. Behind her another bullet spewed into the stygian water.

She sensed rather than saw the ship's hull draw upwards and away from her. Carefully she rose, one hand tentatively ahead to feel the side of the pirate ship. Finally she broke surface and took a deep long breath of cool night air. She was about midway between each end of the ship. Feeling upwards she found a small indentation where she could hold. She pulled herself up quickly, seeking another hold. Above, just out of reach, she could see oar ports with locks. Swinging up she grabbed one of them. She waited for a second and then pushed herself upwards.

Above the oar locks were the gunports. Seven each side. A fancy array of hinges and pulleys made her pathway upwards easier. A thick 'skirt' of wood stood above the gunports. Wide enough to stand on, if precariously, and close to the rail lining the deck. Kassi waited. Catching her breath. Listening to the captain above as he grumbled. She had slipped off the shirt she had been wearing and the captain was complaining that he had fired his 'wand' thinking it was her.

As best as she could tell, all the pirates were watching for her on the far side of the ship. Someone even said that they thought she was dead. Drowned.

"That bitch has nine lives. Like a fucking cat. If she is dead I want to see her fucking body," the captain growled.

Kassi deftly pulled herself up the last couple of metres and slipped silently over the guard rail. She took out two slings and dropped a heavy pebble into each. She stood waiting. Feeling the ship tilt beneath her. Drifting back and forth. Instead of trying to adapt she just focused on the deck. This was the sole space she needed to be aware of. Keeping her eyes on the men and the deck, her world narrowed. Whatever was beyond, and it helped that it was still night and thus pitch black, meant nothing. The deck. It was not moving. The people. They moved, but only in relation to the deck. Nothing more.

She took a deep breath and began to spin both slings. One in each hand. A soft brrrrr of movement settled across the silence. No one noticed, other than her. All eyes were forward, on the black water beyond the deck. She noted who the men were. Those pirates who were the most 'committed'. Choosing two she let go of her left sling. The pebble smashed into the back of the man's head. He toppled forward, briefly leaning on the rail as the men looked in shocked silence. Then he fell head first into the water below. Her second pebble hit a man ten feet from the first. He too toppled against the guard rail, collapsing in a heap. Dead.

The fifteen men looked out into a darkness that seemed to envelope them. The ship was alone in the world. A thing of light separated from Ah'kis. Only when morning came and the moonline turned into the sunline would the world outside exist again. Or so it felt to the captain. He had fired his wand yet still the woman had vanished. Then he had seen the pale ghostly shirt and fired again. It had been instinctive, and wrong. Even as his finger squeezed the trigger he knew that she was not in it. It drifted to the surface like a jelly fish. Billowing almost with life. The bullet did nothing to stop its ascent.

He grunted his dissatisfaction. Looking at his men, he wondered. Only five were definitely loyal. The rest were ex-slaves. Working their way up from oarsman to crew. Three had not yet killed. That always taught him everything he needed to know about men. Any slave would be willing to escape bondage. Any slave would pledge allegiance to him, the captain, but until they killed he never trusted them. It was easy to rush a vessel and terrify merchants. Flash your sword, look intimidating. Be loud. But killing. That took much more. It was when a man had killed for him that he knew that he 'had them'. That part of them would be forever his. A dark, hidden part that he could exploit. Use. Manipulate.

He had seen how easily the woman would kill. *That* part would always be easy; but breaking her had been next to impossible. Now she was probably dead somewhere in the dark, but until he was sure...

Someone muttered. "She's dead. Drowned for sure."

"That bitch has nine lives. Like a fucking cat. If she is dead I want to see her fucking body," he growled.

The men turned their torches back onto the water below. They looked. Carefully and slowly. Foot by foot the circles of light merged and shifted. Nothing.

Then Whillhanson just toppled forward. It was as if he had fainted. Stiff like a board he slowly leant forward. For a second he was steady, the guard rail holding him up. The captain saw the bloody mess that was the back of his head. Then Whillhanson tipped over the rail and into the ocean below. There was a dull splash. Before the captain could say a word, Klyne collapsed in a heap. His two best officers after First Mate Jaqu. Dead.

"Fffuuuuuuuuucck!" someone shouted, and then hell broke loose.

A lad little older than Sin swore, as thirteen men turned to face her. She had dropped the slings and now held two short swords. Before the men moved she was across the deck and striking two more of the captain's men. As they fell she darted back and up the stairs onto the aft deck where the steering wheel sat. She really needed to figure out these nautical terms. Still, first she needed to live long enough to do so.

Five men leapt forward, swords in hand. whilst the remaining eight took long steps decidedly backwards, away from the fight; away from the captain. Smart men, she thought. The captain fired his pistol once but she was already dodging behind the steering wheel thingy.

{It is just called a wheel Kassi luv.}

She kicked the first man who ventured above the level of the floor, knocking him and the others on the stairs back.

{Thank you Sebastian. How I have missed these sparkling interjections}

{Someone got out of bed the wrong side this morning.} Sebastian said in a huff but remained silent afterwards.

{How can there even be a wrong side t... Never mind.}

She stood and swung a sword, catching one of the men ascending the stairs across the brow. Blood arced through the air, followed by shreds of skin and some grey looking brain matter.

God, she loved swords.

The next man she skewered with her right hand sword before kicking him into the men waiting. Two of the eight had been cajoled or had decided to throw in with the captain so she still faced five men. Well, the two were either very stupid or thought very highly of their own skills. Why else leave the safety of a crowd to face a madwoman with a sword?

Kassi leapt from the helm in a bid to find out. She rolled mid-flight, landing on the front two men. Even as she managed to avoid their own weapons. her sword slid down the neck of one of the men and she managed to bring her knee up with all the momentum of her fall into the balls of the second man. Something seemed to explode a little. The second man went exceedingly white and wished to fight no longer. A result in anyone's books (other than the second man's for sure.)

She darted left, feinted right. Chopped at legs and cut through two other men. The remaining stood. A terrified look in his eyes. Like a frightened rabbit that had just had visions of a pot and heaped firewood.

"Boo!" she said.

The fifth man dropped his sword and ran.

She turned to the captain who stood uneasily at the rail, gun in hand.

"I know what you're thinking," she said casually.

"Pardon?" he asked with a tone dripping in indolence and confusion.

"I know exactly what you are thinking right now. That's a mighty fine replica of an old six shooter. Am I right? Of course I'm right." As she spoke Kassi moved subtly forward. "And what you're thinking now is; how many shots did I take? Was it five or was it six? To be honest, in all the excitement I really have no idea myself.

What you have to ask yourself right now, right at this point is: Do I feel lucky?"

She smiled a bright beam of sunshine. "Well, punk? Do you? Do you feel lucky?"

The captain froze. His eyes darting from Kassi's face to the barrel of his pistol and back. Then she stepped forward and hit him.

Five days later the ship rolled with the waves. Kassi was used to it again and stood at the bow, watching the waves undulate. Little flecks of white appeared and disappeared. Sebastian came to her side.

"Was that really necessary?" she asked. "That whole 'do you feel lucky, punk'?"

"It felt culturally appropriate. Besides, it confused him just enough for you to close the gap."

"I could have just thrown the sword," she replied.

"And he would have shot you. Never bring a sword..."

"I know. I know. Never bring a sword to a gunfight. It's not like I had any choice is it?" They both watched the waves for a few minutes. She continued. "I knew. I can count. He had a bullet left."

"Perhaps a bullet but no confidence." Sebastian placed his 'appendages' on top of her hand. She had forgotten how comforting his presence could be.

"Now the decision has been made," he said briskly.

"Great. Can I kill them slowly or do I have to do it quickly?" she said with a laugh.

The mech merely sighed. "It is that sort of puerile humour that makes people distrustful of you, Kassi. They actually think you mean it!"

She snorted.

Sebastian continued. "The damaged skiff has been loaded with provisions and hastily repaired. It should hold for a while at least."

"And we've been sailing from the island since that first morning?"

"Aye. When we freed the oarsmen, and women, they were grateful to you. And of course we have some of the crew from the *Sant Maria del Costa*, so sailing this is fairly easy. A ship is a ship is a ship, after all."

"How many want to leave?"

"A dozen or so. They have families or loved ones. Often someone who is both. They have not been slaves for long and so have a life to return to."

"Fy?" Kassi's voice was dripping with emotion.

"The WatchMother will stay. Says you need an adult to look after you."

Kassi laughed. "Just me?"

Sebastian looked suitably admonished. "Alright. The both of us."

The barbarian woman from the far south stretched. "So let's get on with this. We leave the pirates in the skiff with no oars, correct?"

"Yes. The people onboard thought that we should reciprocate what they did to the passengers of the *Sant Maria del Costa.* Leave them adrift with an equal chance of surviving."

"So." Kassi waited for her big moment. "This is like 'Piratic Justice' Right!?"

"It is Poetic Justice, Kassi." Sebastian replied wearily.

"Come on! How can it NOT be piratic justice? They're pirates!"

"No. I will not have you mangling."

"Mangling? Who's...."

"I say..."

"No..."

".."

HYPERBOREAN BOOKS

THE FOREST GOD

by Rex Mundy

THE BARGIS
by Shreyas Adhikari

She has hair as black as night. Skin as sable as night. Eyes as dark as obsidian. She stands beneath the arched canopy of intertwined mango and apple branches, framed against a dark entrance. Behind her the passage leads to only the gods know where. Perhaps the very womb of the earth.

The girl raises her hands towards me. The fingers are sticky with blood. Red blood, redder than a cherry, redder than a wood rose, redder than a ruby. Her pale, chapped lips open wide like she wanted to devour the entire world. An unearthly shriek tears out of the tender throat.

"Pandurang! You moron!"

He woke up with a jolt. The sunlight seared into his eyes like a hot knife, robbing him of all senses for a full moment. Had this been the hinterlands of the north, some dirty Rohilla would have stuck a dagger beneath his chin right then and laughed maniacally all the time. He berated himself silently while rolling onto his belly and shaking his head several times. It was unbecoming of a warrior to fall asleep on the eve of a mission.

Raghunath sneered at his comrade. He was a handsome man, tall of stature, green-eyed and blessed with a healthy peach complexion that dropped maidens in his lap like fruits in summer. A long, jagged scar ran down the side of his face. Earned during the campaign in Palkhed when he had lost his footing fighting a grizzled Pathan. Raghunath did not think it marred his beauty in the least. On the contrary, women always thought it lent him an air of the mysterious, battle-scarred soldier.

"Should have slept on the way," he remarked.

Pandurang yawned and waved it away. The road had been long and arduous and the Pindaris—the god-awful Pindaris—played dice and sang bawdy songs endlessly. Marathas could sleep while riding; it was a speciality bred into every son of the empire since Shivaji. A very useful trick indeed. But in the hot, humid air of the east it was nigh impossible. He twisted his neck around to check on their companions. Ten warriors in their unwashed tunics and loose trousers, knives held between teeth and eyes roving everywhere, stretched out behind him in a semicircle. Pandurang was rather uncomfortably aware of the fact that they could very easily slit his throat, loot his corpse and vanish into the marshlands and dense towns around if the fancy caught them. Pindaris were not exactly known for loyalty like a regular infantryman from the rest of the realm.

"Kaal Kothri lies just ahead," Raghunath continued, stung by the silence of the older man and filling the awkward silence with his own voice. "It will not be well-defended, but the Nawab must have sent his men after the last time."

Pandurang crawled forward like a child, dragging his rich white uniform along the wet, maggot-ridden mud of the slope. Once he had reached the top, he produced an ornate telescope beset with small sapphires and peered through it. It had been purchased from a French sailor and could carry the sight over a large distance indeed.

There, just beside a sluggish river that trickled like blood in the veins of a giant, stood the village. A cluster of huts with thatched roofs and walls covered by cow dung patties, encircled by a palisade of wooden stakes. Smoke rose from a dozen cookfires. Oxen lowed, donkeys brayed and a lone horse munched on grass in someone's backyard. A gaggle of children played around the well, producing loud, carefree shrieks. A dread seized Pandurang's heart. He had fought enough battles to know that once the blades started singing and the bullets flew, it was the innocent civilians who died first.

But then he saw the soldiers sent to guard them. Bearded, turbaned men possessing arms of corded muscle and thick bull necks. They leaned on spears and muskets while scimitars dangled from their belted waists. Unlike irregular militiamen, these did not dawdle about idly or smoke ganja around a fire, blissfully unaware of the storm that was about to burst upon them. They were grim faced and alert, sweeping the treeline with keen eyes to spot any attempt at an ambush or an attack. It was a testament to the Nawab's fabled hoards of gold that he could afford to hire such talent for his subah.

"Baluchi matchlockmen," Pandurang muttered, replacing the telescope. "Twenty in all. Sharp and well-rested."

The Pindaris hissed foul oaths while Raghunath merely smiled. The former were little more than thugs for hire who preferred to cut a man's throat while he slept. The latter had been trained by the finest war masters of Nagpur and wept if a foe fled before offering a good fight. Both had their uses. Pandurang called two of the Pindaris who carried rifles with them.

"Ali, creep around the edge of the slope and reach that huge banyan there," he pointed out the landmark. "And Mahmud, take the other side directly facing your friend. When I give the signal, fire and keep firing until the skirmish is over."

The scrawny young man named Ali nodded but looked daunted. "Sardar, what is in it for me?"

"Don't you bloody sellswords think of anything other than money?" Raghunath snapped. His righteous anger threatened to bubble to the surface yet again.

"Honour doesn't put food on the plate, sardar. Money does."

Pandurang raised a hand before the situation could worsen. Warriors were a strange lot. They always kept their egos before the success of an expedition and often sacrificed the need of the hour to vainglorious urges. He could not afford a single mistake now.

"Five more shivrais. If the barracks whine about it, I will pay you from my own salary. Now go."

The two Pindaris hugged their slender rifles close to the chest and rose, running away in crouched fashion like apes. The rest huddled closer to him and made their own assumptions about the village. Some tested the edge of their steel. Others whispered prayers to protect themselves against bhut-pret and ifrits. Pandurang did not blame them. For a decade now, bands had been sent to this precise village for raid and plunder. None of them ever came back. The Senapati had once reported to Raghoji himself that there lay some ancient, vile curse upon the region, something that worked its way beneath the skins of men like flaying knives, and corrupted the flesh. That a man of logic could make such conclusions was shocking for the king, who immediately decreed that more raiders would be sent to Kaal Kothri to raid the village and any surrounding hamlets. So more warriors took up the tulwar to prove their valour and vanished forever in the maw of the jungle.

"Do you believe there is indeed a curse here?" Raghunath asked.

Pandurang snorted. The trilling of crickets, the chirping of songbirds and the rustle of the breeze seemed oppressive to him suddenly. All smashing into each other, becoming one horrendous cacophony. He wanted to escape it. Wanted to escape one unholy circus created by nature to another created by mortals. The clangour of freshly honed swords cleaving shield, arm, neck and belly. Watering the earth with gore.

"We'd have been chewed up and spat out by now if there was indeed some monster roaming around. Kaal Kothri has clearly not been touched by one of our bands, meaning calamity befell them well before they could attack." He coughed up a little bit of the dirt that had gotten inside his throat from all the crawling and lying prone for hours. "There's no bogeyman here."

"Do you think the Bengalis are training tigers and panthers to attack us?" Raghunath remained unconvinced.

The other officer shot him an exasperated look. "Time to go to war."

Ali and Mahmud had taken up positions on the high ground, half-hidden by the bushes. The remaining Pindaris had finally girded their loins and firmly clenched dagger and sabre in fists. Raghunath kissed an amulet dangling from his neck and laid a hand upon his tulwar. The screams of birds and monkeys just increased in pitch instead of fading into a sudden silence as usually happened before a fight. It was as if they were trying to warn the people about some calamity about to crash down from the heavens.

Then a brief moment of quiet. The calm before the storm. A bowstring drawn to the ear. The hammer of a musket cocked.

One of the Baluchis below sniffed something and moved forward, one arm raised to warn his comrades. His eyes raked the spot where Pandurang had hidden himself. Once. Twice. They widened in alarm. The Maratha cursed. Damn turbans and their tendency to give away the wearer.

"Har har, Mahadev!" He roared and drew his tulwar in a smooth flourish. At the same time the Pindari sharpshooters opened fore and the Baluchi who had spotted Pandurang died, his skull exploding into bits of bone and brains. The man immediately behind him was thrown back with the force of the bullet slamming into his belly. The other guards wasted no time in readying their weapons and rushing to the front, but by that time the raiders were already charging.

Pandurang and Raghunath led the warriors straight into the middle of the enemy vanguard. When the bards spoke of battle, they tended to gloss over the filthy bits and weave poems of silver words. Only the rank and file soldier knew what a horrifying, gut churning affair it really was. Some of the matchlockmen got off shots but the velocity of the charge saved the Pindaris from getting skewered before they could land a blow. In a heartbeat Pandurang was among the Baluchis, laying about with his elegantly curved sword and slicing off limbs. Raghunath watched his rear and fought like a madman, mixing thrusts and backhands with the dainty footwork of European fencers. He swore like a madman as he slew. Cursing their mothers for giving birth to milksops. Their fathers for teaching them combat well enough. He screamed at them to come forth and experience the honour of falling to a Maratha's blade.

The Baluchis fought well. They were a hardy bunch and loyal to the man who had paid them, but the terrain and the gods were against them. The raiders had pinned them against the palisades of Kaal Kothri and engaged them in savage hand to hand fighting. Their famed, long-barrelled guns were of no use here along with their spears. Men strove breast to breast for supremacy. A Pindari ducked beneath a *pesh-kabz's* slash and drove his own *chhura* into his foe's belly, drawing it to the side so that the resultant gash violently vomited loops of innards. Raghunath got scored in his shield arm and avenged the insult by pushing his scimitar inside the Baluchi's open mouth, angling it so the point burst out of the back of the head. Pandurang was spat at in the eye and blocked his assailant's desperate swing more out of instinct, pulling out and firing a small pistol from point blank range. For his pains, he received a spattering of dark red blood and bowels all over his boots and trousers.

The skirmish lasted about twenty minutes. Three Pindaris died and one had his leg taken off at the knee by a lucky cut. All the Baluchis went down fighting and cursing their killers, gargling blood and thoroughly disembowelled. Pandurang sank his tulwar into the soft soil and panted like a dog. His face was a mask of sweat, grime and gore. A veritable Rakshasa's face. Raghunath wiped his scimitar on a dead man's collar and returned it to the scabbard, grinning triumphantly at Pandurang. Then his face became sombre once again.

"Look."

The villagers had come out of their houses and stood in the middle of the village like lost sheep. Men in dirty dhotis and vests, or bare-chested. Frail women, young and old, clad in saris so repeatedly washed that all the colour had seeped out of them. Children that had been playing just some minutes ago now peeked out from behind their mothers, frozen at the sight of the hard-eyed men glaring back at them. Bathed in the remains of those supposed to protect them.

For a full minute the Marathas and the residents of Kaal Kothri looked at each other. Each gauging the other. Raghunath strode forwards to stand beside his captain, tilting his head so he could speak to Pandurang without taking his eyes off the villagers. As if he did not trust them for even a second.

"What do we do? They are shit scared and unarmed but there is a garrison just three miles north of here," he growled. "If we let them go, they will only inform the Nawab's men. Perhaps they will send cavalry after us."

"No. We ask them to surrender their valuables peacefully and then gallop away before they realize they have been robbed," Pandurang replied. His arms felt like lead. There was an ache somewhere in his groin. He desperately wanted a few hours of uninterrupted sleep.

Before his lieutenant could protest, Pandurang pushed open the rickety gates to the village's entrance and sauntered in. Oddly, the people did not move. They stood still like wax statues and gazed at him with bovine eyes. He found it just the slightest bit; people in most of the villages he had raided in the past either took up whatever tools they could lay their hands on and fought the warriors or simply ran, sobbing and wailing like banshees, towards the nearest outpost where they could hide behind a solid wall of shields and spears.

Pandurang cleared his throat. His Bangla was not as good as his Marathi or Hindi, or even Persian. But he could speak a sort of pidgin. "If you have any gold or silver, give it up now and spare yourselves."

A fly settled on an old man's eye. He did not blink. Pandurang's brow furrowed in curiosity. *What on earth is going on?*

"Do you understand?" he called out, panic making his voice louder unintentionally. "Do you wish to die?"

Raghunath pushed him aside roughly at the same moment that one of the women uttered a guttural scream and ran towards him. In her right hand she clenched a *dao*, like the ones used by Javanese pirates. Her teeth were bared like those of a panther and she looked like she wanted nothing more than to drink his blood. Pandurang crashed down to the ground, jarring every bone in his body the moment Raghunath stepped forward, swiping out his scimitar. The charging woman stepped right into the path of the blade and her head flew off her shoulders, bonking dully of a banana tree and dropping to the ground.

The villagers followed the execution as one. Then they looked back at the Marathas. Growls rumbled out of their chests. Lips began curling back over startlingly white teeth.

"Fire! Fire!" Raghunath screamed. "Kill them all!"

It was a massacre. Pindaris had a nose for trouble and they had already primed their rifles for use, training them upon the mass of villagers. At their officer's command they pulled the triggers in rapid succession. Then dropped the cumbersome guns and pulled out pistols, discharging them at once. The villagers of Kaal Kothri stood no chance. With bestial howls, they tried to rush the raiders but could not get to within even an inch of them before being cut down. Even the little children, half naked and begrimed, transformed into feral cats, hissing at Pandurang and Raghunath. It was like mass hysteria had gripped the populace.

Raghunath gripped Pandurang's arm and pulled him up, upon which the latter simply stared at the pile of corpses before him in utter shock. In all his life and so many battles, he had never seen such an event. There was a ringing in his ears. A sound that sucked in all other sounds and made it a thousand times worse. Like the little, ant like demons banging drums and blowing flutes near the giant Kumbhakarna's head to wake him up.

The Pindaris surged ahead with wild whoops. They knew what they had to do. People who had been warm and breathing just seconds ago were kicked away unceremoniously, some after being checked for bangles or rings. A woman's bloodstained necklace was ripped from her throat and stuffed into a Pindari's pocket. Doors were broken down and huts ransacked. A couple of oxen shied away from all the blood and piss, bellowing in indignation as one leering youth even stabbed the piles of hay for hidden valuables.

"What do you think happened to them?" Raghunath asked, pointing at the corpses. Many of them still had vicious snarls frozen upon their faces. "It's like they were possessed."

Pandurang had his reservations. The Maratha Empire was young but it already placed a huge emphasis on science, arithmetic and logic. He had spent an entire month the previous year at the Pune College, the first of its kind in India, debating theology with a learned pundit from Kashi. Ghosts, spirits, disembodied souls, witches in the woods and rakshasas who lived in the twilight of the world... they were all easily dismissed. Most had not been witnessed by a large number of people, and many who had seen them or claimed such were either under the influence of *bhang* and *afeem*, or they had grown up with tales of monsters lurking in the forest. Forming a preconceived notion from the very beginning. Think there is a demon beneath your bed for two days and you will hear snarling on the third.

But what explained an entire village going mad and attacking fully armed warriors with hands and teeth? He could still see in his mind's eye how all the men and women and children had glared at him with unconcealed malice. Without a flicker of emotion upon their faces. How the fly had landed on the old man's eye and he had not even blinked.

"I have no idea," Pandurang replied softly. The air was ripe with the stench of death. A flash of movement in the distance caught his eye. He shushed his friend and drew a *bicchwa* dagger from his ankle sheath, moving stealthily across the red ground. There... in the dappled shade of a banyan. There was a small shrine, very much like the thousands of little dedications housing idols of gods and goddesses where pilgrims, soldiers or travellers could pray. And someone was hiding behind it.

Pandurang locked eyes with Raghunath and nodded meaningfully at him. Then he counted to three, raised the dagger high and stepped around the shrine quickly. Ready to kill whatever was concealed there.

A girl. Barely ten summers old. Slender as a willow switch. Brown as a nut. She looked up at Pandurang with terror writ large in her doe eyes, shrinking further into herself.

Something made the Maratha stop. He was never a wanton killer of men anyway, but now his hand locked into place as if ghostly fingers had clamped it. He breathed hard, then lowered the *bicchwa* into its sheath again. His arms rose on their own accord and spread towards her in a placating manner.

"Don't be scared," he whispered to the girl. "Don't be scared. I will not harm you."

We probably just killed her parents, he added ruefully in his head. The girl licked her lips and trembled. She had probably heard of Maratha Bargis raiding the rich Bengali countryside before from bards and legends. To see one towering over her, sword hanging at the side and pistol tucked into a saffron cummerbund... must be mind-numbing. He half expected her to bare fangs and jump upon him any moment.

"What is your name?" Pandurang tried again.

She blinked. "Kali."

A smile cleaved his face from side to side. His mind was already racing back to the fields and fens of Bengal to Nagpur, to his estate, the villa with hypostyle halls and muslin curtains skirting large French windows. The chamber he had set aside for Padma. Beloved Padma. His darling, the apple of his eye. A nurse had been begged from the local infirmary to look after her for hefty fees. Doctors had arrived from Travancore, from Paris, from London. All of them had mixed their enzymes and elixirs, measured her temperature, and in the end shaken their heads sadly.

This girl, Kali, reminded him so badly of Padma that it was all Pandurang could do to control his tears. A terrible urge to spring forth and envelop her in a bear hug reared inside him like a snake. He resisted it. The smoke of battle had not settled yet. And she was still frightened as a rabbit caught by wolves.

Kaal Kothri was not as wealthy as some of the other villages in Bengal. Its wealth lay primarily in its fields of wheat and paddy. Crops did not qualify as plunder anymore so the Pindaris had to make do with whatever thin plates of bronze and silver they could find in the humble homes, a piece of anklet here and a necklace of pearls there. Everyone was disappointed. But a bit of glimmer was better than jack squat, as the saying went. One man named Krishna fetched the party's horses from a gully about fifty paces away where they had been hitched. The meagre loot was loaded into saddlebags.

"Kill her and be done with it," Raghunath said. He had come to see what occupied their leader so much. "The king will never approve and the gods will frown upon us forever, but it is an act of mercy."

Pandurang slapped his thigh in anger. "Mercy? Tell me you feel merciful while ramming a knife into a nine year old child's guts."

"There is no mercy in leaving her here. She can't fend for herself. Who will feed her? If you can't kill her then at least bring that nag over here, seat her upon it and send them both galloping to the north. Let them find a larger village. Or a garrison." Raghunath had lost his earlier swagger. Probably because all the sounds of nature had suddenly stopped. The birds, the insects, the frogs. All deathly silent. Overhead, the sun had been swallowed whole by the serpent Ketu and night crept over the land. With night came unease and even men who would trade jokes and sing merrily under usual circumstances found themselves mired in doubt. Goblins were seen behind every rock at night. It was imperative to move out before complete darkness smothered them.

Pandurang made a snap decision. He gently placed his hands on Kali's waist and scooped her up in his strong arms, making for the Kathiawari stallion that one of the Pindaris was holding for him. The other Maratha officer shook his head in disapproval and followed him. "She will not survive, sardar. Where will you keep her? Certainly not a nautch school? Or god forbid, a whorehouse."

He did not answer. Just placed Kali on his horse's back and swung into the saddle. Nagpur was a bustling city. One of the centres of the empire where traders, philosophers, adventurers and people of a thousand different callings and faiths crossed paths daily. One could very easily start their own story there. The stews and nautch schools were a profitable business no doubt, but as a Brahmin he would lose his caste and honour immediately if word got out that a *shiledar* of the Maratha Army had sold a child to one of the perfumed, voluptuous dames who ran these shady institutions. No, he would use his contacts at the College and get her into one of the new-fangled classical literature departments that were springing up from the ground these days.

Deep in his heart he knew he was desperately seeking some sort of redemption. Some respite from the ache that gnawed on his soul day and night.

"We make for Nagpur!" Pandurang called out.

With a flick of the reins they were off, one of the last Bargis sent to plunder the Bengal subah as part of an alliance between Raghoji Bhonsle, Lord of Nagpur, and Rustum Jung, whose brother-in-law had been deposed by the current Nawab. Times were changing. The French had defeated the British in a series of wars to the south. The *Compagnie francaise pour le commerce des Indes Orientales*, also called the French East India Company, had signed a treaty with the ever growing empire which granted them monopoly trading rights in exchange for the promise that the Europeans would remain firmly within their enclaves. Lessons were learned from earlier debacles. The best minds from the dying Mughal Empire and an impoverished England had migrated to Pune to help native Maratha engineers to bring about what the world was calling a stunning feat of modern science. The Industrial Revolution. Soon there would be steam powered carriages and repeating cannons, if the daily rags were to be believed.

The age of savagery and plunder was fast becoming extinct. The Peshwa knew this. His various sardars and generals knew this. The Marathas could no longer be viewed as the horse-warriors of the past who mounted lightning fast skirmishes upon the enemy and vanished hours before an adequate response was organized. When the Europeans looked at India, there should be wonder in their gaze. Not hatred once reserved for the hordes of Genghis Khan or even Attila much farther back. Hence the Bargis were recalled in twos and threes and then altogether. To hell with alliances that corroded reputation.

They rode for ten miles before it became impossible to see the land around them. Pandurang called a halt and camp was made, mostly a fire near a brook and a circle created by the horses. Everyone sat inside the circle and chewed dried strips of meat. Nobody spoke. The recent *firman* that all bandits were to be recalled and absorbed into the army again, hung heavy over their heads. The Pindaris especially. Irregular horsemen and roughshod mercenaries that they were, there were scant opportunities for them to prosper in the coming time.

Kali sat near Pandurang, playing with his horse's mane. The girl had not opened her mouth ever since she told him her name. He carved off pieces of meat from his own rations and gave them to her, and Kali ate them without a word. But apart from that she did not offer any more conversation. The men cast dark glowers at her. None dared question the *shiledar*; he was a gentleman and officer who possessed his own horse and sword. But he knew they did not approve.

Raghunath finished counting his shivrais and tied his pouch tightly to his waist. Then he warmed his hands at the fire, stretched his legs, and cracked his joints. Pandurang watched him keenly. Sure that the man would utter disparagement now. Remind him how he was a fool for bringing along a village girl to a city like Nagpur, where the cultural shock could be crippling for her. But Raghunath said nothing. After a while he simply wished his captain good night, pulled a thick blanket over himself and went to sleep.

The others dozed off soon after that. Pandurang stayed awake for a long time, poking the embers of the fire with a stick and trying to glean scenes from it. The human mind found patterns in the most random of occurrences. In inanimate objects. It created people, cities, seas and animals from fallen leaves and burning faggots.

"Do you want my blanket?" he asked Kali. She had already fallen asleep on the bare grass. Arms acting as a makeshift pillow. Legs folded close to the belly. Smiling as fond memories touched his mind,

Pandurang snuggled beneath his own blanket and closed his eyes.

I see the girl again. This time she is naked, feasting on the carcass of what appears to be a rather large animal. She dips her head into a nest of exposed ribs and tears out great gobbets of flesh. Pink strings of gristle dribble from her mouth. She pays no attention to me, fixated on the act of eating.

I take a closer look at the carcass. The legs are bent at a strange angle and the head is too oval to be a deer or buffalo. The ribs... the hands... I realize not with any particular surprise that it is a man. So badly eviscerated that his features are almost unrecognizable. Even the blood has thickened on his rotted clothes and the loam around him. The girl rips out a long tube of intestines and sucks on it in delight. I cannot be sure in the failing light but it appears to me that the corpse is wearing the white and crimson of a Maratha footman.

Shouts in the morning. Pandurang woke up blearily, head packed with the dense fog of the confusing dream. The camp was in utter disarray. The Pindaris sounded panicked which in itself was not a rarity. Usually they would just pack up and run if a challenge appeared too daunting for them. It was the anxiety in Raghunath's voice which alarmed him.

"What is the matter?" Pandurang asked while rising to his feet in a fluid motion. Kali was also awake. She had taken out a brush of boar's bristle from one of his saddlebags and was brushing the horse's coat with it, crooning a Bangla melody.

Raghunath looked distraught. "Mahmud is gone. We woke up this morning and his pallet was empty. Like he got up and walked away sometime in the night."

Pandurang quickly checked the corral of horses. Mahmud's mare was very much present, stamping her feet and snickering in nervousness. In fact, every beast present was skittish. "He did not take his horse. Or his gold. What kind of a Pindari leaves his gold behind?"

He was at a loss for words. The others checked the bushes and behind the rocks for him, wondering whether he had passed out drunk on rice wine in the night. Pandurang threw a curious glance at Kali but got rid of the subsequent thoughts. The idea that such a small girl could slit a full grown man's throat, drag him to a faraway location and dump the corpse in some muddy ditch was fantastic. Rolling up his sleeves, the officer joined the hunt for the missing *bargi*.

They found him after just an hour of searching. In five different places.

The arms had been ripped off with deliberate slowness and tossed aside like a couple of twigs, bones jutting out of the frayed muscles and skin. In a patch of tall grass. The legs were a mile downstream in the opposite direction, half eaten and crawling with maggots. A copse of mango trees held the intestines which looped around their branches like some macabre garland. Parrots pecked at the pinkish stuff and mocked the warriors as they gazed back with consternation. A large portion of the torso had been abandoned just beneath the tree, propped against the trunk listlessly. Bits of his clothes still stuck to Mahmud's torn, scratched, body.

In a clearing beyond the copse, the Pindari's head stared in abysmal horror at Pandurang from a wooden post which perhaps in some bygone age had served as a road sign. The tongue lolled out, lank and dry, and the low-lidded eyes accused his comrades of not being vigilant enough. The beheading had not been clean.

The less hardy men vomited their dinner and rushed back to the camp, clawing out prayer mats and beads to beseech the heavens for succour. Raghunath said nothing but chewed on his moustache. Pandurang shook his head in sorrow, then removed the head from the post and brought it back, burying the grisly object in near the brook. As far as he knew the man did not have any close relations or next of kin save his band. He would not be missed much. But the manner in which he had been killed... butchered like a sheep. Almost as if the beast which had committed the crime wanted some perverse pleasure out of it.

Kali did not show much interest. She glanced at the severed head mutely for some time before turning back to the horse she was brushing. The Pindaris glared at the child with open hostility now. They were certain she had something to do with the killing.

Pandurang felt doubt himself. He took the girl by her arm and walked a few paces away, kneeling down so he faced her directly. "Child, do you know anything about the man who died? Do you know who might have done this?"

Kali played with a knot in her dirty skirt. "Why did you kill all of them? She did not like it."

The Maratha scowled hard. "Who is she?"

A shout snatched his attention away. Raghunath had discovered something in the ground and he crouched over it, his moustache wobbling furiously. Pandurang jogged over to him. There, on the dark, rich earth fragrant with new rain and rife with the rats and voles and toads who had died with the rain, were a set of hand prints. Wider than a man's palm and longer than an average human's fingers. There was an extra digit which curled backwards from the wrist like a cheetah's dewclaw. Raghunath poked a finger in the print and it sank around two inches in.

"It was here last night," he remarked. "Huge and bloody strong. Armed with claws. And definitely related to us."

Pandurang considered it for a moment. If only the teacher of mathematics could see him now. Dallying with monsters in the vast Bengal subah. "Are you sure it is not a wild beast? Tigers can grow up to terrifying sizes in these parts."

"You have hunted tigers in Kashi. Tell me, does that look like a pug mark to you?"

It did not. They covered up the strange mark with earth to not spook the Pindaris and told them nothing. Kali watched them from a corner of the camp. Her eyes unblinking, filled with neither dread nor alarm. It was a case of cold irony. Hardened soldiers who had fought and slayed countless foes in battle were on the verge of collapse but a slip of a child remained calm. That itself was unsettling.

Pandurang gave orders to mount up and start riding west at full speed. They would reach the borders of Nagpur the next day if the current course was maintained faithfully. Nobody needed any encouragement. They knotted the reins around their hands and drummed their horses' flanks cruelly, sending the animals thundering down the plains. When twilight painted the sky purple about seven hours later the party halted, once again made a circle of horseflesh and lit four fires. One at the centre of the camp and the rest arranged like a triangle around the perimeter, blazing brightly to chase away the phantoms of the night. Meat was passed around along with a hip flask of whiskey. Men settled down to brood.

Raghunath told Pandurang about an incident from ten years ago. A party of *bargis* had set out from Nagardhan to do their lord's bidding, thirty men strong and each one of them a cavalryman of the army. It was time when the ministers still advocated maintaining close ties with Rustum Jung and political correctness was yet not discovered. Out of the thirty men only one ever came back to Nagpur. Deprived of his warhorse and turban, sword and lance. Gibbering nonsense about the night attacking his brothers and carrying them away one by one. Upon examination by doctors from the college, he was declared insane and confined to a sanatorium.

"He kept blabbering about some creature of the night that had four arms and ten heads," Raghunath recounted, gazing dreamily into the dancing flames. "Poor man had had his wits addled by whatever ungodly thing had killed the rest of his band."

Pandurang nodded. Sleep threatened to engulf him. "Maybe he had been tortured. The Nawab's men ambushed them and left one alive to tell the tale."

"Damn it, *shiledar*. You are still thinking like a soldier. Get down from your high horse. Scrounge among the witches, the medicine-wives, the *vamacharis*."

"Are you suggesting our adversary is supernatural in nature?" Pandurang asked.

He tried to inject some contempt into his voice, but drowsiness robbed half of it. The other half was barred by his own confusion. He wondered whether bringing Kali along had been a good decision. By allowing his heart to rule his head, he had actually condemned himself and his men to a doomed fate. But the girl lay curled up at his feet even now, and abandoning her in the wild would be an ever greater sin.

"What else could it be?" The younger man spoke. "Should have taken a priest along. Or at least one of the *vamacharis* who sell charms for a song nowadays everywhere in the empire. Did you see Mahmud today? He was toyed with, Pandurang. Wild animals don't do that."

There was a truth to his words that could not be denied. The man had been utterly destroyed. And whatever took him had come very close to their camp, probably broken his neck to prevent him from crying out in pain, and then dragged him away. The thought that a hideous cannibal monster had been just inches away while he slept gave the Maratha shivers. He took extra care to post two sentries around the camp while all of them slept side by side in a row of pallets. Covered with a thick wad of blankets and weapons close at hand. The slightest rustle, the faintest click of claw against stone, and blades would come singing out of their sheaths. Kali huddled close to Pandurang for warmth and comfort and promptly fell asleep. Regarding her with wary eyes for some time, he willed himself to slumber as well.

The girl stares long and hard at me. I have disturbed her meal and perhaps she considers tearing into me with tooth and nail, tearing out my liver and plucking out the eyes from my head to eat like grapes. The thought stirs my loins. The naked girl resembling a Greek wood nymph, flecked with blood and smeared with mud, hair cascading down the bony shoulders and small breasts. A medley of expressions stamped upon the face. Hunger, caution... lust.

A loud crash yanks her head abruptly to the left. There, something is watching us. From the shadows of the undergrowth. Something tall and black, merely a suggestion of a form. Unmoving. Silent. I squint to see what it is, but the girl seems excited. Dropping the hand she was eating with relish, she darts away into the darkness like a deer. An ululating howl of delight rips out of her lungs.

Raghunath's yell of fright woke everyone up.

In a trice tulwars were rasping to life as warriors sprang to their feet and rushed hither and thither, crying out challenges to various demons. It was still an hour before dawn. Pandurang armed himself with both his sword and pistol and scanned the surroundings, heart hammering in his chest. Raghunath was staring madly at the spot where they had set sentries scant hours before. Both the men no longer stood.

"I saw it!" he cried out. "I saw the fucking monster! I was pretending to sleep when it appeared from there!" A shaky finger pointed at the long line of trees that had flanked them all the way from Kaal Kothri. Seemingly endless. Tall, ancient towers of leaf and bole that hid only the gods knew what unspeakable horrors in their midst. Pandurang felt a frisson of primal fear as he gazed upon them. A raven shrieked back at him, as if daring the brave warrior to explore its home.

Instead, he caught hold of his lieutenant and slapped him viciously across the face. "What did it look like? Where did it go?"

Raghunath gulped. He looked shocked out of his wits, which was quite unnatural for a man of his flamboyance. "Like the night come alive. Too dark."

There was no use getting anything out of him. Pandurang gave the man some whiskey out of his own flask and sent him to sleep while he inspected the dead sentries. Krishna and Ali. Two of the best Pindaris he had fought alongside in many campaigns. Hard men, one from Mirzapur and the other from Indore, who had faced hissing, spitting, much better armoured soldiers of twenty different lands and races and forced them back with sheer muscle. Torn apart like rag dolls now. Cleft open from chin to groin, eyes gouged out leaving black pits behind. And arms broken so badly that nubs of bone protruded from the skin in many places. Their swords were still inside the scabbards and the powder was still dry. Meaning both had been dispatched at the same time or one after the other but so swiftly that they did not have enough time to even comprehend what was happening.

And scattered all around the site were the same abnormally large, humanoid hand prints.

Pandurang dragged the corpses away from the camp and tossed them into one of the bigger fires, adding a load of faggots and some black powder from his store of cartridges to help the process along. The stench of burning flesh charged the air. He came back and ordered the remaining men to stay awake for the rest of the night. They were only too happy to agree. Every man sat with his back to the other and clenched blades tightly, rifles loaded and placed on the ground before them to enable instant firing.

Kali crawled forwards and tugged at Pandurang's sleeve. He stooped low, and she whispered in his ear. "She is out there. Hunting you. I can smell her."

Keeping his voice low so the others could not hear him, he questioned who she meant. "Is it someone from the village?"

"No. She was there when my grandfather decided to found Kaal Kothri with his companions. She was always there, sleeping in caverns beneath our feet. Hunting pig and nilgai in the forests and fields. The occasional child. My grandfather made a deal with her."

Pandurang's curiosity was inflamed further. Could it be that a savage, primal cross between man and monster dwelt in the wild lands around Kaal Kothri? One intelligent enough to understand the various emotions of human beings and feel them itself?

"Tell me more about her. Please."

"We made offerings to her every week. Sometimes a buffalo. Sometimes a mule. Sometimes a couple of chickens. One year she refused all other animals we set before her and took to destroying our fields, so a child was given up." Kali said it so normally that it did not seem she was affected by her people sacrificing livestock and offspring to a barbaric entity. It was quite natural for her.

"And she protects you from bandits in return?" he pressed further.

The girl nodded. "My mother told me once that she is actually a goddess who favours us. So we modelled our lives after her mannerisms. Filing our teeth once the thirteenth year was reached. Eating raw meat."

"What is her name? How do you know she is a female?"

Kali was mute again. She did not have the answers to these questions. Pandurang abandoned the line of inquiry and bade her sleep while he held vigil. The night suddenly seemed to stretch on and on, smothering them all in a veil of Stygian darkness. The trees in the distance swayed as the breeze caressed them, silent and sinister. It seemed like one mammoth trap. Designed to crush men who breached the womb of Bengal with sharp iron in hand and murder in their hearts. One wrong step and the jaws of wood and steel would snap them all up, chew them into bloody bits and spit out what remained.

The day dawned grey and morose. Raghunath had developed a fever which ravaged his body. He shook off all help and mounted his horse himself, though once he was seated firmly in the saddle he simply rested his head on the stallion's neck and closed his eyes. Pandurang drew up beside him with Kali in front of him. The last four Pindaris formed the rear guard. They were bristling with weapons harvested from the dead, primed and ready to go. The riderless nags and mares were also brought along because if nothing, they could fetch a good price in the bazaars.

After an hour Pandurang spotted the post which marked the end of the Bengal subah and beginning of the Maratha Empire. The land dipped unusually, undulating like the coils of a giant subterranean serpent, skipping and hopping till it met a vast wetland where snipe and ducks honked noisily. The air became sweet and light.

Pandurang breathed it in, letting the honeyed taste linger at the back of his throat and spread all the way through his limbs like a balm. Driving out the sense of corruption and unease that had accompanied him since the plunder of Kaal Kothri.

Kali squirmed in her seat. She winced all of a sudden and tried to get down, frantic in her efforts. At the same time the Kathiwari neighed in panic and started rearing; Pandurang retained his seat and his neck only because of his rigorous training at the military school. His hand strayed to the hilt of his tulwar even as he wondered what the matter was.

All the other horses were snorting and whimpering now, striving to break away from the column and bolt. Kali clapped hands to her ears and began writhing. Like in the throes of a seizure. Beside Pandurang, Raghunath slipped down from his saddle—nay, he was pulled down! "Bastards!" Pandurang roared while swinging his legs over the horse's back. He landed on the ground and drew his tulwar, eyes hot and bright as live coals. The Pindari called Kaak stabbed Raghunath multiple times with a dagger in the spot where his shoulder met his neck. The warrior was too weak to defend himself. He just glared at his killer as if that was enough to burn him to ashes, and then died quietly. A tiny stream of blood bubbled out of his mouth. The other Pindaris stood in a circle around their comrade. The swords had not come out of the sheaths yet but three rifles pointed his way. French in design, grooved barrels, premeasured cartridges making it quick to reload. Pandurang made a mental note to ask all the quartermasters of all the Maratha houses to forbid mercenaries from taking weapons from the state stock.

Kaak wiped his bloodied dagger on a length of his own turban and stood up. He did not have the malicious glint of treason in his eyes like most mutineers did. On the contrary, the man looked scared to death. His face was pale as a sheet of mill paper.

"Sardar," Kaak began. "Your reputation as an honest man is well known in Nagpur. If we deserted, you would have come after us with a large troop of *shiledars*."

Pandurang watched his friend and lieutenant lying lifeless upon the ground. In a different land, not even the minarets and stews of his beloved home. He felt despondent and bemused at the same time. Despondent because it was a terrible loss to the army and humanity in general. Bemused because for all his talk of sexual prowess, Raghunath had ultimately died a bachelor and his heart belonging to no woman. He hefted the tulwar in both hands and half-crouched, slipping smoothly into battle position. Kali hid behind him.

"It is all because of her," Kaak continued, pointing at the little girl. His comrades nodded in sullen agreement. "She is cursed. Give her to us."

"You have already committed treason, Pindari," came the growling reply. "That's why the Peshwa advises us against hiring your kind. Unclean, barbaric, uncivilized. And bloody cowards. Don't add to your sins by slaughtering a child."

"Don't preach morals, Maratha." Kaak had grown bold with his act of rebellion. "Two days ago, who ordered us to open fire on a village full of civilians? Your own friend."

He launched into a diatribe against how the empire was a juggernaut that crushed those who defied it underneath it. It was a monolith carved from the bones of a hundred kingdoms and dynasties, a million people. It was the rakshasa that had beggared honest folk in the name of employing them. And while he cursed and spat, the birds fell silent all at once.

"She comes," Kali whispered. Pandurang heard but did not acknowledge it. He sensed the shift in the air as well. The sweetish smell of decay. A feeling of cold dread in his gut. His grip on the sword turned clammy and nigh slipped, but he maintained the posture anyway. If they opened fire he would become paneer cheese within a millisecond and die before he knew he was hit. But before that could happen, an unearthly shriek rang out of the last neck of the woods.

Kaak broke off mid-rant and turned in that direction, all the bravado seeping out of his bladder in a trice. He shouted at his friends to aim muskets and hold. Pandurang had to smile. Lesser men always sought to become leaders in the middle of a crisis by eliminating the ones above them. He bid his time for a lunge that would kill the obnoxious Pindari and save him from getting shot due to knee-jerk reactions from his friends.

Something emerged from the treeline and leaped towards the group at incredible speed. It was taller than the tallest man Pandurang had ever seen, black as boiling pitch and possessing a skull which angled steeply towards the front. The creature's hair billowed like a horse's tail as it ran towards them on all fours, long and braided with little trinkets that appeared to be gold and silver from this distance. Full melon breasts swung wildly from a ridged chest. *Holy Durga, it is indeed a female. A woman almost.* Pandurang fought to keep his rising panic in the nether regions firmly and rooted his feet to the ground. Whatever happened, he could not afford to let his wits be overwhelmed now.

A Pindari fired his musket. The ball slammed into the creature's arm but she did not falter. With a wolfish howl she launched herself upon him and began ripping into the unfortunate man with long, spider like arms. He screamed in mortal agony and bawled like a child, the sound cutting off suddenly when she ripped out his throat. There was blood and excrement everywhere. Another Pindari fired from point blank range and hit again, only to be disembowelled with a casual swipe of dagger like claws. The last Pindari threw away his gun and started to flee. The monster snarled and skewered him with a finger, twisting it inside the wound while blood leaked out like a rivulet.

Kaak twirled his tulwar once and decided he would go down in history as a man who had slain a monster from the bowels of hell. But before he could take even one step forward, Pandurang exploded into action, lopping his head clean off his shoulders. Doing so, he came face to face with the huntress that had stalked his party so long. So close that he could count the wrinkles in her hide.

She had hair as black as night. Skin as sable as night. Eyes as dark as obsidian. In her sharp cheekbones and flabby chin he found a feral beauty. A beauty that only a bard could appreciate. The thin mouth, lined with yellowish fangs, dribbled blood and bits of flesh. She smelled of birth and death and afterbirth. Mould and morning dew, burning wood and freshly turned soil, the salty ammonia odour of piss. The mixture of scents reached inside Pandurang and brushed away his fears, igniting a lust he had not felt for years. He felt his groin harden.

"Don't kill him, mother," Kali chirped. She ran up to the monster and hugged one of her fleshy, elongated legs. Some of the bestial hunger drained out of that alien face. "He's a good man. He protected me from the bad ones."

Pandurang breathed hard, leaning on his tulwar's hilt for support. He felt euphoric and depressed at the same time. As if he had one foot each in two boats, sailing down the holy Ganges. The monster growled once and nuzzled Kali like she was her child, keeping her eyes on the man all the time. She did not trust humans. Violent humans.

"You can go, uncle." Kali turned around to speak to him. There was a smile upon the girl's pinched face. A bright smile. She was with someone she loved and trusted. "She came for me. And she will not harm you."

Perhaps it was the sheer outlandishness of the scene in front of him or something else, but suddenly Pandurang snapped out of the reverie. A watchful god had grabbed his hair and pulled his head out of the pond of honey he had been drowning in. The Maratha officer awakened. Priorities were asserted again.

"If I go back to Nagpur," he told Kali. "I will have to file an official report with the Senapati. Word will reach the Peshwa and he will hastily commission a huge army to march into Bengal and capture, or kill, your... mother."

Kali played with one of the hooked fingers and buried her face in the creature's downy chest. "You will all die. No matter how strong you are. Mother was out hunting in Morshidabad when you arrived. You escaped her. The next time fortune may not favour you."

His eyes narrowed. "The Empire has some of the world's best warriors. What can one creature do against a thousand full-blooded soldiers?"

The smile turned sinister. "Who said there is only one?"

CHORDS
by Lamont Turner

Hal Spencer stared at his hand and scowled. He spread it out on the table, took the cleaver in his other hand, and brought it down on his wrist. He passed out immediately.

"What do you make of it, Doc?" Maggie Taft, a reporter for the Enquirer asked, watching the orderly adjust the straps securing Spencer to his bed.

"Hard to tell," Doctor Richmond responded, prodding Hal's stump with the tip of his pen. "We've had to keep him sedated since they brought him in."

"It isn't everyday a famous guitarist hacks off his own hand," Maggie said. "Think he was high?"

"The toxicology report says he wasn't," Richmond said, scribbling something on his clipboard. "Although he did have that reputation. It's possible the years of self-abuse caught up with him. That kind of life style can have long term effects. He went on and on about some old bluesman who'd sold him a guitar, and how a ghost had seeped from the strings into his hand."

"Whistling Bill Toombs," Spenser groaned. "I cheated him on the guitar. He died and came back to punish me."

"I'm sorry, Mr. Spencer. I didn't realize you were awake," Richmond said, nodding at the door to signal the orderly to get a nurse. "We're going to have to up your medication."

"I'm fine now," Spenser rasped. "It's all over. He can't make me play those chords anymore."

"I understand you believe you were possessed by some kind of spirit," the reporter said, earning a dirty look from Richmond.

"Haunted!" Spenser shouted, straining against the straps. "At first it was in the guitar, making me play his damn songs! Then, after I smashed the cursed thing, the ghost jumped into my hand. After that it was the same no matter what guitar I played!"

"What kind of songs?" Maggie asked as a nurse appeared, to nudge her away from the bed.

"It was his songs—only they were weird, like he'd added to them after spending some time in hell. It scared me to hear what I was playing, but I couldn't resist. I had to play!"

The nurse loosened the restraints to adjust Spenser's I.V. while Richmond went out into the hall to signal the orderly to return in case there was any trouble.

"What did the music sound like?" Maggie asked from the corner she'd been pushed into.

"It was horrible, like the screams of the damned!" Spencer said. "I can almost hear them now..." He suddenly blanched, his remaining hand clutching the rail of his bed.

"Calm down, Mr. Spencer," the nurse said, laying a hand on his chest. He didn't seem to hear her.

"My God! I can still hear it," he whispered, staring up at the nurse as if looking for confirmation. "I didn't get rid of him. He's in my head now."

Before the orderly could make it across the room, Spenser had slipped his restraints, pushed the nurse aside, and hurled himself through the glass of the window.

"What have you done?" the doctor shouted at the reporter as they both stared through the broken pane at the body crumpled on the street below.

"I wanted to see how he'd react," Maggie said, trying to silence the blues riff coming from her phone. "I never imagined he'd be able to move so fast."

She had to tap on the screen of her phone several times before the music stopped, just as the sound of the guitar was replaced by harsh, taunting laughter.

THE LUCK OF IT
by Joseph Farley

"Probability. That's what it comes down to, isn't it?"

"That what the prophets wrote."

"Right. How does anyone know they really exist? How do they know they really are here?"

"We know when others affirm our existence. We cannot trust our own thoughts on the matter."

"Sounds silly when you think about it. A lame excuse for philosophy."

"We have all felt that way at one point or another, but..."

"...But reality is what it is. I've seen it happen. You've seen it happen. An individual begins to doubt their own existence. No one intervenes, and, puff, they disappear in a cloud of dust."

"It is so unlikely that any of us could exist. It boggles the mind that we are here."

"Only if you think about it. That's why we meditate. That's why we laugh. That's why we go to wild parties, drink too much, do other things, and wake up in strange places."

"Yes. It all helps. But when you wake up a day or two after the party..."

"It's twice as bad. That question of meaning. The pondering of existence..."

"I've lost so many friends after a crazy weekend, and not just from accidents."

"Still, we are what we are. We think what we think. And, sometimes, we do what we have to do."

"It's a pity there are so few of us left."

"There used to be billions of us, running about, distracted by work, hobbies, entertainment, the pursuit of pleasure."

"It was a golden age."

"You can't put off the big thoughts forever, no matter how high you get. It had to catch up with the world sometime. Heavy thoughts."

"It was as if it all accumulated in the atmosphere over generations then rained down on ours."

"Not just our generation. It has been going on for many generations before ours. We just had the opportunity to notice because we were goofing off at the time. Before then it was just 'Where's Harold gone?' 'He must be on vacation' or 'Maybe he called out sick' or "He's been talking about moving to California, maybe he finally did it.'"

"The absurdity of it. Who would want to move to California?"

"I'm talking about before the eruptions, before California turned into a volcanic wasteland. No one would want to live there. California is strictly a tourist thing. Now where was I?"

"You were talking about the world before people realized that every moment was a matter of chance."

"Before people realized that they could suddenly disapparate."

"That too."

"Fortunately you are still here."

"As are you."

"What? What? Why am I fading?"

"Sorry. I still have my doubts."

"You little bugger. Two can play at that game."

Fewer than two hundred remained. All were members of the order. It was the only club around.

They stayed together all day, every day, in the great hall, giving each other hugs, telling jokes, reassuring one another that they mattered, and that they did, in fact, exist. It was a tough sell. Even the Grand Master and his Chief Acolyte had succumbed to the blight. Their dust had joined the swirling clouds outside.

Ungla was tired of the jokes. They had grown old and stale. There was nothing new to amuse her. Meditation no longer worked for her. It just made her fall asleep. She began to doubt. The doubts grew.

A figure saw what was happening before the rest of the survivors. Mugwum jumped over a row of chairs, ran to Ungla, and put his arms around her.

"Don't go," he said. "You exist. I love you. You exist. I need you. You exist. I want you."

It did no good.

Ungla's final words were, "Ew! Get your filthy hands off me, you spotty bastard."

Ungla turned to dust, a small swirling cloud that blew towards the door, quietly opened it, closed it behind her, and merged with the storm outside.

Mugwum wept as the dust ran from his fingers.

"What's the point?"

He too turned to dust, fumbled with the door knob, but eventually got out of the Great Hall and joined the storm.

Those who still lived patted each other on the back and passed out certificates of appreciation.

Panglot refused to accept his certificate.

"Sorry," he said. "Have enough of them. Don't know what to do with them. I only have a small cell. Barely enough for a cot."

"You need one. It proves you exist. You are not ignored."

"You could burn it when winter comes to keep warm."

"I've got enough already to burn for the next ten winters," Panglot said.

This was not a lie. Thanks to greenhouse warming winter only lasted a few days before the weather returned to searing heat. Winter was, at most, a mild chill in the air. With proper training, you did not need a fire to stay warm. You could be naked through it. Or put on a sweater.

"You could smoke it," said an encouraging voice. "Hemp paper."

"No thanks," Panglot said. "Got plenty."

Panglot stared at all the well-meaning faces. He was tired of the hugs, the pats on the back, the participation trophies. Meditation bothered his knees. And none of them understood his humour.

The more he thought about it the more he realized he really did not like any of them. Never really had. He'd just gone with the flow, followed the crowd, what little there was of it. So he had joined the order. What else could he have done? Outside was nothing but heat and the dust storm. There were times when he wanted to disappear like so many others had, but he could not, no matter how hard he tried. He believed too strongly in his own existence, whatever that was. He wasn't so sure about the rest.

Doubt is contagious. A shudder went through the Great Hall.

Come to think of it, I would probably be happier by myself. Probably get along nicely.

Did I think that or say it out loud?

This was ultimate blasphemy. Its sinfulness sent out ripples. People began to wonder and disappear.

This made staying in the hall with the rest of the order even less appealing.

"I think I'll just go outside for a bit and walk around," Panglot announced.

People clung to him.

"You cannot go!"

"It's too hot!"

"You'll turn to dust!"

"Fine with me," Panglot said. "Better than being stuck in here with you lot."

He shook hands and bits of dust off his arms and legs and walked to the door. He ignored the pleas and puffs of dust behind him. He opened the door, went out, and closed it behind him. Panglot smiled and walked into the dust storm. He disappeared.

For a long time there was only dust. Then the dust thinned out. Panglot emerged from the storm. The sun was out. It was mild. There was grass. Green grass. And trees. An amusement park stood in the distance. There were no ticket takers or security guards at the gate. The rides were running. Best of all, there were no lines.

HYPERBOREAN BOOKS

THE MISSIONARY DIED AT DAWN

by Rex Mundy

RARE
by Toban Barnes

The butcher glared at me from the corner of the funeral home. He was tall and pale and wore his wrinkled skin like a wet rag over protruding bones. Over a black suit and tie, he wore a spotless black apron. It was this attire that earned him the title of butcher.

The funeral home was full of family and friends all making their way in a line toward my father's coffin. I got in line alone and tucked my hands in my pockets. It smelled like the smell you get when a swimming pool has just been cleaned, mixed with the sweet scent of perfume and cologne. The carpet was a flat, faded red.

"Oh, Harvey." I heard my aunt before being wrapped in rolls of fat. "I was wondering when we'd see you."

"Yeah, sorry about that," I said in a tight breath, "I had some issues this morning."

She loosened her grip and moved her hands to my shoulders. "That's what your mother said." Her neck fat flung like a chicken's wattle as she looked toward the chapel.

I followed her gaze and saw my mother on a wooden pew talking with my Uncle Ken.

I felt my eyes pull to where the butcher stood. He was watching the crowd, but his eyes moved to mine. He gave me a slight nod.

"Hey," Aunt Malissa grabbed my cheeks. "Don't you worry about him. This is your father's funeral. Don't let him take your mind off what's important."

I nodded and felt some relief when my aunt went to bug some other family member. This relief soured into regret when I saw the butcher walking straight for me.

I looked for another family member. They could talk about dad, hug me, or grab my cheeks. Anything to avoid the man in the black apron. But everyone was aware of the butcher's movements and avoided eye contact.

"Can I wait in line with you?" the butcher asked.

"Y-yeah, that's fine." Up close, I noticed his lips were the colour of frostbite and he reeked of a strong spice.

"Thank you." He tucked himself next to me, so our shoulders brushed together. "I haven't seen your father since the mortician got him all cleaned up."

I couldn't help but cringe in discomfort.

"That wasn't appropriate," he said, putting a skeletal hand to his lips, "I apologize."

I looked at him; his dark green eyes locked onto mine. "It's fine," I said, "There's no point in hiding what you did to him. Everyone here already knows."

He scoffed, "I'm not trying to hide anything, Harvey. This just isn't the place to talk about such things."

When we reached my father's coffin, I hoped that would signal the end of our conversation.

My father was cleaner than I had ever seen him. As my eyes examined his stiff corpse, I couldn't help but look for an indent in his grey suit. "What piece did you take?"

"Harvey," the butcher hissed in my ear, sending chills up the back of my neck, "don't ask that now. Not yet."

"Then when? When are we going to do it?"

"Your mother didn't tell you? How strange."

I glanced back to see people keeping their distance. "Well, it's not something that comes up. Especially over dinner."

The butcher chuckled. "But you have no issues bringing it up at your father's coffin?"

He had a point; I didn't know why I wanted to know. The suspense just felt so heavy. And I didn't know what else to say.

"Your mother scheduled the transfer immediately after the service." He rested his cold hand on my shoulder, and I felt ice bleed through my shirt. "I promise I'll answer all of your questions then."

I nodded and turned away, "Fine."

I kept my eyes straight ahead, forcing myself not to look back. I went into the chapel and found my mom still sitting on a wooden pew, now talking with a small group.

The chapel walls were covered in panels of rustic wood and wooded beams held the roof at a point above us. My mother must have said something because once she saw me approaching, the group dispersed. She looked like a Victorian ghost in her white flowing dress.

"Hey, Mom."

"Hey, Harv."

I bent down and hugged her. Her body felt thin. "How are you feeling?"

She shrugged and her eyes became glassy. "How are you?"

"I'm fine." I gritted my teeth and looked back toward the coffin. I didn't see the man in the black apron. "It's just hard to think about Dad when that butcher is glaring at me."

"He's not a butcher, Harv, he's the funeral home's memory transfer official." Mom grabbed my hand and jerked it toward her. "You don't have to do it, Harv, you know that, don't you?"

"I don't want to." I teared up at this confession, "but it's like what you said this morning, it's a tradition."

My mom's eyes scanned my face.

I took a deep breath. "I know it's important to you. It'll be okay."

She rubbed my hand with her soft fingers, "You're brave, Harv." Then she turned her head away, "In a way, it keeps your father alive. Thanks to you, we'll always have a piece of him with us."

I pulled my hand from my mom's grip, "Yeah, I know."

I sat with my mother, greeting family and friends until the services started.

The service was standard. Some of my dad's friends told stories. One man spoke briefly about how "Dave will still be with us." He looked right at me when he said it.

As the service approached its end, I felt anxiety build inside me. I was like a kid waiting in a doctor's office for a shot.

I helped carry my father's coffin into a hearse with crowds following behind. Family and friends moved to their cars, and I considered running to mine. But my mom grabbed the back of my sleeve like she knew what I was thinking.

"Listen, the burial isn't for another hour. If you're feeling okay, you can come. But please, if you have any side effects, just head home and get some sleep."

"It won't be very long, Miss Shepard." It was the butcher; he was standing next to my mom. "While side effects vary, he'll probably feel fine." He gestured back toward the funeral home. "Are you ready?"

I swallowed the emotion that was crawling from my stomach. "Yeah, let's go."

The butcher led me back through the chapel and downstairs into a hallway. Lights hung from chains, leaving enough space between to create curtains of shadow across the hall. He stopped at a door with a silver plaque reading, IOBA Memory Transfer Office, Do Not Enter.

The butcher produced a key and fidgeted with the knob. The door cracked open to a room concealed in darkness.

"Go ahead, Harvey," he said, waving his arm into the door.

As soon as I stepped in, the lights flashed on with a buzz. The room was cold. The walls and furniture were a smooth chrome that reflected light like a mirror. There was a table, two chairs, and a black door in the back. It smelt rusty, like the inside of an old metal lunchbox.

The butcher stepped in behind me and shut the door. "Please, take a seat."

I obeyed, sliding into the smooth metal chair. I could hear him messing with his key in the lock before he joined me at the table.

He sighed in relief. "Well, Harvey, now is your chance to ask your questions. I promise I'll do my best to answer them."

"What's with the room?"

"You don't like it?" he said with a chuckle.

"No, it's freaky. And it's cold."

The butcher nodded, his blue lips slipping into a smile, "It's designed to show cleanliness." He gestured a hand across the room, "The floors are shining white, you can see your reflection in the walls and furniture," he leaned in closer, "and not a drop of blood in sight."

I pushed myself back in my chair.

"I don't mean to scare you, Harvey. But when people think about what we do, they imagine a butcher's shop, which as you can see, is not the case."

"But you don't do your work in here, do you?"

"The most important part of the procedure is done here. I, of course, do the preparation elsewhere." He glanced back at the door behind him.

"Does that room look like a butcher's shop?" I asked, folding my arms.

"I'm afraid not," he winked. "I'm quite clean."

I stared at him, the sound of lightbulbs buzzing in my ear.

"Well," the butcher stood, "if you have no more questions, I'll go get to work."

"Wait," I said, "will I lose anything? Like a part of myself?"

He smiled softly and tilted his head. "No, Harvey, you will only gain from this procedure."

"But what will I gain?" I asked. "What if I get something I don't want?"

"I don't know what you'll gain. But almost everyone who undergoes the procedure has received good memories." He approached the black door and cracked it open. "Besides, even bad memories can be beneficial." He slipped through the door and shut it behind him.

Five minutes passed until the man in the black apron returned. In one hand, he carried a plate topped with a silver cloche, in the other, a white folded napkin.

He set the plate in front of me, and I could see my reflection on the silver cover. He took the white cloth and unwrapped it. Inside there was a silver fork, spoon, and knife. He removed the utensils one by one, then picked up the white cloth and held it up like a magician about to cover a birdcage. "May I?"

I nodded, keeping my hands in fists at my lap.

With his bony hands, he tucked the napkin's corner down my shirt. He stepped back, admiring the scene, then returned to his seat.

In one quick jerk, he removed the cloche. "I'm sorry I can't offer you water, but liquids seem to interfere with the transfer."

The plate was the colour of cream and hosted a small filet of red meat and a clump of white potatoes. A small pool of red testified to the rawness of the meat.

I swallowed hard. "Where's the meat from?" I asked. "What part of him?"

"I'm obligated to answer your question by the rules of my organization. But I must advise against it. I think it's best not to think about such things."

I could feel my brain twirling in my skull. "I still want to know."

He sighed as he brushed his hands down his long black apron. "The cut is from your father's left thigh, heated but not grilled. Grilling can damage the memory transfer."

I picked up the fork and poked at the potatoes.

"You don't have to eat those, but it may help you with the meat if you eat them together."

I jabbed my fork into the meat. Blood bubbled out like juice from a grape. It rushed across the plate, turning the white potatoes pink.

I dropped the fork. I couldn't cut it, not when it was this raw.

"Close your eyes," the butcher said, reaching for my fork.

"Hey, wait," I said, moving for the fork. But he beat me to it.

"The quicker we get this done, the better off you'll be." He spun the fork in his fingers.

I took a deep breath. He was right, and I knew I couldn't do this alone. I closed my eyes and could hear the tinkle of metal and the scratching of glass.

"It's just a steak," the butcher said, nearly whispering. "It's rare, but it's just a steak."

I could feel the presence of the fork at my lips but couldn't open them.

"It's alright, Harvey, it's just a little potato."

I loosened my lips to speak, and the fork was shoved into my mouth. It scratched against my teeth and was flicked out between my lips. It was done in an instant.

I let the chunk of meat sit on my tongue for a moment, but once I felt the crimson juices stir into my saliva, I chewed.

At first, I chomped it like a piece of gum, pushing the meat around my mouth. But once the first flecks of flesh made their way down my throat, I felt my body begin to tingle. I got goosebumps and my arm hairs pricked up.

I smelled my father's cologne. I could see my dad talking to Mom on their front porch. It was cold, and Mom smiled in a way I'd never seen. It felt like warm water was being poured over my muscles and was pooling at my feet.

"How is it?" the butcher asked.

I opened my eyes. The fork was resting against my plate, the tips a slight translucent red. I reached for the utensils and cut into the flesh.

The feelings returned with each nibble. One bite, I saw my dad in rush hour traffic, the next, he was in a classroom—the knowledge he had gained was becoming mine. Another, and he had a bloody man pinned to a brick wall. I could smell copper and sweat. I could feel the excitement.

I shovelled in bite after bite, like someone desperately feeding a furnace. The meat was gone after a minute. I then went for the potatoes, focusing only on the parts soaked in blood, but they didn't give me the memories, they didn't do anything.

For an instant, I thought about asking for more, but I realized how wrong that would be.

The man watched with satisfaction on his face, "You did very well, Harvey."

I could feel my father's memories becoming blurrier, like a weakened signal. "Something's wrong, I, I can't remember. I'm losing them."

"It's all right," the butcher reached for my plate. "They will return slowly, and more memories will come. Give it a couple of days to allow your body to fully absorb the flesh." He lifted the plate and examined it with a smile. "Still some potato, but not a scrap of meat left."

THE DEVIL'S DOWNFALL
by Andrew Bell

"My spirit shall not always strive with man."
— Genesis 6:3

David Corbin, 42, crossed the room, cut through the square of light, and took his place in his seat. On his desk stood a Disney World cup, dirty with neglect. A small chip along its rim caught the light sometimes. There was also a chip in one of its big ears that jutted out the side. It was a gift from Marcy, the girl from the front desk. She had legs and... that was it, nothing else; a pair of legs at the desk, answering phones and shuffling paper around. When she brought the little trinket back with her, it was like the Holy Grail to him, it was a step closer on that illusive ladder in her stockings. That was, until a week or so later, that David found out she had visited the place with her new boyfriend. He still drank from it, but it rarely got an oil change. Sometimes pens and pencils sat in it.

He sometimes thought he carried a plague, and that something was growing on the side of his body; and people usually put two and two together to make thirty five, thought it was catching. Giving him a wide berth, their eyes often met, but he would never engage in conversation with them. Often times they would nudge each other accidentally by the water machine, apologise; grabbing a pen or a ream of paper for the Xerox machine. They'd acknowledge each other, say sorry then get on with things. They'd look, then, hurriedly, turn away.

You see, David was one of those people that never seemed to be busy, yet always got things done. He'd never broke a sweat in ten years, that's how cool he was. There was something not quite right about him.

"So, how you're going to get to the bottom of this one?" asked Detective Stevens, coughing into a hand-kerchief. He quickly looked at its contents, grimaced and then stuffed the rag into his back pocket. "Huh?"

Detective Corbin looked up from the ripped stomach of the corpse. He wasn't listening. His attention was for the creature sitting beside him on the rock. Silently, it had surveyed the woman, that seemed older than her appearance would imply, and it screwed its face up in deep concentration, before shaking its head. It looked at him, tears forming at the corners of its eyes.

"Could you turn around—"

"I always thought you were like that," replied Stevens dryly, lighting a cigarette.

"—and go as far away from my scene as possible, please?" he finished his sentence. "Don't smoke near here, you dick!"

The other man clicked his teeth like a petulant child, and walked off, drawing deeply on his cigarette.

Skin cracked like salted leather, as features appeared in the creature's oval face. Something akin to a mouth formed, like a tear full of jagged and blackened teeth. Its eyes lacked pupils, and veins spread across them like wild ivy. The eyes wore cataracts like the skin of an old hound; hung loose, pulled down by a great weight. It never slept, just hid within the folds of the detective's clothes when it got weak. And each day it was getting lighter, losing weight, it seemed. It was humanoid in form, it featured the appendages that the pictures depicted; two arms, two legs, but no sexual organs. This way, try as they might, the human host could never understand its emotions. It was the one thing that distinguished them, gave them identity, a soul. These creatures were the stuff of a child's nightmares, even though they were real. Everyone had their misconceptions, but this seemed to fool Corbin.

When the stakes had been high, almost as high as everyone around the table, through the haze of still cigar smoke, the little critter didn't look so bad. Of course, it had taken a while before he had accepted it instead of hard cash. After all, God only knew what it would do once it left the room. It had been a gamble alright. Instead of a jaw full of broken teeth, he had gone home with the creature. Days passed into months, and the demon had been faithful. He had been happy.

Now it was starting to feel the burn. Restless, it moved about a lot. Like a lizard on sand, it lifted its limbs from the ground. And when it cooled, rested them a while. This behaviour had occurred only recently, like the constant reminder of time.

"Any ideas?" said Corbin, under his breath, waiting for Stevens to get out of earshot.

Hands cupped and covered its eyes, pulling skin, like a tight hood, over its face. The hood hid its eyes and mouth. Tiny, razor fine nails dug into the grooves there; that had been designed over the years. Corbin could see a slight inflation, as though it were breathing. But he knew that it was already dead. At least it didn't have a pulse when it was offered. Air had no right in its lungs, in fact, it didn't have any. The skin was membranous and clotted in various areas. The flesh was as thin as a bat's wing, gossamer thin. Thick vessels throbbed, like veins pumping blood, around its being. It hunched its shoulder-like parts, and it folded down into a small ball shape, like an egg. Then it suddenly unfolded, and stood upright, reaching almost nine feet, He first feared it. Then he grew to see it for what it really was; beneath him.

"Woman... here... open... man... had... advantage... took... what... machined... her... insides..." it spoke in slurred clicks and clacks, and croaky here and there, like fingers scrabbling through pebbles at the bottom of a fish bowl. And Corbin understood every word.

"All I need is a name and address."

"Take... you... there," it replied, climbing onto his back, up his sleeves, slowly crawling underneath his jacket. It wrapped like a long snake, around his body, overlapping itself over and over. To others, Corbin should look obese, carrying this extra being everywhere he went, but his clothes hung loosely. It couldn't be seen by any other person. That was what the guy at the table had said. The thing had been a "great weight" to him. Corbin couldn't understand that; it had been nothing but a massive help to his investigations. "Brian... Thompson... 43... Cornhill... Street."

Corbin nodded, smiled, then made his way to his car. He passed Stevens on the way.

As he turned the engine, the younger man relaxed in the passenger seat. "Got an address?" he asked.

Corbin didn't say a word, just reversed from the kerb, and drove away.

It waited until late then went to the library. It was a place that only it knew of, at the shoulder of a black hill. No living man went there, for he would have to see God's face first. It was invisible. And when the detective was in slumber, it could just reach that damnable place. It took the book from the shelf on high.

The page crackled like bones, and it enjoyed the smell and dryness of the parchment. The tome was bound in flesh, hidden amongst the dust and dead insects of the furthest shelf. It needed to stretch as far as it could to reach it. It was not human hide, it was thicker and heavier. Hairs dotted here and there, and if you looked closely one would see it move, its pores breathe.

The demon smiled as it read, moving its strange mouth, soundlessly, its claw tracing the jagged writing. It read the words, moving its ragged mouth, and its smile wavered. It knew time, and it was quickly disappearing, like sand through a glass. It had to act, and fast.

The book spoke of a distant land that had no name. Four earthbound spirits had supposedly spoke with the Creator Himself, and scribbled His words down. It was a way from this damned existence, a place of purity, and goodness. The Holy Bible was its name, and it had to wear gloves when it touched its butterfly wing pages. It spoke of an insistency; that once the ball was set in motion, there was no turning back. Passages warned of a heat that would approach until it had passed through this time and space. To the end it would drift, taking all on its way as though it was air.

The creature had been a plaything for too long, a human had owned him before Corbin. It had been a slave, a creature even lower than its human counter-part. But this excuse inherited it because he could not shake off the things he had done. The card game had lasted all night, and it was one of the desperate player's last resort. From "misplaced" mortgage deeds to a being in a box. Anything went. It all depended on a card. A demon in a will, captured by law. It was cursed to be passed from dead hands to the damned. Five hundred years, or maybe more, it had curled about a human thing's waist, just because of the things it had committed in some past existence. Then it was put in a box, to be used or forgotten. To be at a human's beck and call.

It understood how a soul had to live with its history, how the past had a way of creeping, or pulling one back, but now it was time to exit. It had had enough.

It followed the words, reading voraciously, turning the pages. It read every night. There was so much to learn, it thought. Yet it came down to one thing, just one simple thing, to break free. It just might work. And when it was done, it gently, slowly, put the book back. It sat until dawn, thinking over its plans. And when Corbin was about to stir, it climbed in beside him, like a lover returning to the warmth of his beating heart. It was a while before its smile faded. It knew that a fire was coming. So it had moved, feeling the heat move beneath its skin, as if maggots writhed there.

It had to catch him first.

Detective Stevens watched the officers escort Brian Thompson to the waiting police van and let the handcuffed man get comfortable in his seat before climbing in beside him. Then they drove away. Stevens lit another cigarette. He looked over at the obligatory twitching curtains of the homes along the street.

"How many of you knew he was here, eh?" he mumbled, almost whispered, the words. The clouds were filling with rain, and he felt the first needles of it touch his cheek. Corbin's little mole had to be hiding somewhere close. He shook his head, then climbed behind the wheel of his car, and broke away from the kerb.

It wrapped its arm around his waist, slightly tight for comfort, thought the detective, walking away from the coroner's office.

Her name had been Billy Danes, and her parents had identified her by the small home-made tattoo of a hummingbird on her wrist-

We told her not to go to her friend's that night. How we argued to her about catching something with that tattoo

-other than that, she had been unrecognisable when the police had dredged the river for her missing remains.

He had passed the killer's details onto other detectives then called it a day. He passed the Danes' family in the hall. They were a bunch of arms and legs, a heap of human being, cuddled-up and crying for their daughter, their sister...

Corbin entered a well of sunshine, descended the steps, and left gloom behind him. He patted the creature, affectionately.

It waited, patiently.

That night, it woke up from its bed on the curve of the man's body. The dream had been too real. It cried silently, in pain, rubbing its flesh with its nails. Walking across the carpet, back and forth, leaving small patches of skin where it had moved, it remembered how time was quickly making it its own.

The dream was like any other. Around its waist, like cement, holding it in place, was a chain. It was made from fire. Orange and red flames licked around it as it tried to pull away, but it was futile. It knew sin. It had for thousands of years. But this one, this discrepancy, was a tale it would never tell and get away with. It just couldn't fathom out why. Despite trying to remember the details, it knew that now was the time to act. It set its plans.

Corbin felt the hood removed forcibly from his head, his black hair caught in his eyes. The darkness around him was palpable, and he could smell thin dust floating in the motes around him. He tried to move his hands, but they were chained fast, with handcuffs. The same went for his feet, he realised, trying to kick. Then he froze, the familiar scent of rotten fruit and dead flowers filled his surroundings.

"Show yourself, I know you're there," he said, his voice thunderous in the small room. For it had to be a small size, after all, his voice was ricocheting off the close sides

"We're alone, my child. I swear," said the voice.

The detective jolted furiously at the sound. It was a loud but gentle voice, one that was strange to him. It spoke with a heavy, old, tone. It was slow and deliberate, as though with tiredness and resignation.

"Nothing will leave this place," said the voice. "Whatever you want off of your chest, this is a little archaic, but the right place to do it."

"Just... tell me," said Corbin, his throat as dry as freshly fallen leaves. "Where am I?"

"There has to be something on your chest, if you don't know that—"

"Where is this place, please?"

There followed a moment's silence, then the person spoke.

"I've never stepped in a church before, let alone a confessional booth," said Corbin, trying to pull at his restraints.

"Here at St. Anderson's, I understand," the voice chuckled, dryly.

"... say... hello... to... the... priest..." the creature said, its face appearing in the darkness.

The air caught in the detective's throat, and he looked down, to see one of the creature's large razor-sharp claws press against his belly. "I... said..."

"Hello-hello, father."

"Please forgive me if I don't ask you your name. I won't tell you mine," the older man said. "Here, we are anonymous. Nothing will leave these walls; you have my word on that."

Corbin looked into the face of the demon, saw the saliva drip like living wires from its scabrous mouth. It was smiling.

"I... I... don't know why I'm here..."

The claw pressed even further against his tummy, threatening to break the skin. The face was an inch from his now, spittle almost touched his chin.

"Confess... to... the... nice... man... and... you'll... never... see... me... again," said the creature.

"Confess what—I don't—"

"Just talk," said the priest, softly. "All will be well."

"You... heard... the... man," said the demon. "... I'll... tell... you... what... to... say... or... else..."

"Or else?"

"You... die..."

Silence as Corbin sat still, the claw pressed in his side. He watched its edge break the skin, a tiny pearl of blood appeared, and ran along the serrated bone. Breath caught in his throat, afraid of the damage it was capable of. Then he saw the gauze, and the faint outline of a face behind it. Like a cameo, he saw its profile; wondering if he was there at all.

"I... say... words... you... copy... what... I... say... yes?"

Corbin nodded, fear in his eyes. He could feel the beads of sweat roll from under his arms.

Slowly, the demon chose his words.

Corbin did as the creature asked of him, having to sit in silence for a faint spell, as the priest, hearing such filth, couldn't help stepping out for fresh air now and again.

"I cannot believe what kind... of man, he must think I am?" the man whispered, hearing someone throw up noisily, beyond the confessional booth.

"I... don't... care..."

"He's coming back in," said Corbin, trying to keep his voice at a low level. The sound of hinges moving in the confessional booth beside him, broke the solemnity of where he was, like a heavy boot through thin ice. He didn't just feel small, he felt insignificant.

"I'm sorry," stuttered the priest, his voice hoarse. "You... can carry on, if you... really have to."

If you wish. He was meant to ask if I wish to carry on.

Corbin took a deep breath, asking the other man if he was okay to hear the last of his words.

"I've had to sit through worse stories," the priest lied, trying to sprinkle the place with his version of humour. But it wasn't working. "Erm, please. Go on, son."

"That... was the first time I—" Corbin started, looking at the creature beside him, "that was the first time I had eaten human entrails. But that wasn't the worst thing I had been ordered to carry out."

"Go on," the priest, eventually. There was an air of trepidation in his voice, as though he needed to hear the story, yet his stomach was turning with revulsion.

He heard the words but could not believe he was relaying them; it was soul-destroying. Tears ran down his face, but he wiped them away, before the creature could see them. Corbin sat up straight and cleared his throat. He noticed the ever-widening patch, the deep red stain of blood, in his shirt.

"The room was at the bottom of the garden. Tools adorned the dusty shelves. It was a shed that had small barrels of home brewed wines and beers here and there.

Mouse traps and rotten lumps of cheese dotted about the dusty floor. In the window, a fly hung lifeless, in a spider's cobweb. When it was time to raise the dead from beneath, the place had been the perfect hiding place. Nobody knew they'd crawl from there, nobody believed.

"I knew not what was required of me... until I led the victims there. Then one by one, the others came. Knocking their dead fists against the wooden boards. I had to rip up the floor, let their blood-red eyes see the dimness of the room. They looked like me... they could have been from the same spawn... but I threw... I threw the young... I threw the victims, their throats freshly cut, at the ground. The dead lapped their tongues like thirsty dogs, at the open arteries... then they pulled their meal... down into the ground. I recovered the ground as best as I could. He rewarded me with the freedom of a human man... and I went in to the dark and stole from... from cribs—look, can I stop for some fresh air? I... I think I'm going to be sick." Corbin wanted to throw open the doors of the booth before the priest or the demon had time to answer. But he had been bound, and nothing could stop the helplessness he felt.

The creature leant forward in the dark oppressiveness, smiling at the outline seen in the gauze. The old man held a cloth to his mouth, and his thoughts were as visible as a candle burning in the umbra. He wished the old man could hear him, surely, he had that power? But the detective would wear his sins for him, and he shall be worthy again... the book said so.

Corbin saw a bar of sharp autumn light lance through the shadows, and the demon quickly looked away. Dust swam about in the motes, like microscopic atoms.

The demon grimaced, covering the hole where its nose should be.

"What the hell do you think I eat? Roses?" mumbled the detective, getting comfortable.

"You're... ready—"

"Let's just get this over with," Corbin, replied. His nose was almost touching the creature's face. He didn't think hate could burn through his skin, to rise this far to the surface. And he wanted the creature to see it in his eyes.

"I am... running... out... of... truths..." it said, a tone of sorrow in its voice. "My... time... is... short."

"There's a bottle of whiskey waiting for me back home," Corbin replied, his voice barely a whisper. "It's the only spirit I want to see."

It turned to the gauze patch in the wall then started to speak, and the detective closed his eyes, and repeated what he heard; a tear rolled down his cheek. Then he stopped, suddenly relaxing somewhat, although what he said turned his stomach. He realised that... no matter what he said, everything would be okay. He sat up straighter in his chair. Whatever he said wouldn't go anywhere, no matter what it did to his reputation as a man. He looked around in the darkness, smiling wanly.

"What could... you... be... smiling... about...?"

"Say whatever you want," Corbin chuckled. "Say whatever you want."

It looked over at the square on the wall, the sound of breathing, just beyond.

"Before we go on," said the priest, "I must warn you that, to save a soul as yours, you should seek the help of the local constabulary—"

"I've heard it all before, old man," said Corbin. "No offence." He looked at the creature he had won in a card game and felt something akin to pity for the shrivelled-up excuse. "I say my piece, walk away, all's forgotten and forgiven. I know the hypocrisy, so do you."

There was silence in the next few seconds, and as the faint outline moved behind the gauze, they relaxed in their seats.

"Your... time... is... almost... done," the demon said in Corbin's ear. His gravel-like voice was followed by the softness of laughter, almost too human, he thought.

Corbin closed his eyes, feeling the rise of the pores in his cheek; the smell of burning hair tangible in the small confines of the booth. He readjusted his position to get more comfortable, but again, he felt the burning sensation slowly spreading across his clothing. Now was not the time for awkwardness, he said to himself. Soon it would be over, he just needed to stay still. But he couldn't help feeling as though the room was changing into an oven. He felt the beads of sweat zigzag down his back.

"Nothing... can... hinder... my... progress—"

"What's wrong with you?" hissed Corbin, his breath rattling in his chest. Blotches swam before his eyes in the darkness.

The face stared blankly at the detective, a lump bobbing up and down in its throat. It stood still, suddenly remembering. As though his crimes were far too heinous to tell. But the thoughts were of a different kind.

"You wanted me to... say those things," the detective said, under his breath. "They can't go back now."

Then it started to speak once more, but this time, it shook with fear and something akin to dread. It grabbed Corbin by the lapels and squeezed them. No words came, just the heat from his face. It was as though it wanted to say something, something it couldn't quite recall. And slowly, it loosened its grip, letting him fall to the ground.

The detective instinctively put his hand to his throat, a tightness there.

"What the hell is wrong with you, huh?" he said, breathing deeply.

The creature curled into a ball, holding its head, and shook. Corbin reached out, but pulled back his hand. The cuffs rattled in the darkness. The heat of the small confessional booth was almost intolerable, and it was getting hotter.

Corbin turned to the door to let in some air, but he stopped, his eyes widening.

Small tendrils of smoke licked at the air around its shoulders as it hugged itself. It was as though it needed to generate heat in its body.

"I don't know what to do."

Suddenly, the demon looked up. Tears coursed down its cheeks, its body continuing to rock back and forth.

"It's... too... late," it croaked, a flicker of flame appearing in the smoke on its shoulders. "I... was... there... I... saw... the... miracle... I... didn't... believe..."

"I don't understand."

Already the flesh was starting to crisp and blister on its face. A small eye quickly covered in cataracts, popped, then ran down its cheek. As if it was made from wax, its face started to misalign, and fall to one side. Corbin could hear the bones break, and grimaced.

"I... was... in... paradise... when... it... fell," it said, trying to manipulate its tongue, but what looked like teeth fell onto the floor. "I've... no... way... in... now..."

"I'm atoned, isn't that right, father?" said Corbin, almost choking on the smoke. He felt the twang of his heart strings almost. "Surely what I've told you will... atone for... my sins?" he added, looking down at the thing in the corner.

"I've... read... the... good... book," said the demon. "It... is... over... The... Nazarene... healed... the... weeping... the... suffering... I... didn't... believe..."

Corbin wanted to sing and dance, to cry the place down with the relief he felt inside. He also felt a kind of sadness. If he was to carry on and relay the creature's sinful past, he thought, and to a priest of all people, then it was on the right road to Heaven? Right?

"You... have killed," said Corbin. "Now that's a sin."

"Yes... but... that... is... pardonable..."

"No," shouted Corbin. "This is insane. The worst sin is cutting a man down? Surely?"

The demon shook its head, curling into a foetal position. Smoke continued to rise from it, and this time the detective had to kick out with his feet, to push open the booth's door to clear the air.

He made his way down the aisle, coughing. The chains there hung on to his skin like claws. And when he reached the large oak front doors, he threw them wide, and took the steps three at a time. The air felt delicious in his lungs, he didn't look back.

The priest slowly opened the confessional door and peered inside. There weren't even the signs of a struggle. The floor was as highly polished as always. The small seat was warm at his touch, but apart from that, it was as though the place hadn't even been occupied. He looked inside once more, but there was nothing there. He looked over at the entrance, the doors still closing slowly, then he shut the booth.

The creature burst into flames, yet nobody could see it. In the corner of the booth, tongues of fire licked at the body, devoured it. And like ash, it fell apart.

Corbin looked everywhere for the creature, but it was nowhere in his apartment. He even checked all of the closets, to see if it was hidden amongst some of his old junk. But it had gone. Although he was now free to live his own life, the detective could still feel a loss. He even pined for it. He remembered its final moments, trying to make sense of the madness. After all, it had almost got to where it wanted to be.

With this thought, he switched on his laptop, and found some whiskey in an old bottle, pouring it into a dirty mug. He waited for the laptop to boot up, then searched for old quotes. There had to be something there, he thought, taking a long draught of the hot liquid. He was about to retrieve some ice from the kitchen when he stopped in his tracks.

"But..."

He read the words, then switched to another site, just in case they somehow had it wrong, but...

He leaned in closer, and read the quote:

"Therefore, I say to you, every sin and blasphemy will be forgiven men, but the blasphemy against the Spirit will not be forgiven."

Mathew 12:31.

CREMATE YOUR DEAD

by Carl Bluesy

Lem's eyes were sealed shut and felt heavier than when he lay down for bed. He found getting back to sleep was a more laborious task than he expected. As he attempted to re-position himself, Len found this to be as impossible as his attempt to fall back to sleep.

No matter how hard Lem tried to roll onto his side, his body refused to move. As fear took hold of Lem, he tried to open his eyes to see what was holding him in place. Lem's eyes refused to open. Sleep became the last thing on his mind as fear became a full-blown panic. With great determination, Lem concentrated on forcing his body to move in any direction. With no success, he lay in bed in a petrified state as minutes passed to hours. The longer that Lem lay there, the more his clothing irritated him.

The singing of the birds gave way to people driving their cars and mowing their lawns. Lem's confinement became a vicious cycle. The more Lem panicked, the more his bed aggravated him. This made it hard to concentrate and calm himself. After lying in a state of fear for a long period, Lem was able to relax, despite not understanding his situation. The itching sensation in his body became more of a tingle. Having a loved one on the way to help offered Lem some solace.

A wave of relief flooded his body when the doorbell rang. "Help is here," he thought.

The voice of Lem's daughter's echoed through the halls. Lem tried to call out to her, only to find he could not move his lips. She made her way to the bedroom. Rebecca dropped her keys to the floor and ran the rest of the way to her father. She grabbed Lem by the shoulders and shook him to wake him. What had begun as gentle rocking with her soothing voice soon became a violent shake with her heartbreaking screams begging Lem to wake up.

"Wake up, Dad! Wake up!"

Lem was shocked to hear his daughter call him Dad. He had lost the title of dad long ago. Finding him in such a predicament was not the best way to start the birthday he had promised her. Lem told her he would make more time for her since he was had been forced to retire. At first, it hurt when she rejected him. Although he could not blame her. He knew he was a poor excuse for a father. After a few months of calling her, she agreed to meet up with Lem for breakfast on her birthday. Rebecca didn't waste time once it became clear Lem wasn't going to wake up. She ran out to the phone Lem kept in the hall; it was the only phone Lem owned.

In less than ten minutes of Rebecca's phone call, the paramedics had arrived. Lem felt so thankful to feel their helping hands examining his body.

"They'll get me back on my feet," he thought.

Lem tried to think about how he was going to thank Rebecca for getting the help he needed.

"I will treat her to dinner, a spa day, or buy her a house," nothing seemed big enough. This was when Lem overheard the paramedics pronouncing him dead.

"DEAD! DEAD? That's absurd," thought Lem.

He tried to yell at them, to let them know he was alive. All the effort he gave was for nothing since Lem was unable to move his lips. Rebecca sobbed in the hallway outside of Lem's bedroom as the paramedics removed Lem him from his bed. A zipper was pulled up from his feet and past his head. Soon they lifted Lem onto a gurney and pushed him through the front door of his house. It sent a shock through his body. Lem found himself in disbelief at what was happening.

A crowd of people gathered in front of Lem's house, they murmured to one another when the paramedics rushed him outside. No vehicles passed by Lem's street as they moved him. He found this odd since this was a busy street in the morning. The quiet allowed Lem to listen to the pleasant chirps of birds once again. The birds singing drowned out the sound of the gossiping community.

A sweet song of birds calmed Lem and gave him the hope things would be okay, despite how bleak it seemed in the back of the ambulance. The irritating babble of the crowd at the front of Lem's house soon drowned out the pleasant sounds of the birds. When the ambulance doors shut, Lem wondered if he would ever see his home again.

The ride to what Lem assumed was the hospital seemed endless. Upon his arrival, they rolled him in and did not stop until what Lem believed to be an elevator. From there they rolled him into a cold room. Lem was sure he would end up with frostbite. His inability to move his body made the cold spread much faster.

Not only was Lem freezing, he was experiencing hunger pains, leaving no part of him free of pain, from his chilled exterior to his internal organs.

Lem could feel his stretcher being pushed, he could only assume he would be presented to a physician. He heard a ding and the sound of mechanical doors opening. He was now sure he was on an elevator.

Following another ding, the stretcher began moving again. People yelled out from every direction. It was all so overwhelming for Lem. He then found himself pushed into a room free of chaos.

A man with an authoritative voice entered, he gave directions to all around him.

"When did he get in? Bring the tray over here. Pass me my gloves," he said.

"This must be the physician. Thank God, there's still hope for me to survive," Lem thought.

The doctor asked the nurse to prep the patient.

"Soon I will be put to sleep.

"When I wake up, my life will return to normal, then I will put this harrowing experience behind me where it belongs."

Lem assumed they would soon put a mask on his face. Why he was surprised when they gave him nothing for the pain, he could not say. A cold scalpel cut into his skin as if he were a piece of raw meat. It was like nothing he had ever experienced. All he could do was lie there and accept it. With no sedative or painkiller, they cut his chest open with force. Lem's body might have been unmoving and silent on the outside. But on the inside, he was screaming in agony.

The excruciating pain remained constant from start to finish. In a unique way, he felt his insides as their hands and tools entered him. Lem's insides chilled as they pulled his organs from his body in a way he never expected to be possible. They dug deeper into him than he ever thought they could, it was as if they were cutting into his soul. Soon there was nothing but air filling the region where his innards had been. The breeze inside him sent chills through both his body and his soul.

It was as if Lem's mind was trying to repress the memory even while it was happening. The pain was still unbearable after regaining awareness. When Lem's eyes opened for the first time since the ordeal started, he got a glimpse of the white room. He could see a surgeon standing over him, bloody scalpel in hand. That was before a bright light blinded him again. His eyes were too sensitive to light after having them shut for so long.

When they finished removing Lem's organs, they pierced his skin with what he assumed to be a needle as they stitched him back together. It did not take long, but it was a wasted effort. Without his organs, Lem would be dead before any infection or disease could kill him.

When they finished sewing Lem's body back together, they pushed the gurney back down to a freezing room. Lem was sure he would be dead in a matter of minutes. They had taken him apart, he thought to himself.

"I will need a miracle to survive the next hour."

Lem tried to come to terms with his fate. He reflected on his accomplishments, his kids, his career, and all the wonderful times he had enjoyed. A calming peace washed over him.

He should have stopped his thoughts there, with the happy memories, and not let his head fill with the dark images. All Lem had never done. The moments in his children's lives he would miss. Lem dreamt of the day he might walk Rebecca down the aisle, a dream he realized at this point would never happen.

Lem continued to reminisce, wishing he could relive his life with less regret. As he lay there motionless and freezing, he hadn't a clue about what was keeping him alive or if he even was alive. He could only assume his sense of time was off. With nothing to keep him distracted, all the pain worsened.

"Just a little longer," Lem kept telling himself. Each time he believed it a little less.

"What an outstanding length of time for a body to carry on functioning with missing organs," Lem thought.

Lem assumed he had passed away and transcended into limbo until someone pushed their way past the door and grabbed onto his stretcher. He was moving once again.

Lem was loaded into a vehicle. The sounds of the vehicle's engine along with the hum of voices was a pleasant change from the sounds of silence he had become accustomed to. When the vibration from the ride ceased, Lem was clueless about his destination.

They moved him into another quiet room. Hands manipulated Lem's body as they dressed him, the clothing, and the new surface Lem was placed on were soft and comfortable. The room was a comfortable temperature, Lem was thrilled his body had a chance to warm.

The sounds building in the room worried Lem. As people entered, they came closer. He did not recognize the voices until they came closer to his body, at which time Lem recognized the voices of many family members. Still, some remained a mystery to him. It broke his heart to listen to them as they sobbed, relating past events they had shared.

After a few guests had a private moment with Lem, the voices quieted down to a whisper as selected people gave their speeches. Nothing shared was even close to how Lem thought he would be remembered. He lay there coming to terms with the fact he had died, he would never see his friends or family members again. Lem listened to their last goodbyes. This brought him great emotional pain, surpassing the experience of his organs being removed.

A gentleman talked about the time they had spent on the golf course. He spoke of how Lem always kept his cool, even in the hardest of times. It must have been a co-worker speaking, Lem realized. Anyone who knew him in his personal life knew Lem was quick to anger. He would always yell over spilled milk. Those things seemed insignificant to him as he lay there.

There was a brief break between speeches in which they played Lem's favourite song. No matter what the situation was, the old folk song always rang true. This situation was no different.

The speeches ceased. Lem never thought he would experience this part of life. Or death. So many questions about what comes next filled Lem's head. The doors opened as they wheeled him outside. He enjoyed the sweet lullaby of the nearby birds, singing him down to his last sleep. The songs of the birds were cut short by the shrill, wailing sound of bagpipes playing an old cliché song. Lem lay there like a scared child, as the priest said his last prayer. They lowered Lem down into his grave, a slow and dreadful process.

When people faded away one by one, Lem found himself surrounded by silence again. Yet the darkness was worse, as he knew it surrounded him. Still better than freezing to death. Lem reflected on all that had transpired in his life. His life seemed to happen in an underwhelming flash, filled with missed opportunities. There was a rhythmic pounding above him. It did not take long to understand the source of what struck his coffin was dirt being thrown down on it. Lem tried to keep calm with peaceful thoughts, but they were soon replaced with anxiety and fear.

The sound of a small fly buzzing inside his coffin broke his solitude six feet under. The fly became a great annoyance, making it hard to focus on anything else. Lem was searching for something to kill his anxiety in the dead silence. But this buzzing wasn't a suitable method of relief.

"The fly's life will be short," Lem told himself. "And it will soon be dead like me."

The buzzing of the fly did not cease, instead, it grew, as the annoyance gained company. Various parts of Lem's body itched from the incision wounds. The pain worsened as time passed and became impossible to ignore. Lem's skin was moving, the parts in motion grew sore. The skin on different areas of his body broke open. The skin around his neck was the first to break, causing fluids to leak out. As it continued, Lem noticed a sensation to it, as if it were squirming its way out of him.

Lem felt little legs crawling all over his body. He was aware of something still buried under his skin as flies picked away at him. He could not understand how so many flies had got into his coffin. Dozens of flies seemed to surround his body. With a sickening thought, Lem realized they had been with him since their birth as maggots. They rose from the dirt, followed by them eating their way into his skin and back out again in a cruel cycle. They feasted away at what remained of Lem's festering body.

The discomfort grew to tremendous heights as they broke more ground, eating away at his body. Lem lay there with an empty stomach as breakfast passed to lunch, and lunch to dinner, and dinner back to breakfast.

"When will this nightmare end?" Lem wondered.

His body had died, but his thoughts were still very much alive. What would happen when these flies and time completely removed all his flesh until nothing but bones remained? He did not know for certain, but it couldn't happen soon enough.

"The end must be near. Please, let the end be near!" Lem begged.

Lem thought back to the days leading up to his death. If he could have one last conversation with his loved ones, he would tell them to "Cremate your dead!"

EMPIRE OF THE MOON AND STARS
by Simon Bleaken

Our lights pierced the thick darkness of the shaft, those deep depths where the only sounds were the distant echoing drips of moisture and a faint furtive scurrying of unseen things. Kaz flashed me a glance and I read the alarm in her eyes. We both hoped it was rats, but we both knew it probably wasn't.

There was fear down here, a palpable terror that hung in the air. It smelt like sour sweat, and it mingled with the damp musk of the tunnel network. Another smell hit us then, the stomach-wrenching stench of fresh vomit as Delv staggered into view, wiping his mouth with the back of his hand. His face was pale and greasy in the light of our torches, and his boots and the bottoms of his fatigues were spattered in puke.

"You need to work on your aim," Kaz ribbed him teasingly, but the humour fell flat. Nobody felt like laughing, not down here. Not after what we'd just seen.

It was finding the missing patrol that had done it, those shredded fragments covering the tunnel floor, each so torn apart it was impossible to even be sure how many bodies we were looking at. The leeches hadn't done that, which meant there was a stalker down here somewhere. We were on the right track at least, but that didn't make us feel any better. It meant we were in more danger than we cared to admit. These tunnels were normally the only safe way to move about during the day. Okay, safe was a relative term, but they were definitely far less risky than the surface while the sun was out. Nobody could survive up there during the day anymore, not out in the open at least. You could thank the leeches for that, for forcing human beings to become nocturnal, for stealing away our daylight world and forcing us into a new empire of the moon and stars.

In truth, we called them leeches, but nobody knew what they really were. They were slimy segmented things, covered in greasy scales and spiny hooked appendages, with mouths like lampreys. They only came out during the day, at night they slithered away into cracks and burrows, and seemed to shy away from dark spaces altogether. The darkness apparently activated a natural sleep-cycle in the creatures, made them vulnerable, so they hid and slept until the sun's warm rays woke them once more. But what made them truly terrifying was the speed with which they could swarm a person, and those jaws, once they clamped on, were nearly impossible to prise off.

These sinister new additions to the fauna of our planet were the unfortunate side effects of a disastrous first contact with the only alien visitors to have openly made themselves known to humanity. Things had not gone well, we barely avoided war with them, and when they left, they left their cockroaches behind. Some felt it had been a deliberate contamination, perhaps the first stage in a long occupation. Nobody knew for sure.

That had been three years ago, and we were still learning to adapt to the changes in our world. Whole cities had been rapidly abandoned when it was discovered that during the day there was no reliable means of keeping the leeches at bay. Walls were scaled with alarming ease, chimneys became a feeding chute down which the creatures could tumble unharmed and cat flaps also provided an all too easy means of ingress. Only locked doors and sealed windows would keep the things out, and entire houses and office buildings had frequently been encrusted with a coating of the writhing things trying to reach the warm meat hiding inside. Settlements quickly became closed and secured as the inhabitants shifted to the nocturnal lifestyle of their new midnight world.

As scary as the leeches were, the things that hunted them, the things we called stalkers, were worse still. At least the leeches only came out during the day. Reports of stalker attacks, although fewer in number, seemed to indicate they were active both day and night. Trouble was, nobody had so far got a clear look at one. They seemed to possess some kind of natural camouflage, but body parts had been brought back to the settlements for study—sinewy limbs covered in clumps of wiry hair and ending in hooked talons. It gave us an idea of what we were up against, but we still needed to know more.

That's what brought us down here, into the old transit tunnels outside Newstone Settlement. We were following the spoor of the stalkers, one of six small teams of reluctant 'volunteers' tasked with bringing back a live specimen. It was hoped that a better understanding of these omnivorous predators would enable us to develop defences against their attacks. As it was, stalker attacks were swift, deadly and unpredictable. They struck out of nowhere, vanished just as fast, and so far had evaded all attempts at capture.

Our reward for undertaking this dangerous assignment was the promise of extra food rations and a larger water allowance. Right now, just the thought of stripping off these damp, sweaty clothes and having a proper hot shower was almost making it all worthwhile.

"Going down?" Kaz asked grimly, and I saw we'd reached a ladder leading into a deeper section of tunnels. Kaz shone her light into the darkness below, illuminating grimy rungs slick with moisture.

"Jeez, it stinks down there." Delv wrinkled his nose.

Kaz flashed him a withering look. "We ready for this?"

I gave Delv a sympathetic glance. He had looked like a rabbit in headlights since we'd come down into the tunnels, and clearly wasn't cut out for this kind of work. None of us were military, but Kaz had some former experience in private security and was one tough cookie. I'd seen her punch out the lights of a drunken guy twice her size after he made a racial slur towards her one night in a bar, and I knew she could hold her own in a crisis. I had formerly been in the fire service, and was no stranger to dangerous situations myself, though this was a whole new one for me. Delv on the other hand had been a parcel courier, and so must have been crapping his pants since drawing this assignment. But everyone had to do their Civic Duty. It was a requirement of admission into a Settlement. Citizens were put onto a rota, each required to take shifts at whatever jobs needed doing, everything from planting and gathering food to security patrols and repairs and maintenance. The rotas were originally intended to be tailored to suit skills already possessed by the citizens, but often the reality was that everyone just mucked in with everything.

"Let's just get it over with." I clapped Delv on the back. "Sooner it's done, sooner we can go home."

We started down, Kaz in the lead and Delv bringing up the rear. The going was slow and awkward, the rungs slick and dangerous. We gripped the ladder so tightly our knuckles were white, our boots threatening to slip off at any moment. The metallic clanging of our slow descent echoed into the darkness, and some part of me morbidly wondered if we were just ringing the dinner bell for whatever waited below.

"That stench..." Delv whined from above. "It's making me heave."

I suddenly wondered if having him go last was a mistake.

"Puke on me and I'll shoot you," I warned him, but in truth, part of me felt the same way. The stench rising up from below was nauseating, the sickly smell of rotting meat coupled with something like spoiled vegetables.

"Hey, Delv, you could have held it in," Kaz joked.

"She who smelt it, dealt it," he grumbled back.

Kaz suddenly let go of the ladder and dropped into the darkness. For a heartbeat I wondered why—then heard boots splash into stagnant water after a drop of only two feet and realised we'd reached the bottom. She moved off to the right, torch dancing across tunnel walls, and I heard her exhale loudly: "Jesus!"

Moments later I joined her and understood why. The tunnel was a slaughterhouse lined with ragged carcasses, ribcages stripped of flesh, bones that had been gnawed upon and cracked open for the marrow, torn fragments of old shoes and shreds of bloody clothing; all of it crawling with insects that were quickly cleaning up any remains that had been missed.

"Is it some kind of a nest?" I asked, pressing the back of my hand to my mouth.

"Something like that," Kaz nodded grimly. "This is definitely not leeches."

"Look at the size of these teeth marks." Delv shone his torch upon a human femur riddled with deep striations. Under normal circumstances, I know Kaz would have made a smutty joke about the size of Delv's bone, but here, in this subterranean abattoir, even her normally unflappable sense of inappropriate humour was silenced.

"Guys, there's fresh kill over here." Kaz's voice sounded strained. "It's Bravo team."

Those words sent a jolt of panic through me, the kind of nervous terror that flips your stomach over and makes your balls crawl up into your body. I glanced at Delv and saw his eyes were wide, his lips pressed so tightly together he no longer seemed to have a mouth. We were silent as we joined her, our torches adding to the illumination that now showed us the pile of fresh bodies. The limbs had been snapped like dry twigs, the torsos and faces shredded beyond recognition, and still-warm piles of congealing entrails squelched underfoot. The blood had already coagulated, but there was no getting over the fact that those remains had been up and walking less than an hour before.

"That's two teams dead," Delv whispered. "Two."

"Hold it together," Kaz warned. "We start doing anything stupid, we end up the same."

"This—this is stupid, running around down here like this!" Delv's voice rose to an unsteady shout, and I put my hand on his shoulder.

"Keep it down," I urged. "Whatever did this could still be close."

"I'd better radio this in," Kaz said. "You two, keep an eye out."

Delv and I backed up against the curving tunnel wall where foul water dripped like icy tears onto our heads and backs. We shivered as we strained our ears, listening to the soft ambience of the tunnels—the drip of distant water, our own breathing, and the faint echo of things shifting and scuttling far away.

Is this what the other teams had heard before the end fell upon them? Had they too thought they were safe and alone down here? Had there been any warning before death had claimed their lives? I looked at the gore-spattered guns still clutched in dead hands. It didn't look like they had even had a chance to fire a shot off. How was that possible?

"Delta team reporting in." Kaz's voice sounded strained in the gloom.

"Report." Stoker's reply cut crisply through the still air from the central control room in the settlement.

"We've just found Bravo team. No survivors, looks like they were ambushed. That's Bravo and Echo teams down."

"Any sign of the quarry?"

"Nothing yet, though..."

"What is it?"

"Well, there's something moving around down here. We've discovered what looks like a nest at these coordinates. There are a lot of bodies here; looks like it's been established for some time."

"Understood. Retrieve Bravo team's cameras and weapons, then proceed with your assigned patrol route."

"Yes sir, but..."

"Is there a problem, Wilde?"

"Well, no sir. I just wondered if it might be wiser to join up with the other teams before heading on. From what I'm seeing, the smaller teams are being overwhelmed. If we had greater numbers, we might..."

"You have your orders. Stick to them. Stoker out."

Kaz's face was pinched into a tight grim line when she turned to us. She gestured at the torn and scattered bodies at her feet. "Okay, you heard him, give me a hand here."

We set to work retrieving the cameras and guns from the corpses. It was a grim task, and we stayed silent as we did it. I saw

Delv's hands were shaking and I wondered how much longer he could hold up down here. Our hands and boots were soon slick with gore, and we cleaned them as best we could. After we were done, Delv stumbled out into the other tunnel for a few minutes. From the sounds of retching that reached us there was no doubt why he had gone. We should have stayed together, it was a foolish risk to allow any member of the team to wander away, even into the adjoining tunnels, but neither Kaz nor I made any attempt to stop him. We were all struggling to cope. When he returned, looking drained and paler than I had ever seen him, we put the retrieved weapons and cameras into the pack on my back, and without another word we pressed on.

The tunnels down here seemed tighter, narrower, and the dripping of moisture formed an almost constant background sound. We felt more on edge too. Those bodies were a clear warning that we were not alone, and that we were wandering through territory that had been claimed. It was why we were here, of course, but the ease with which the two teams had been slain was terrifying, and only served to highlight how vulnerable and ill prepared we truly were. The unknown pressed in all around us, filled with a sense of growing threat, and I looked back several times at Delv; partly to reassure myself he was still there—that something hadn't clawed him off into the darkness without our knowing—

and partly to make sure he was holding up. His eyes were wide, his lips moving soundlessly as though reciting something over and over, and the hands holding his gun were bloodlessly white.

"Head's up," Kaz called. The light from her torch had picked something out in the tunnel up ahead. It looked like a doorway, probably some kind of maintenance access, but there was a thick smear of blood on the wall next to it.

"Delv, take the left. Stu, go right," Kaz instructed. We did as she said, positioning ourselves either side of the door, while Kaz stood against the wall opposite, readying her weapon and torch. At a nod from her, Delv reached out for the handle and pulled the door open, whilst Kaz aimed both gun and torchlight directly into the opening.

"It's clear," she announced, lowering her weapon.

That was when I saw the wall beside her ripple.

I went to call out, but something dark and fast barrelled into her, knocking her sideways. She landed heavily and then the air was full of the coppery taint of blood. It all happened so fast. I swung my gun around, trying to focus on whatever was attacking, but all I could see was the frantic writhing as Kaz rolled and squirmed and kicked on the floor, ragged chunks ripping from her clothes and skin as she screamed. I caught swift and sudden glimpses of something stocky and dark, covered in coarse hair, but it seemed to vanish as soon as I saw it, like some kind of deadly chameleon.

"Shoot!" Delv screamed. He stood like a man frozen before the headlights of an oncoming train, his own gun forgotten in his hands.

"At what?" I called back. The thing could either mimic its surroundings perfectly, or had some other means of becoming invisible to our eyes. If I fired blindly, I'd hit Kaz. If I waited any longer, it would all be over for her.

Even as the thought flashed through my mind, Kaz gave a horrible gurgling screech, and I already knew I was too late. She slumped back against the damp stone, throat torn open and the front of her stomach glistening where she had been brutally disembowelled. A sick cold shock shivered through me, my heart thudding dully in the back of my throat. For a second that pulsing throb of my own heart was all I could hear. I tried to swallow but all the moisture had dried in my throat and mouth.

"Where is...?" Delv said faintly.

"Shut up!" I hissed, trying to focus my eyes on the shadows and dark spaces around where Kaz's body now lay.

Had the thing moved, or was it still there, hidden and watching us?

"Shine your torch!" I hissed again, and that finally coaxed some life back into Delv's useless frozen form. With a click his beam shone fully onto Kaz's ravaged face, then flicked quickly away, shining into the darkness around her. I was grateful for that, because I was sure her dead eyes were staring accusingly at me, as if asking why I hadn't saved her.

I kept my gun trained on the darkness, listening to the silence of the tunnel.

"Stay there," I said at last, "I'm going to try…"

From the corner of my eye I saw something move. I staggered back and the dark shaggy mass of the stalker slammed into me, throwing me back against the wall. My head cracked hard enough to burst white stars in my vision, and my mouth filled with the taste of blood as I bit down onto my tongue. All of that was eclipsed by the agony of the talons that now shredded into my stomach, parting cloth and skin like paper. With a shriek of shocked pain I tried to grab the writhing mass, to pull it off of me, but it was like trying to grasp a shadow. It was a physical entity, but it moved and flowed as if it were liquid, evading my grasping fingers as it sank teeth into my shoulder.

Dimly, I was aware of the sound of someone running; a thin wail of terror going with them. In that second I realised Delv had abandoned me and was fleeing back along the tunnels.

That was all I knew before the camera fixed to my helmet discharged with an electrical burst that lanced needles through my body and consumed my vision in a bright white blast. It was as if every tendon in my body had jolted violently. I bounced and clattered against the stone convulsively, and I struggled to draw breath into my lungs.

Then there was only darkness.

I must have blacked out, for the next thing I remember was trying to sit up, my head pounding. My body was a shrieking mass of raw agony, my lap full of blood, my shirt hanging in tatters, and my lungs feeling as if all the air had been slugged out of them.

I also realised I wasn't alone. Four armed figures were standing over me, torches lancing through the damp darkness as they loaded something limp and hairy into a metal containment cage. One of the figures saw me moving and swung his torch-beam into my eyes, blinding me.

"Stay down," he ordered. "Medics are on their way."

"Did the bait work?" I heard Stoker's voice crackle over the radio.

"Yes sir, they drew it right in. Your rigged cameras did the rest. The electrical discharged knocked it right out."

My brow furrowed at those words. Bait? We had been the bait?

"Any survivors?" Stoker asked, coldly.

"Bravo and Echo teams are lost. It looks like their cameras malfunctioned; they never discharged when they were attacked.

Probably all the damp down here messing with the systems," the figure reported. "One survivor present from Delta team. He's pretty torn up."

"No," I wheezed, trying to pull myself up using the wall, but my blood-slick fingers kept slipping off the bricks. "Delv..."

"Get the specimen back up here ASAP," Stoker barked. "Retrieve the guns and cameras too."

"And the ETA on the medics?"

"Forget the medics," Stoker answered. "We don't have the supplies to spare. You know as well as I do, nobody survives a stalker attack."

"Wait..." I called, anxiously trying to stand. "Wait!"

But they ignored me, stopping only to take my gun and the pack from my back, and then they took their caged prize and retreated the way they had come. I listened, trying to ignore the growing pain in my chest and the desperate pounding of my heart as their sounds grew steadily fainter and more distant.

That was... how long ago? It's hard to say. After that, I just lay here in the dark, listening to the shadows. It's getting hard to breathe, my lungs feel like a fire is burning inside them, and my legs are so numb I'm not even sure they're still there. I hold out a secret hope that Delv might come back for me. I imagine that he's just out of sight, hiding around the next bend in the tunnel, waiting until it's safe to come and get me out. If so, I hope he hurries up. There are sounds out there in the darkness, getting closer. Scurrying sounds, like claws on stone. I don't think they're rats.

In the darkness I can see Kaz watching me, a sad smile on her ragged lips.

She knows I let her down when she counted on me the most.

I hope Delv comes back soon.

The sounds are getting awfully close.

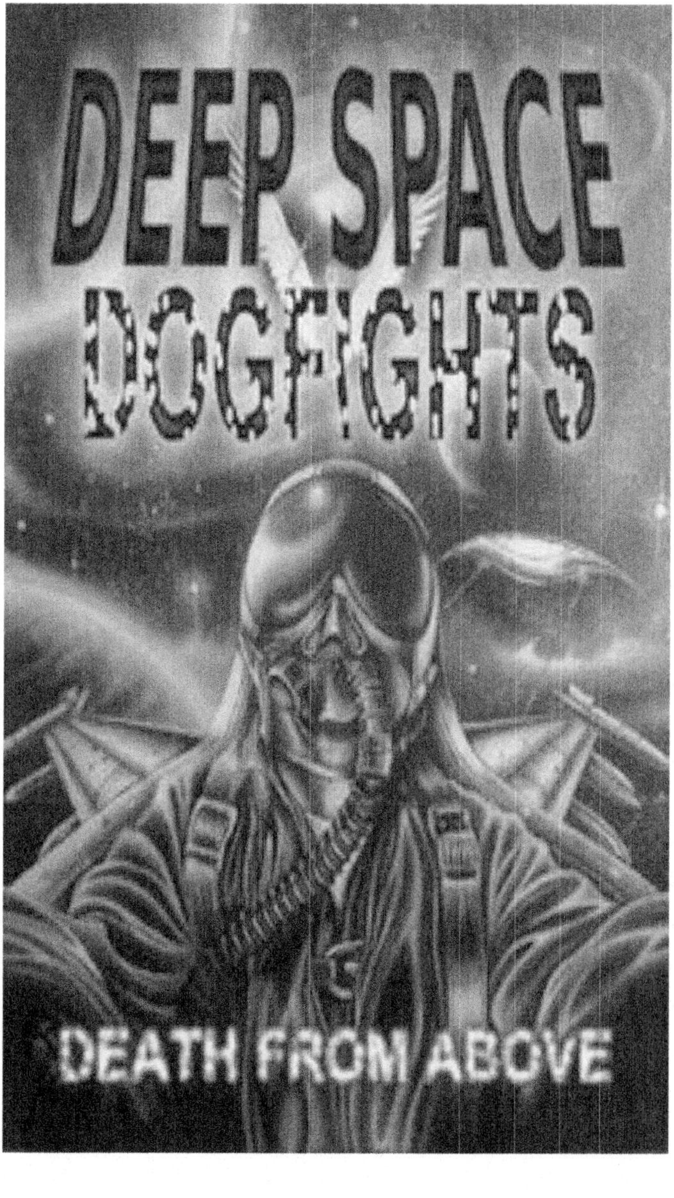
DEEP SPACE
DOGFIGHTS
DEATH FROM ABOVE

THE TESTIMONY OF JESTER THOTH
by Scott J Couturier

Due to the torture-backed insistence of certain avid and arcanely inclined historians, I endeavour here to set forth a brief chronicle of my life. Herein the reader should expect no depictions of unparalleled valour, no account of daring escapes and mystical interludes; my existence is that of a jester, a clown with malformed limbs and spirit. Once my soul was bright, but time and circumstance have worked their perfidies, leaving me a drooling, shambling husk. Where once I savoured the ecstatic poetries of hallowed Xeru, now I spout profane limericks and crude, perverse jokes. I leer and belch and fart and shit on the floors, to roars of profane amusement. My motley is smeared with faecal matter, my hair home to a thriving microcosm. Yet once—once I was a lover, and even before that a child.

I shudder to recall such things, yet recall them I must. The probes of the Mysteriarchs await me should I fail in my task to properly record how all this came to pass.

I was born in a small village in a primeval wood, just north of the once-sprawling ruins of Eld Sama. I was raised simply, by simple folk. They taught me how to gather herbs and sing songs, showed me the Great Wheel and the names and interrelations of the telling stars. The slow, mumbling river T'Pua (its name in after-eras) flowed past the village, curving off sinuously through halls of virgin oak and ashwood. My people had no writing or concrete symbol-language, yet they maintained a vigorous trade with other communities up and down the river's length. Transactions were marked on small clay tablets, hen-scratchings predating the most elemental mathematical thought; again, I find myself uncomfortable recalling these things. Both the world and its inhabitants have changed unutterably since that distant age. I quiver in horror to think that I have lived through each permutation, each cycle of life and death, still bound in this same debased, infernal flesh—truly, jesters are never allowed to cease their capering.

There was an old mystic in the village, a teller of fortunes and curer of ailments. Some called him a wizard, but there were many half-formed words for his vocation. My mother simply called him Grandfather. I became closer to him as I grew to manhood, drawn in by the webs of his stories and chants. Often we wandered the great forest together, seeking the deeper haunts of its vast green dream. Some of the trees and animals could speak the language of my people, while others only spoke in tongues ancient or wholly foreign to the mind. Wise beasts and strange, half-material spirits haunted the inner gloom; the air was full of a constant, capricious muttering, as if the very wind conspired to mischief. Frequently we strayed across mouldering ruins or circles of vast, vine-choked stones, their surfaces graven with images half-worn away by the march of time and element.

The legends Grandfather told me hinted at the origin of these places. He said they were the work of another race, alien and long-vanished. Once, he took me into a small chamber beneath his hut, showing me a collection of curious objects bound in mummified leather. "These are books," he said, the unfamiliar word flooding me with an inexplicable elation. "The ancients recorded their knowledge in this way." He opened one of the objects, and I saw that it was full of yellow sheaves with weathered, time-blackened edges. "Paper," he told me. "Made of pressed wood pulp. The symbols on the paper represent speech."

I was enrapt. The idea that words could be preserved in an imperishable form obsessed me, and after making careful study of the books I began developing my own written language, intent on capturing the quicksilver speech of our people. In the process I came to work very closely with Grandfather, and share in some of his darker, deeper secrets; suffice to say that ten years later my alphabet was complete, and I had become a magician.

In that time I also fell in love. Her name was Ilas; she was beautiful, skin dark as the

New Moon, with the promise of regeneration in her laughter. She often haunted the banks of the sleepily moving T'Pua, the lilt of her golden voice luring eager fish into her nets. For this reason she became known as Fish Singer.

Inspired by the title, I worked for many days and nights to design a symbol expressing her use-name. Revered ancestors were called upon, bones cast, the spirit world inveigled. When finally I had the symbol, I showed it first to her, then to the other villagers. All were in awe, and immediately began demanding their own personalized glyphs. I had much toil advancing my alphabet, though Grandfather helped me when he could; my initial scratches and marks developed with rapidity into a bewilderingly complex hieroglyphic system. As for Ilas Fish Singer, she became my much-cherished wife.

In those first months our bounty was great. Fish Singer was soon with child. Having dispensed with the task of divining symbol-names for my clan, I turned to more esoteric pursuits, roving naked and fasting through the ruin-littered forest for days at a time. I slaughtered small animals, daubing new-wrought symbols onto my flesh with their blood, and at each full moon sacrificed a stag to the orb's awesome power. Gods had not been conceived of yet, let alone God-the-singular; these were some of my later innovations.

I pause here to doff my many-belled cap before the reader, with a bold release of flatulence. I am grotesque to look upon, hideous to sight, touch, smell, taste. For untold millennia I have loathed my own image, loathed this deathless flesh that I cannot disinhabit. In writing of my past, my origin, I find old memories and sensations awakened, flickers of feeling I'd thought lost to atrophy. When I think of Ilas, tears gather in my eyes. Yet you will not see them staining these pages.

She died, did my delightful Fish Singer. Down by the water, at night, alone. I could only comprehend that she had been murdered; a fine swimmer, she was found floating face-down, her bruised body forced against an embankment by the river's sluggish flow. I wept and shrieked and cried out, draping my senseless body over the blue bulge of her belly. I dragged her corpse back to my hut and kept it overnight, chanting strange songs that came unbidden to my fevered brain. Grandfather protested, calling my impulses abominable, but I would not listen. When morning came the other villagers stormed my hut, respectfully restraining me as they bore Fish Singer's body away. I kicked and hissed and spat at them, uttering a hex that struck blind all those who touched my beloved. My hair went from auburn to shock-white, half of it falling out at the roots. It was then that Grandfather forced me to choke down a rich, heavily herbal fluid. I collapsed into slumber.

Days later I awoke to find myself bound. Grandfather was at my side, as were my brothers; they told me they had taken Ilas' body and burned it. I feigned acceptance of their tale, knowing that, according to my people's belief, burning a body consumes the spirit inside. When I had recovered enough sense to convince them to free me, I began roving the forest by night with a dowsing rod, seeking my wife's burial place. I was not disappointed. They had not burned her, risking her soul's dissolution, but inhumed her between two great roots of an oak tree. When I disinterred her she was reeking and half-rotten, her eyes and tongue gone, belly split open to expose the gelatinous remnants of our child.

In recent months I had made some headway in translating the books of the ancients. How I cannot say; I knew no practical means of deciphering them, but long hours of meditating on individual words and symbols led to certain inexplicable revelations. I understood, or thought I understood, the purpose of the great stone circles and the humped, black-stained altars they invariably circumscribed. The ancients had perfected a complex system of controlling nature that they called Magic—the stone circles were augmenters of will, connecting-places to other spheres and influences. There was much talk of raising the dead, of the hunt for a divine stone that imparted the possessor life everlasting. Life everlasting... my body trembled as I secreted Ilas' befouled corpse in a narrow, deep cave some distance from the village. I spoke to her as I carried her, went back to retrieve one of her legs when it tore free on a bush. I loved her. I still love her, though now it means less to me. Jesters must never take the cosmic joke too personally.

Over the next few weeks I sealed myself up with the rotting corpse of my wife, blocking the cave mouth with heavy stones until no sunlight or intruder could penetrate. I pored over the ancient texts, reading by brazier-glow, and made offerings in deep pits below the main cavern, operating out of some hideous instinct. The magic of the ancients unfolded before me, until I could read the books as if they were written in the tongue I had devised. Frantically I began a translation, seeking any means of returning Fish Singer to life.

The villagers were alarmed by my absence. At first they assumed I had gone mad and wandered off into the forest, but Grandfather sensed what I was doing. He led the villagers to the disturbed grave, then gathered his divining tools and set out in search of my secret workshop. He was aware, it seems, of certain shadowy prophecies from up-river, portents of doom spewed from the lips of a famed oraculist's severed head. Why he kept these auguries from me I can only guess; not that the knowledge would have deterred me. Destiny has an odd way of fulfilling itself, especially when propelled by the torments of base mortal grief.

I fended off Grandfather's seeking for weeks, weaving a cocoon of bewilderment about my hiding place. The books were translated at a frenetic pace, my hand gripping the stylus with such force blood leaked from beneath my fingernails. Autumn had come, imparting a brisk, numbing chill to the air; I started coming above ground after dusk to seek the nearest fully erect stone circle. My plan was to use the coming night of Sowen, as it was later called, to summon a considerable amount of energy from the Outer Spheres. The books insisted that the reanimation of long-dead tissue was possible under such rarefied conditions, and I didn't think to question them. Already I had used incantations gleaned from their pages to reverse the aging process of Ilas' corpse. She lay in a shallow depression in the stone, her skin blue-tinged and waxen but unblemished by decay. I had removed the leavings of our child from her womb, and painstakingly stitched up her belly and severed leg with all the prowess of a latter-day mortician. I slept by her, in those rare instances that I slept; often I would talk to her, and sometimes I made love to her.

Do you recoil, gentle reader? Never forget that, as the jester apes for your amusement, it is you who are mocked above all! I have told this part of my story often in the black courts of my mistress, and it never fails to elicit a certain appreciation from the rutting hordes. The undead pretend offense, of course, citing their disgust at the conjoining of deceased and living flesh, yet I know more than a few among them who maintain vital harems. That these toys are eventually drained, turned, or devoured does not detract from the hypocrisy of such affected disdain.

As Sowen drew near, I readied the unclean instruments of my craft in secret. This demanded most of my focus, the glamour of bewilderment weakening from negligence as a result. My oversight inevitably drew Grandfather's attention—such a wise, well-meaning old fool. Gathering the men of my village, he led an assault on the barrier of confusion veiling my workshop, the troop singing wordless ancestral songs to maintain orientation and focus. I was, I will confess, now wholly consumed by a spirit of rank necromancy—a puppet of the grave, unwitting servant to Death Divine. Yet, there were no words for these things among my people, no true fear of the dead returning to life. It had been an innocent age before Grandfather showed me the books; I, in my thirst for knowledge, plumbed atavistic pathways long given over to the Abyss. What I discovered in those blackened straits was a recrudescent power, ancient and malefic, hungry for a vessel to contain and express it anew. Yes, yes, eternally a pawn of greater wills—such is the jester's plight. Perhaps my chosen profession is becoming more coherent to you.

At any rate, I repelled Grandfather's attack. Summoning a trio of demonic genii, creatures long-banished from the world, I destroyed the men of my tribe, wiping out utterly the masculine flower of my own generation. So dedicated was I to the resurrection of Fish Singer that I saw only more resources to use in the upcoming ritual—truly, I was driven to a black madness by my grief. Little did I suspect this grief had formed a wound, through which something ulterior had bled and infested...

Infusing the fallen dead of my tribe with a rude animacy, I set them to work preparing the stone circle for Fish Singer's resuscitation. The eve of Sowen came two sleepless nights later. In the distance I could hear the wailing of the women and children of my village, carried on the chill wind; rather than stir my humanity, their lamentations drove me to a frothing rage. That night I dispatched a legion of my rotting kinsmen back to the village to silence their caterwauling, compelling them to return with fresh corpses for the ritual. As they embarked on their loathsome errand I descended down into the cave, to attend to Fish Singer's body and read a final time from the Book of Power I had tirelessly worked to pen in that abysmal place.

Writ on mummy-flesh made pliable by vivifying sorceries, bound with a spine of inhuman vertebrae pilfered from the crypts of Eld Sama, the words and symbols recorded in the book were almost wholly exotic to my waking mind. Frequently I found the need to consult my own hastily recorded revelations, yearning to catch a glimpse of what had, for the briefest of flashes, appeared so clear and succinct. I had recently donned my first suit of jester's motley, moving perhaps on some subconscious recognition of my own self-created doom. Here too I innovated a new role, or rather resurrected one long-forgotten, for there were no jesters among the people of the river. Strong and sublime and young my race had been, free from the avaricious oppression of gods and daemons, magicians and emperors; yet now, my desperate love for Fish Singer had summoned up the world-marring powers of a lost aeon. I was as helpless as the corpse of my beloved to alter what happened next.

Fires flared in the decrepit, long-forsaken fanes of the Black Gods as the night of Sowen drew down, lit by no human hand. As the Great Moon hove zenithward I unsealed the cave's entrance and made for the readied circle, the rigid body of Fish Singer clutched tenderly against my breast. I made love to her, implanting life's seed, as the dead of my village gathered in a reverent ring inside the standing stones, women and children now among the men—ah, still I hear the wild, orgiastic shivering of the bells on my new-stitched cap! Once-innocent ornaments, fashioned by a peaceful tribe downriver to adorn their painted canoes... raising my hands and intoning a series of incantations so horrible the words seared from my mind even as I spoke them, I appealed to both Nature and the Grave to overturn the finality of their rulings. I tempered my supplication with copious sacrifice, offering up several virginal youths brought yet living from the village. Winds howled, and the gathered undead moaned in a despicable chorus, their voices catching and reverberating among the stark menhirs. The corpse of my love lay in glorified repose, her midnight skin now laved in blood. Crying out a final word, I leaned down and kissed her, imbuing her body with the Black Breath.

I felt something leave me, departing forever, while at the same time something entered me, never to depart. Reeling back, I stared down into the ebony face of Fish Singer, her exanimate beauty now distorted by a fresh, baleful life. Rising from the altar, the black-gleaming body of my love parted her lips to reveal a set of fulsome fangs. Her eyes gleamed with an otherworldly abhorrence, multifarious fires displacing the lifeless glaze of death. It was not Ilas Fish Singer that peered out at me; some monstrous intelligence had transplanted itself into her meticulously prepared vessel, something that should never have known material incarnation in this sphere.

The half-mended rift dividing my race's brief paradise from the recondite past was torn wide and weeping. The Black Goddess had returned, but she did not come to haunt the heavens, to inflame the minds of seers and tyrants, to build great temples through the vicarious labour of devout flesh. Instead, wearied by her great decay in the Outer Dark, she came to rule. And for that, my lover's body was chosen as her sovereign containment.

From here, mere summary should suffice. Surely the Mysteriarchs know enough of the Necromantic Night to make my recounting trivial. A thousand years of perpetual darkness, wherein a culture of decadent, aesthetic undeath evolved and flourished. The Bloodlords reigned from their onyx-paned pleasure eyries, enrapt by primal night unending, whilst lich-lords animated swarming kingdoms of the dead and set them to toil at tasks of boundless, insentient ego. The perpetual night was no place for living creatures: rats were dug squealing from their holes, drained or devoured nearly to extinction. The blood of lepers was considered a rare (and ambitiously cultivated) delicacy. Humanity was bred in caverns under the earth as bloodstock for Death's unceasing appetite, countless generations spawned in a deep-sunk warren called The Marrow. Those few chosen to receive some variant of the dark gift were singled out accordingly, but the mass served foremost as fuel for the Bloodlords and their underlings.

Over all this profanity presided the Black Goddess, incarnate in the hideously reanimated body of my love. I, in turn, found myself hideously alive—Death departed from me forever in the moment I kissed the body of Fish Singer. My heart beat, my mortal hungers persisted, yet I was beyond mortality, as such being unpalatable to the creatures my monstrously misguided sorcery had unleashed. Dressed in my jester's motley, I became a fixture in the court of the Goddess: the progenitor of words, the first human maker of symbols and sorceries! It gave the assemblage great delight to mock at my capering. A living man doomed to abide forever amid the debaucheries of Death—what hideous fate, you may say. Yet I performed my jests and slaked my yearnings as readily as I was able. The dark sorceries I had mastered, the written language I constructed were burned out of my mind, leaving charred remnants fast-subsumed by a centuried decadence. For a time I became a genuine madman, an unaffectedly gibbering fool. I watched the civilization of Death rise and fall, spawning poets and despots and dreamers and lovers and dull fools as assuredly as any mundane mortal cycle.

However, mortal cycles came in due course. The power of the Goddess inevitably waned, the Great Darkness dispelled by new gods manifesting via the minds of certain prophets among the bloodstock, wreathed in flame and cleansing wrath. I admit, I had fallen into the habit of absconding to The Marrow, performing nonsensical shadow-plays for the chattel as a sick amusement. From these humble origins sprang the triple-godhead of Viran the Just, Salann the Liberator, and Chron the Virtuous. Let the Great Wheel mark, when finally I expire, how I have time and again—all unwittingly—greased its rapid turning.

There was open rebellion, and the sun shone anew on a starveling landscape, blighted and lean as a corpse. I went into hiding in the deep places for an unreckoned span, hunting blind cave crickets to appease my hunger, my own eyes eventually devolving to become gelid, useless orbs. For a time I was parted from the Black Goddess. I thought her material form destroyed, Fish Singer's long-blasphemed flesh finally laid to rest.

However, after several thousand years of stinking darkness and protean grasping, I was called by the faint-but-irrepressible whisper of my mistress, into whose service I had sworn my pathetic soul. I crawled forth to jest in her court through three later renaissances before the sun's eventual dimming, though none could match the Necromantic Night for sheer arch-depravity.

It was betwixt these latter periods of service that I most regained my human-ness, even managing to shed my garments of self-mockery for a spell. I revered Beauty, listened to the poets, and even aspired to become one myself. For a brief while, in the halls of Xeru and later imperial Philatia, this idiot jester laid aside his motley and dreamed of becoming something more. I did manage some fine verses, but none that will outlive me.

It was all at the whim of the Black Goddess, of course. Cold, cruel, and potent she reigns, a creature of inhuman tastes and unclean passions—often I caper and cackle merely to distract myself from the utmost profanation I have wrought, all for the absurd sake of love. Sometimes, though rarely twice in a century, I am taken to grapple with Fish Singer's infernally imbued corpse. During these nightmarish sessions of lovemaking the demon will pretend to recede, exposing flickers of the woman I so long ago adored. Inevitably I appeal to Fish Singer as if she were truly present, only to have the Goddess's foul laughter pour discordantly from my dear lover's mouth. The deep whorling scars marring my flesh are the result of her talons. Still hideously in love, I have spent uncounted nights dancing and gibbering for her amusement... even now, as the world advances into its final benighted age, I remain her willing, or rather willingly will-less, slave. Needless to say, profanity has long since displaced poetry in my mind.

I have endured it all. Through pestilence and bounty and exile, through unnumbered wars... waves of generations I have seen go to dust in my dirge of protracted existence. Again and again I behold the cyclical aegis of civilized idealism collapse weeping into the tarn; I have seen the indignity and cravenness with which the deathless die. Severed from the universal fate of all life, I at turns have courted madness, meditation, magic, art, sex, and sybaritic release as balms, though nothing has long assuaged the endless malady of my living.

Now, confronted with an ultimate end, I can only cry relief to the livid firmament. To finally not be myself... a haunting and enticing possibility, sweet as cool water to a throat eternity-parched. As the world grows sere with unending cosmic night, I am called to make this testimony to a congeries of interdimensional magi, who have threatened me with torments unknown in even my detestable expanse should I fail to adequately record my part in these matters. Currently I fulfil my sacred purpose in the court of the Black Goddess, who reigns in faded majesty over the last feeble Necropolis of an already-dead world. The sun glows a dull umber, swollen to a size that eclipses half the sky. I only pray its continued expansion will finally burn away the hideous weft of enchantment that binds me to this flesh. But perhaps, after the world itself is annihilated, the particulates of my body will yet cling to consciousness in the new-made void. And perhaps, too, those culminant fires will purge the Black Goddess from my love, and our disparate matter can at last commingle in a serene, silent oblivion... but, these are a jester's dreamings, and as such of perilously little import.

OCCUPATION
by Michael W Clark Ph.D.

"Stand up on your legs." Jack Call hung in the air. He liked manipulating gravity as foreplay.

"I am standing on my legs. I have four of them," Ovula snapped out in English. She spoke English well for a Pe-li-too. Her fur was silken despite its durability.

"Hind legs. The backmost ones." Jack Call moved the controller up above zero. His bare feet touched the cold of the carbon fibre deck. It would warm automatically with touch, but for an instant it was as cold as vacuum space. Jack Call loved contrast. It made him laugh.

Ovula stood. Her ventral side was smooth and silky too. The fur there was a lighter shade than on her dorsal side. "You will never fertilize me. No matter how often you try," her mouth prevented a smile. Her two sets of eyes did twinkle with glee.

"Never my intent. Ever. With anyone, human or non-human. More sentient beings around than needed." Jack Call had just retired from the Service. Foreplay was what filled his time now. The Pe-li-tooians were a very agreeable species. It was why he requested his last tour of duty on Pe-li-too. He wanted to stay. The Service needed civilian admin. He could get his Service pension and a civilian admin salary. Plenty of funds, plenty of time, for foreplay and full-play.

Ovula grasped Jack Call by the neck with the four hands she had on her forelimbs. "I will squeeze, which you like."

Jack Call chuckled and turned the gravity negative. 'Strangled in free fall', they called it. A total loss of control. Total submission was so much fun to a soldier. It just wasn't reality and that was what fantasy was all about. Ovula squeezed slowly. Her hands were small but each had a thumb and three fingers. They squeezed every part of his neck. Jack Call smiled with the pressure as he reduced gravity further. Despite the mass, the two floated into the air. A civilian admin's dwelling / office was small, so they touched the ceiling almost immediately. Ovula squeezed continually. Jack Call's smile faded as his face reddened. He tried to reach up, but Ovula had restrained his arms with her hind legs. They too had two hands each. Jack Call had never panicked in his career. But he did struggle unsuccessfully. Ovula continued to squeeze until Jack Call had neither resistance nor life left in him.

Ovula released Jack Call. His negative gravity kept him on the ceiling as Ovula dropped to the deck. She typed on the wall keyboard. During foreplay Jack Call turned off the voice control. Ovula was happy about that. It switched off the security access protocol. Jack Call wasn't too trusting, he was too condescending. He thought Ovula too unsophisticated to understand technology. All the humans thought Pe-li-tooians simple minded. They were all wrong. Jack Call just discovered; too late, how wrong he was. Ovula wanted to install an access point in the Service central net. It was the last day for Jack Call's Service authorization codes, so it ended up the last day for Jack Call. "Your semen is too soft to fertilize a Pe-li-tooian, Jack Call," Ovula said as a goodbye to Jack Call's floating corpse. "It has to be in an arrow shaped packet to pierce the body wall. Your semen is like snot, just another mess to be wiped away."

Ovula had reduced the temperature of the dwelling / office to prevent decomposition. The corpse would freeze eventually. Ovula left an app running on the terminal to make it appear that Jack Call was fulfilling his duties. It would last long enough for the campaign to be well under way before any human wondered about the fate of Admin Call.

"Because we didn't resist," Ovula stated to the other occupants of the meeting place. The Pe-li-tooians preferred to hang than sit, so the walls were full.

"They will be surprised," was the chorus reply.

Ovula hopped to her favourite wall fixture. "Net access was established. The Service code checkers are as smug and lazy as the rest of the Service. It might be a month before they find it."

Ovuto was much older than Ovula and thus had much more authority. "The campaign should have a foot hold by then. So good. So good. Humans are so disgusting."

Ovula nodded.

"Disgusting they are," was said by all on the walls as a reply.

"The state of the Pe-li-too infrastructure is so deteriorated that most of the humans stay on orbital platforms." Fagigbe was an Academic and thus of low status to the Service. He studied what they conquered. That was the way the Service put it. "The humans generally think the Pe-li-tooians just let things go. The cities are mostly abandoned by sentients. The formerly high technology civilization which had developed on the planet has gone native. Rejected tech for a life as hunter gatherers in the planet's dominating jungles. It could have been a religious reawakening? It could simply have been economic pacification. The jungles are so dense with abundant resources, the present Pe-li-tooians are pacified by nature. With no limit on food, hoarding is unnecessary. Greed was unnecessary too. Most hunter gatherer societies only own what they can carry. Possession of territory confuses them. When you have picked all the fruit just move on. Next season there will be more. Most of the early human merchant traders thought Pe-li-too was the planet of suckers." The audience's laughter was growing. They were here for the same reason Fagigbe was. The annual report. Every division had to give and receive. Fagigbe was usually bored with the Service boasting of battles which never happened. Pacifists have no winning strategy in battle. Not being involved was an attitude, not a strategy. When the Service moved into a new area on the planet, there was no battle, just troop movements. The battles were mostly with the dense vegetation.

"Weak suckers, at that!" someone shouted from the audience to more laughter.

"The microbes here put up more of a fight!" someone else shouted.

Fagigbe sighed. He wanted to stop right then but if he didn't finish, he didn't get paid. "Cultural norms. Alien cultural norms are, well, alien. But there are analogies between them and us. Human society had to become spacefaring. The global metropolis which ancient Earth had become drove humans out into the galaxy. Ancient Earth was used up, resource-wise. We could only look for other resource sources. In many ways, the Pe-li-too fled their cities back to the jungle, much like humans fled the Earth."

"Humans expanded into the galaxy. We didn't run away!" It was an angry shout.

"Our civilization is aggressive in that expansion, then." Fagigbe was calculating how much money he would lose if he ran away. He wasn't afraid of being afraid. "When our outposts have harvested all that can be had from a planetary system, it moves on. Much like the natives here, eat all the fruit and then move on."

"No analogy I can see!" Everyone recognized the voice of the Commander. "Academician Fagigbe? Are you nearing the end of this, ah, report?"

"If the Commander wishes it. The end is near." Fagigbe knew that annoying the Service officers always terminated any interaction. The Service irritates, it does not get irritated.

"Make it nearer," the Commander commanded.

"Like any rainforest." Fagigbe nodded. "All nutrients are caught in the cycle. There is very little mineral excess. Everything is being utilized. The sentients are the only resources of any abundance, in a manual labour force."

"They give great massages. Those eight little hands. Now that is a cultural achievement," someone stated to the applause of all of the Service personnel.

"Not good head though, too many teeth!" someone else shouted. Laughter rained.

Fagigbe warmed with embarrassment. "Well, I think I have said enough."

"More than enough," the Commander verified.

Fagigbe's immediate superior was tall and thin from being born in space. He was a microgravite. An MG. So that was what everyone called him. It was better than his other nickname, Gravity Unwell. MG never left the space platforms. It was a valid excuse for not being at the annual presentations. Fagigbe had been born in a gravity well of 0.85 G. Fagigbe thus had no excuse, as well as no status. "Tradition." It was MG's answer to most of Fagigbe's frustration-oriented questions.

Fagigbe had let his hair grow while he was on Planet Surface. It had gotten longer than he had thought. He hated how his hair floated around his scalp in microgravity. He would get it shaved off right after this meeting. He called it, 'Frustration Hour.' "Why do they bring us, if they ignore what we say or laugh at it?"

When MG shrugged, his entire body was involved. "Always been that way. It is imbedded in the military budget. No one reduces that. It has been continual growth, so there are never any cutbacks. Gives us non-military types a wage."

Fagigbe frowned. Exo-anthropology was his field. Exo-anthropologist? That wasn't his title. Planet Surface engineer. That was his title, his position, but it had no job description. It was a job title only. He did mostly whatever he wanted. "I want to add to human understanding of alien cultures," Fagigbe muttered. "I feel no one else cares but me."

MG looked pained. "Whatever made you think anyone would? The Service's unofficial motto is, 'It's not exploitation if you need it.' Does that sound like they care about others? As a MicroGravite, I know outer space. 'There is limited space in space.' That is our unofficial saying. Resources are always limited. You have to learn not to worry too much. Disaster was always possible, so why worry about the inevitable?"

Fagigbe hated this talk. They had it over and over. It always ended the same.

"Don't worry, be happy, because tomorrow you might die." MG had a little tune he sung it to.

These talks were why Fagigbe called it the 'Frustration Hour.' He was frustrated going in and frustrated going out. The only difference was the reasons for his frustration. It was all very unproductive. Happy and unproductive didn't mix with Fagigbe. "I need a haircut." He stood up slowly, getting used to microgravity again. He didn't want to hit the ceiling.

MG nodded. "Yeah, looks like a halo. Ha! You no angel."

Fagigbe had thought he liked MG, but maybe he didn't? Maybe he had just grown tired of him and it? There weren't usually

Pe-li-too on the orbital platforms, but there were two down the corridor just past the Vacuum Barbershop. Fagigbe thought he recognized both of them. "Ovuga? Ovufu? What are you doing up here?" Fagigbe pulled himself along the wall for balance. The Velcro soles took some getting used to again. The multiple hands of the Pe-li-too allowed them to move with agility in microgravity.

Ovuga was the larger of the two. "Engineer Fagigbe? We thought you were at Planet Surface?" Ovuga hit Ovufu with his large tail.

Ovufu jerked around. "He's not supposed to be here."

"It is you." Fagigbe came up to them. "I had to come up after the annual presentation. It's deserted up here, everyone else is Planet Surface. My manager can't go down, so I have to come up to report on the report I gave down there. Bureaucracy. You know how it is. Ha! Your fur still lays flat up here. How do you do that?"

Ovuga pushed Ovufu with his tail, wanting her to move. "Oh. I read about your old world. There were birds with feathers. The featherlets had interlocking barbules. Our fur has a similar structure. There is epidermal musculature also involved." Ovuga looked down the corridor. Ovufu had disappeared.

Fagigbe patted his head. "Wish I had that. My hair stands straight out. If it is too long it hits me if I turn around too fast. It stings." Fagigbe liked the Pe-li-too. They were always so attentive.

Ovuga nodded with understanding. "Maybe a better solution would be Planet Surface. Human evolution put your species on the ground. Very two dimensional." Ovuga was hanging / standing on the ceiling.

Fagigbe giggled. "Yes, seven million years ago or more, we came out of the trees. Seven million years is a long time even for geological concerns."

The hindmost set of external ears on the back of Ovuga's head became erect and turned in the direction Ovufu had gone. "Engineer Fagigbe, please return to Planet Surface. It is safer for you there."

Fagigbe was puzzled. "You mean the microgravity? No. The doctors checked me out. Heart's okay but thank you for the concern."

"As you wish. But, but, we have respect for you, Engineer Fagigbe. Much respect for your views." Ovuga waved as he turned. "I must go."

Fagigbe smiled waving back. "Nice seeing you." Fagigbe rubbed his head. His hair developed a static charge. It sparked slightly. "Air is kept so dry up here. Maybe I will go back down on the next shuttle. Save myself the cost of a haircut." He could get a free meal up here too. Food was free on presentation day. On the orbital stations everything was available at the same time.

Day and night cycles were artificially controlled and had little to do with Planet Surface. Everyone had their own cycle. Fagigbe felt like pancakes. They were fluffier in microgravity than one G. It was a good feature to have, to suck down the butter. The syrup was extra sticky for the same reason. Foods needed to stick together in microgravity, with themselves and each other.

Fagigbe wanted to take a nap after his large breakfast. There was an alcove in the cafeteria just for this purpose. It had sound-dampening privacy curtains. Fagigbe napped alone. No cuddle companion for Fagigbe. It was his involuntary routine. He was deficient in both sex appeal and disposable income. He still felt groggy after his nap. He could sleep further on the shuttle down, so he went from the cafeteria directly to the shuttle bay. The corridors were absent of staff. Presentation day usually cleared out the station but not like this. Fagigbe had spent months on Planet Surface. Maybe there had been staffing changes? The Service routines would alter abruptly for unknown security reasons, so he shrugged it off as SOP. Still, the next shuttle was there. It was vacant. That was too strange even for the Service. Someone was always on the move, usually. The shuttle was on but there was no pilot. Fagigbe was curious but cautious. It was basic space training.

There were personnel down at the far end of the bay. Fagigbe waved at them. "Is there a drill?" He was waking up sufficiently to realize the personnel were Pe-li-too, not human. They were emerging from a troop transport. The lead group of Pe-li-too heard Fagigbe's query. They didn't answer but started running toward Fagigbe. Pe-li-too were fast. Their unusual aggressiveness startled him. They were almost on him before he considered evasive action. He was never good at running with Velcro soles anyway. Fagigbe closed his eyes instead of running. He didn't know what was happening. Maybe it was a prank by the Service. They liked humiliating the civilians.

Fagigbe heard barking. Pe-li-too language was difficult to mimic but he understood most routine conversations.

"Leave him!" It was Ovuga's voice.

The reply startled Fagigbe more than anything else. "He must die!" The statement, demand, opened Fagigbe's eyes.

Ovuga stood between Fagigbe and the murderous group. "Leave him to me. Continue with your part of the Campaign!" The group bowed without a word and ran out of the bay. Ovuga turned toward Fagigbe. "My wish was for you on Planet Surface."

"What is happening?" Fagigbe was having difficulty with the divergence from routine. "Why did they want me dead? Do you? Are you my killer?" Fagigbe was very confused. "Why?"

"No!" Ovuga scanned the bay. "No. My request was for you at Planet Surface. You living was the point." Ovuga grasped Fagigbe by the right arm. He pulled Fagigbe up in the air with a rip of Velcro. "I need you hidden."

Fagigbe stared into the multiple sets of eyes. "What is happening? Please."

Ovuga sighed. "Just because we didn't resist didn't mean we lacked a response."

"A rebellion?" Fagigbe was astonished. He had written an evaluation on just such a possibility. His conclusion had been wrong, apparently.

Ovuga jumped while hiding Fagigbe. "Our response is your surprise."

Fagigbe nodded as Ovuga slammed him into a produce stasis locker.

Suddenly time stopped for Fagigbe.

The annual presentation week was a controlled shore leave for the Service as well as a bureaucratic formality. Annual reports had to be produced, reported and filed, but they could be enjoyed too. The Service personnel took every second to enjoy the process. Alcohol rationing was lifted at this time. Anyone who wanted it could be intoxicated to the level they could tolerate. Contraceptives were not required. "Just do it! The Service will need more recruits." Few officers noticed communication alerts. The non-coms weren't noticing anything much at all. Once they were at Planet Surface, they lost interest in the true heavens, to seek the oblivion of intoxication. A spiritual quest of a sort. A quest for spirits.

It was not that they didn't care about the fate of the skeleton crews on the space platforms. They just didn't much care about anything at the time. The Service routine was all about future conquest, the next first encounter, the next occupation of an alien world. All preparations, all activities were for things to come. The annual boring presentations about the past were actually the prelude for the release of tension and order to oblivion. Synaptic disorder. "Fuck the Future," was the drinking salute. "Alive for now."

Another item all the Service personnel and non-Service humans didn't notice was the lack of Pe-li-too. The usual Pe-li-too complement was there at the beginning of the annual presentations but soon disappeared. Those officers who did notice shrugged it off as the simple-minded lazy natives taking a nap. "Fuck the aliens too! When you can!"

Ovula always felt contained by the human's keyboard interface. She would have preferred to speak commands but the Campaign's Code name was Quiet for a reason. Platform internal security monitored speech. The Platform AI would interpret certain words and phrases as security breaches and potential mutineers. The Pe-li-too were well versed in Human 1 and 2 languages but the Campaign was too important to play games with the AI speech monitors. Few humans used the keyboards routinely. They were kept active, though, in case of emergencies. Ovula was thus manually entering the release codes for the newly built troop transports. Pe-li-too was at the edge of human expansion. Human strategy was to build the devices of war on site and then bring in personnel. The strategy was efficient and had been effective. Human expansion had never been stopped by any alien race they had encountered. Blitzkrieg had always worked. Rapid and aggressive. The Pe-li-too had learned. The Quiet Campaign was silent and rapidly aggressive. The access codes Ovula had gotten from Jack Call reassured the AIs. Any orders Ovula entered were seen as valid. The troop transports needed to be stocked and fuelled. Time was the factor here. Ovula watched the clock. Weapons were prepared too. The Urgent category on the orders had the AIs working a top efficiency, by passing all other commands that might come from other sources. The entire space platform fleet was now under Ovula's direction.

There was hand to hand fighting within the corridors of the space platforms. Isolated human skeleton crews lost their struggle to maintain control. Since the Pe-li-too could withstand severe conditions, many corridors were simply opened to space. The humans would succumb to the cold vacuum before any Pe-li-too. Energy weapon discharge could be interpreted by the AI as mutiny. The AI dilemma which the Pe-li-too understood was that the AI had superior intelligence but were limited. They were intentionally limited by the humans as a security precaution. The Pe-li-too used it to their advantage.

Ovula was monitoring the situation but growing anxious. Time was being eaten by the loading of supplies.

"The troop transports need to move soon," Ovuga said from the cabin doorway. He had Fagigbe over his back.

"What is he doing here?" Ovula hissed.

"He was supposed to be Planet Surface but Fagigbe was never a routine human. He will come with us." Ovuga placed Fagigbe on the deck. "He is still recovering from the supply stasis field. We are to be on our way before his complete recovery."

"It is not in the plan," Ovula hissed again.

"A slight modification is all. Like a leaf in the wind, the Plan will not notice," Ovuga hissed back. "The transports have to move now. The evacuation must be successful. That is the imperative of the Plan."

Ovula hissed not a word. The troop transports begun their approach to Planet Surface. "The imperative implementation has begun."

Ovuga looked over at Fagigbe, slumped on the deck. "He will understand. Some humans will understand."

"Most won't. Most couldn't." Ovula typed in commands. "The corridors are clear now. We can move to the command ship."

"He will need an EVA suit. I will get him in it and follow you." Ovuga clicked open an emergency closet. An alarm sounded.

Ovula hissed no words but typed in a command and the alarm stopped. "Hurry!" Ovula left the cabin without a glance back.

"I came to tell her to hurry," Ovuga stated. "I will follow." He picked up Fagigbe and inserted a limp leg.

Fagigbe wasn't in the Service but he was well trained for living in space. He knew never to throw up in an EVA suit. There were training sessions on the repression of vomiting. Stasis recovery always made him nauseous. He just couldn't think about it. Where he was, he should think about. He was face down but moving. He could see very little through the helmet. He saw deck plate and Pe-li-too fur. He was on the back of one. When he lifted his head, he could see the frozen bodies of the Platform crew. There was a hull breach. There must have been an accident. But then Fagigbe remembered the shuttle bay, what had happened there. "No accident," Fagigbe said to himself. He could see the helmet control panel, the comms were off. He was still too weak to move, so he didn't. "If they wanted me dead, I would be."

He was eventually strapped into a seat on a shuttle. Ovuga moved him there. Ovula was piloting. Once the shuttle doors closed, Ovuga removed the EVA suit helmet.

"Fagigbe-man? Are you consciousness?" Ovuga took a neck pulse reading. "You are excited. Heart rate is high. Things are happening. But not a reason for fear," Ovuga said slowly. "But you have to come with us. There is no other way I can keep you alive."

"He knows too much, already," Ovula snapped.

"That is why he has to come." Ovuga patted Fagigbe's chest. "Just be yourself. Your unmanly self. Circumstances will work out. When we get to the command ship, you have to go into stasis again."

Fagigbe nodded. "I can't resist. I don't have the strength."

"You wouldn't, because you will understand." Ovuga checked the seat restraints. "Best to go to sleep. Deniability then, if need be."

"If the Campaign fails, you mean?" Ovula barked. "It can't fail."

"It won't fail," Ovuga soothed both Ovula and Fagigbe.

The General of Service was not pleased with the interruption. "I have officers who deal with communications. Talk to them," the General grumbled at an appropriate level.

"I am one of them, sir." The Captain of Service was a large woman. She was never intimidated by power. "We have lost communications with the platforms."

The General blinked in confusion at still being talked to. "Contact another."

"All space platforms have gone silent. Posted satellites too. There is no communication off surface." She coughed. "That is limited, too. The shuttle crews don't respond either."

A civilian whispered into the Captain's ear. She frowned, which caused the General to frown back at her. "Sir, there are no shuttles planet side. It is not standard procedure, I know."

The General of Service laughed. "Ah, the annual presentation razz. Just a laugh, yes. Good one. My complements. Lost contact with space. Ha! Ha!"

"Not a hoax sir. A fact," the Captain stated without intimidation. The civilian nodded silently with enthusiasm and silence.

The General sighed. "Get me a four hand. They are too simple to have a sense of humour." He scanned the arena for a Pe-li-too. "Where is one? Ah, where the hell. One should be in every section."

The Captain came to attention. "We were wondering if the General of Service had sent them all on a secret errand? They are missing like the shuttles."

"What the hell is going on here?" The General of Service had never lost his voice in his later years. His bellow stopped every member of the Service immediately. They all came to attention the best they could. "Everyone, find the shuttles and a four hand. Find out what the hell is happening."

"Do you think the Pe-li-too took the shuttles?" The civilian broke his silence.

"Why would they do that?" The General turned red faced toward the civilian. "They all go for a joy ride?"

"We will find out exactly the situation, sir." The Captain saluted.

"Find the fuck out fast." The General bellowed again. All the Service members saluted and then scattered.

Nurse Bendora stumbled into the command ship docking bay. Her eyes were red and panicky. When she saw Fagigbe leaning against the wall, she ran the best she could toward him. When she hugged him, Fagigbe gasped with surprise. "They killed humans. They can't kill. They are vegetarians." Nurse Bendora was shivering with fear.

"I saw. Yes. You are the nurse from Planet Surface." Fagigbe said it just to confirm she wasn't a hallucination.

"Bendora," she whispered. "Ovuhela had always been so nice and kind. The Pe-li-too always volunteered at the Centre. They healed, not harmed." Bendora shook violently. She cried out. "We shall die!"

Fagigbe hugged her tightly. "No. No. We are okay. They didn't bring us here to kill us. They could have pushed us into space."

"Hostages?" she whispered into Fagigbe's ear.

"Us? Well, me? The Service wouldn't care about me." Fagigbe knew they wouldn't care if he lived or died. "You are a nurse. They need you."

She pulled back a little to see Fagigbe's face. "I, ah, I'm sorry. I don't remember your name." She pushed her face back down on his shoulder.

"Not important, like I said." Fagigbe scanned the docking bay. There was a shuttle coming in. It was filled with Pe-li-too. "I think we had better move. Ovuga wanted me to wait. I guess for you. And then we go into the supplies stasis chamber. To be certain the other Pe-li-too won't kill us on sight."

"But they are non-violent culturally. I don't understand." Bendora separated from Fagigbe just enough so they could walk.

"Apparently, they are deceitful culturally. Whatever it is, things have changed. We need to get out of sight." Fagigbe picked Bendora up and carried her to the stasis chamber. Bendora wept as he did. "I would tell you not to be frightened, things are okay, but that would be deceitful too. Just hope Ovuga and Ovuhela survive."

"I will hope," she muttered as Fagigbe sat her in the supply stasis chamber beside net bags full of heads of cabbage. She couldn't look at them though, they looked too much like heads, not enough like cabbage.

Fagigbe set the timer on the chamber, entered, closed the door and sat down beside her. He put his arm around her. And then nothing. Stasis felt like nothing. Unfortunately, coming out of stasis held plenty of feeling.

The Captain of Service pointed at the subspace communications array. "You mean it has been sabotaged? We can't contact the other base planets?"

The civilian technician was uncertain of what the answer should be. She decided as close to the truth as possible was best. She was cut off too. "It's in the software. In the millions of lines of code somewhere. Just a do not proceed command. Stops everything. No outgoing or incoming."

"The hardware is functional?" the Captain snapped.

"All diagnostics on the mechanical aspects are nominal. Functional. Just a bug in the code." The civilian knew what was coming next. She tried not to wince.

"Then find the bug!" the Captain ordered.

"It could take days."

"We aren't going anywhere." The Captain of Service pointed at the console. "Get started. And where is the station crew?"

The technician shrugged as she adjusted the seat. "I got here the same time you did."

The Captain stared at the screen. It always had the various satellite camera views up. A quarter for Planet Surface, but the rest of the screen for Surrounding Space. The enemy would come from out there, so watch there. Now the screen was blank. It was switched off. "Who switched it off? There were no warnings. No external computer incursion detected."

The technician was shaking her head as she spoke. "Nothing has been forced. Access codes were valid. A Jack Call."

"But he retired a month ago." The Captain went to a terminal. "Jack Call records." Nothing happened.

"The keyboard. You have to use the keyboard. Vocal has been shut down too." The technician typed. "There. Jack Call. Retired. Access. Active. Someone was lax."

"We have to find out what happened." The Captain turned and left the room.

The technician shrugged but kept typing while answering the departed Captain's question. "Situation normal, all fucked up. SNAFU. And a FUBAR too."

Fagigbe and Bendora were given little time to recover from stasis. They were physically put in a fully stocked shuttle by Ovuga and Ovuhela. Fagigbe was a good pilot. But he felt nauseous as usual. "Are we being abandoned?"

Ovuga shook his head. "Compromise. The rest of the Pe-li-too are gone."

Ovuhela nodded. "To keep you alive, you must become emissaries for the sentient race in this sector. The coordinates are laid in."

"Emissary of what?" Bendora was waking.

"The Pe-li-too had an improper evaluation of Human aggression." Ovuhela looked out into space. "We thought appearing non-threatening and submissive would cause the Humans' aggressive trait to lose interest in us and then you would move on."

Ovuga was wringing his front hands as he balanced on his hindmost legs. "The aggression continued to total dominance. We have never seen such a response in our biological systems."

"Evasion seems the least destructive solution." Ovuhela looked at Bendora with love.

Bendora stared back. She liked Ovuhela very much. "All of you are running away?"

"It is the most reasonable thing to do." Ovuga sighed. "Too many deaths have occurred already. We didn't want more. So, you have a purpose. It is key to your survival."

"We can't come with you?" Bendora frowned at Ovuhela.

"Not in the compromise." Ovuhela looked away. "You need to convince the Su-su-lanar to, ah, run away before you Humans get to them."

"You can stay with the planet or go with the Su-su-lanar when they leave. It is your choice. Since you don't know where we have gone. It doesn't matter." Ovuga backed out of the shuttle slowly. "We have beamed Human language 1 and 2 to them already. They know you are coming but not your purpose. It is best to hear it from a human, humans. The Su-su-lanar are a very practical race. Just the real data should make it clear to them."

"You were, are, a space faring civilization? There were no indications of such technology." Fagigbe's face reddened. "You hid it all? From me?" Fagigbe was almost in tears.

"It seemed the most reasonable of circumstances. All of Pe-li-too thought you would think us too primitive to bother with." Ovuga hung his head. "Our entire populace was wrong. So, hiding from humans was the fallback."

"So, we have fallen back." Ovuhela stepped back out of the shuttle. "We will wait until you are underway. Once you are gone, we will go. Please do not try to follow. Your mission is the most reasonable thing to do."

"Nothing about this is reasonable!" Bendora snapped out. She was restrained to the chair so she couldn't move. The shuttle door had shut already and the engines turned on. "Not reasonable at all." She started to weep.

Fagigbe touched the controls. The shuttle moved ahead. The path was already plotted. He simply touched Engage. "It may not be reasonable but it is all we have. At least we are not dead."

"Yet!" Bendora muttered.

"That can always be said about life." Fagigbe smiled. Another new species. An undiscovered civilization. He would be first contact. "Something to live for." He was just recovered enough to smile.

WHAT MARNIE TOOK WITH HER
by William Couper

I keep the doll. It's meaningless, there's nothing important about the doll. I wish it was something else, like a ceramic cat. It's not, so here we are, staring at this vacant, inanimate creature that sits on the shelf, imbued with a shock of terrible fascination, like your eyes are the thing making it sit bolt upright, the unease it exudes flows through you and back into it.

Or you're just staring at a silly old-fashioned doll. All that's there is a painted porcelain head attached to a wooden body. I have been curious my entire life about it and about an hour after it came into my possession I looked under the yellowed dress and the greying petticoats.

I was never told I couldn't look at it, but the implication was strong, and there would have been consequences for following blind speculation and grabbing the thing from its place in my parent's room. It sits again, blind and still.

'There are a lot of other things you could do with it, you know,' George said, about a week after I got it.

He had been simmering on it for that whole time. I'm not the most demonstrative person, so he hadn't realised I was aware of his growing disquiet. It was like a water balloon being filled from a tap that wouldn't switch off. I could see the thinning of his membrane of patience, the sloshing of his discomfort clear to me. Of course I didn't say anything. I simply let him carry on, not looking at the doll, and when he did he allowed a small flinch to rock him back.

'It's the only thing I've kept from the house, from them,' I said.

I knew it would shock him, I could have lied or waffled, but I was compelled to tell him the truth. Not that I'm some kind of robot or have an aversion to lying. I lie regularly. Nothing that will change anyone's life, just those small statements that smooth over roughness and stop sharper experiences becoming large enough to tear at the flesh. I had lied to George a couple of hours before, something about how I was feeling after lunch. The thought occurred to me at the time about how different the magnitude of the lies was, otherwise, I would not have remembered the older one. Too many memories are dangerous.

His surprise was subtle. His brow furrowed further, his greying eyebrows tried to touch like cursed lovers, destined never to meet, always within sight. I'm not sure what he was searching my face for, his eyes bounced from point to point, stopping to lock gazes with me and going on to rove over my features.

'There were other things you could have taken. What about that painting of the woman and the dog? That could have gone in the hall,' he said.

'I didn't want the painting,' I said.

'Are you sure you wanted the doll?'

I paused then, a stupid thing to do. His eyes narrowed, as though he had caught me in something illicit or taboo.

'I had to have something,' I said, too quickly, too reflexive, too defensive.

'It's not an obligation to take something from your dead parents' house. Keepsakes are nice, but there isn't a law that says you have to have them,' George said.

He sat down in his chair and leaned over the arm so that his face was a few inches away from mine. His eyes were intent and earnest. I tried not to avoid his gaze in case he thought there was something wrong. My discomfort rolled and twisted in my abdomen with all the frenzied enthusiasm of a shoal of piranha stripping a cow down to the skeleton. The time for me to shrug and make a non-committal sound was past.

'We were there and it's not like I'm going to be back in the house. Most of the stuff will be sold,' I said.

'Yeah, that's great. You didn't need to deal with it. You didn't need to go to the house at all.'

'I did. I had to be sure.'

He looked pained, and not for himself. This mild pain became a sad smile, and his eyes went soft with sympathy. My smile was almost involuntary. I could not leave him staring at me like that, and I hoped my response would make him give up. The conversation was already a torture, and I was tired.

'There's that, isn't there?' he said and patted my arm. 'I could still smell that perfume your mother wore.'

'Amazing that you could smell anything over the stench of my dad's pipe.'

'I was surprised, too. The smoke smell hadn't faded at all. Still like that first day we went to their house as a couple. I think your dad stuck that stupid thing in my face just to make me cough.'

'He did. He always did. You made the mistake of telling him you don't smoke.'

'Wouldn't he have done it if I said I did smoke?'

'He would still have done it, but he wouldn't have shoved it in your face while you were eating.'

'Not that I ever ate that much. I can't believe you grew up on that stuff.'

'I didn't know any different. I didn't understand the smells from the school canteen were food until I was seven. The idea that food could smell and taste good was a bizarre concept to me.'

'I remember. The first time you saw a steak that wasn't a couple of minutes away from being a cinder, I thought you were going to faint.'

'It was overwhelming. When I tasted it, I didn't know what to do with myself. I was this close to moaning.'

He chuckled. 'That answers a question.'

'What?'

'I never understood your expression that night. It was so weird, I couldn't get a handle on it, couldn't really describe it.'

'Now you know.'

He nodded, stood, and patted his jacket pockets. He had been preparing to go out for something, I can't remember what. Something small or several things, nothing consequential. It didn't matter.

As ever, I hoped my relief didn't show. After his intense inquisition it seemed as though the subject was forgotten. It was not, it was a postponement, he would bring it up again later. At least now I could prepare myself, formulate some replies that made sense. It would be on my mind obsessively for days, going through everything I needed to smother this line of questioning.

He leaned down and kissed my forehead. He looked into my eyes and smiled, before standing up. Another pat of the pockets and he left. A lingering smell of aftershave and body odour faded to join the neutral smells of our house.

I kept my eyes away from the doll because it was just a meaningless piece of inherited bric-a-brac.

It was after midnight and I sat in the pool of light from the lamp on the side table, reading. The rest of the room was dark, George had gone to bed a few hours before. He had to get up early in the morning.

I had a fleece cover draped over my shoulders to keep off the chill. For a long time,

George had tried to persuade me to leave the heating on while I sat up reading, but I couldn't bring myself to do that. Running the boiler all night filled me with so much anxiety that even considering it brings me to tears. He gave up trying to assure me it was okay and had bought me the cover, along with a blanket, and numerous cardigans.

The quiet suits me. I love George, I do, but there's only so long he can go without saying something or doing something that breaks the peace. Even when the television is on, he will get up and make a cup of tea, fidget with one of his models, or pick up a pen and play with it, drumming or clicking or idly scribbling on a pad. None of it annoys me as such, but when none of it is there, I feel more at peace, a little calmer.

I was lost in the book when I felt something brush against my foot. We used to have a cat called Layton, a rescue animal who was an adult when we got him. It had been two years since we took Layton to the vet and didn't return with him. There was nothing else in the house to touch my foot.

I looked up from my book and cast an annoyed glance around the room. Nothing had changed since George had gone to bed.

The curtain swayed a bit, pushed by the evening breeze. I like having the window open, the night air soothes me. Despite everything that had happened to me on so many nights, the feel of a nocturnal breeze is relaxing. I can feel my heart rate lower as I sit and read, the lazy air that often seeps into the living room wraps me up, a warm embrace in summer and a cooling influence in winter. The only times I considered closing the window was on nights when there was a storm. The window faces into the prevailing winds and it was easy for rain to be pushed through to soak the floor beneath, something we had discovered to our cost. I prefer to watch lightning and listen to the angry gales anyway; those are thrilling and there have been nights I've seen through to the dawn as I wonder at the violent weather.

I rubbed my bare foot, certain an energetic gasp of wind had swirled into the room and touched my toes enough to make me believe something solid, something flesh, had pushed past me. It certainly wasn't the ghost of my years-dead cat.

Tiredness hit me harder than any errant breeze could, and I yawned. It was before one, so it was early for me, since I didn't normally go to bed before two. Still, an unusual early night would be welcome, it is rare that I feel compelled to go to bed at all, even when it's late. I thought it was a good idea to follow the urging of my body.

My hip cricked as I stood and I stretched, forcing out the stiffness that had settled into my legs and shoulders. I froze.

The doll was lying on its side. It had managed to fall over silently. The weight of its body at least should have knocked against the shelf and made even a slight sound. The quiet in the living room is easy to disturb, even cars driving past too quickly can shatter the peace.

The doll's painted eyes stared across the room, mirthful and lifeless, and the small mouth frozen in a meaningless pink grin. There was no danger of it falling, somehow it had tipped over into an even more stable position than when it was sitting.

Without thinking, I reached for it. My fingertips were almost touching it when I stopped. Why did it need to be righted if it was safer like this? The only reason to sit it back in its original position was aesthetic and no one would see it while I was in bed. If it had fallen over so easily in the first place, there was no reason to waste time sitting it up again. My sense of correctness wanted to make sure it could not fall again while in its proper position, but that would be something to deal with during the day, in the light.

Even as I thought it, the concept stuck with me. Why was daylight so important to moving a stupid ornament? I convinced myself it was because I was tired then, eager to be in bed, and messing around with the doll would be an unnecessary delay.

I looked at my hand, rubbed my fingers together, and rushed out of the room.

Penny looked surprised and pleased to see me. I don't get out much, and I rarely visit anyone spontaneously. If there is someone I'm going to visit without a day's worth of planning, it will be Penny. We've been through a lot together, even more than George and I have. She's been there to help or offer support when George and

I have been facing difficult times. I think she's saved our marriage on a bunch of occasions.

'Come on in, Marn,' Penny said. 'I've been wondering how you've been getting on.'

'Been ups and downs,' I said as she guided me into the kitchen.

It had only been a couple of weeks since the last time George and I had visited her, yet it felt like decades had passed. Nothing much had changed in Penny's house since then. There were a few extra glasses sitting on a table, her sink had some dirty dishes in it, and some rubbish was gone, the changeable stasis of every living space. She wore the same dark grey cardigan, and her short white-blonde hair was tousled in the same way it had been since she was seventeen.

'Park your bum,' she said and pointed at one of the kitchen table chairs.

Penny lives out of her kitchen, as a result the furniture is more expensive than anything she has in her living room. The room is always warm and pleasant-smelling. She doesn't neglect the rest of her house, I don't think she could live with herself if she allowed the whole place to go without her attention, but the kitchen is the centrepiece of her life. It has something to do with her mother, who, on the rare occasions I met her, was a wraith who called from behind the closed door and appeared, small and eager, to offer tea. The kitchen itself seemed to be off-limits for everyone but Penny's mother, even her father, a burly, overbearing man, acted as though the kitchen was a forbidden zone. I never saw

Penny enter either and she hinted that getting in was an honour.

Her interest in the kitchen doesn't extend to hours baking or cooking, she likes to sit in there and do other work. When she isn't working, she will read or assemble and paint models she buys from the internet.

'How's Zane?' I said.

'Same as usual. Off somewhere on business for a week. He left yesterday morning. I have to fend for myself again.'

'You love fending for yourself. You're not the lonely neglected housewife, Penny. You told me one of the reasons you married him was because he's hardly ever around.'

'I'm allowed to get lonely sometimes. Especially when work's getting on top of me. Would be nice to have him a bit more available to chat with.'

'You're making me feel like I'm clairvoyant.'

'I'm not going to burden you with my bullshit. Not after what you've been through.'

'I'd like to think about something else for a change. It isn't the only thing in my life.'

'Has your work started to hassle you to go back yet?'

'I haven't heard from them in a while. Compassionate leave and a doctor's note are a guaranteed way of keeping your superiors off your back. I still keep flinching whenever the phone goes.'

'That says a lot. Has Georgie-boy been much use?'

'He tries. He always has. Sometimes he gets it right, sometimes he completely fucks it up.'

'What's the ratio there?'

'About seventy-thirty.'

She looked at me hard as she put my cup of coffee next to me. A slight smile played around her lips and I had to suppress a smile of my own. There are times when it's difficult to tell if she is feeling playful or not. If I crack a joke when she is being serious, she will get sullen. Her sullenness never lasts long, but I find it unbearably uncomfortable.

'Which way do those numbers fall?' she said, her expression still inscrutable.

'He gets it right more often than not. You don't need to be so hard on him. Especially since he's not here.'

'That's the perfect time to be hard on him. I get more honest answers that way. It's good to hear he's not completely fucking up. You should tell him I say hello, by the way.'

'He'll be thrilled.'

'How was the funeral?'

I could tell that she had been itching to ask the question the moment I walked into the house. Penny can be harsh and too straightforward for some people, but she isn't devoid of social skills or empathy. She knows when she is about to needlessly hurt someone's feelings. She is even capable of saying nothing, a skill I've found a lot of other people, myself included, find hard to master or even exercise.

'A funeral,' I said.

'Were there many people there?' she said, ignoring my attempt at evasiveness.

'Not that many. I didn't expect there to be. A couple of mum's relatives, one that she really hated. She would have been pissed to see him there, but I was glad to see him. Mostly it was dad's scummy drinking mates.'

'No pub landlords?'

'They were never allowed to drink anywhere long enough to get to know any landlords. There weren't many places him and his friends were allowed to drink, before he died.'

'From what you told me about the shit they got up to, anywhere that let them drink deserved what they got.'

'My theory is that they had money and there are still plenty of pubs who will tolerate a lot while a bunch of pricks is handing it over. And they spent a lot of money at a time. Dad would come home so drunk some nights...'

Penny's expression reminded me of George's, pained and sympathetic. I wanted to tell her to pack it in, but I could also sometimes use that under-used skill of not saying something hurtful. I had let my mouth carry on without the full consent of my brain, and now I was the victim of more sympathy than I was comfortable with, certainly more than I felt I deserved.

'Your dad was an arsehole,' Penny said, a metallic zing of anger in her voice. 'I've always said it.'

I nodded. She had hated my parents from the moment she had seen them. I remember something in her eyes changing when I introduced them, before either of my parents spoke. I don't know what she could have seen in them after only a few seconds. Their words, sneaky put-downs and unfair criticisms, and their actions, the nasty little pranks, cemented her hatred and she made sure she was out of their company quickly that day, making an excuse about work. In the years after, she only met them again once or twice.

They didn't like her either. My mother, in particular, was obsessed with trying to put me off Penny, to drive a wedge between us. Some of the lies she told about Penny were insane and desperate. My father would make threats against me or her whenever he heard her name. I pushed it all out of my mind, annoyed that I had allowed the memories to intrude.

'Why did you go to their funeral?' she said.

'For whatever else they were, they were my parents. It's something I had to do.'

'I'm not sure you did. I saw some of the shit they put you through and I don't think they deserve the acknowledgement. You should have used the excuse to forget about them. When was the last time you spoke to them?'

'I've had this from George already.'

'So, he's smarter than I give him credit for. Those people might have given birth to you and whatever, but they didn't act like parents.'

I couldn't look at her. Her gaze was too intense, it was hot enough to make my cheek burn. I took a sip of the tea she had given me and stared out of the window next to the back door. She would not stop staring.

There was a clatter outside, something heavy had fallen. She tutted and sighed. I could feel her reluctance to move like a heated brick pressed against my skull. It was getting harder to keep my gaze locked on a nothing outside of the window.

'I'll be back in a minute,' she said.

As she opened the door, she skewered me with a glance, it was not angry or disappointed. The best I can describe it as is determined. A determination to carry on the conversation, perhaps, but it was more than that, deeper. Going to places I was not prepared to go. I should have welcomed it, been pleased that my friend was willing to do that for me, but I was terrified.

She hovered there for a second before her concern for whatever had fallen became too great and she went out. When she saw what had made the noise, she became annoyed, swore, and marched to deal with it. She went out of sight and for a moment I felt relief.

A cold feeling quenched the relief, sluicing it away in a wash of uncertainty and exposure. I became aware of how open the two kitchen doors were. The one in front of me that I could see every bit as much of a threat as the one behind me.

Penny grumbled and complained, rattled the metallic objects that had fallen. Clanking, scraping, falling again. I don't know what garden tools she wrestled with. I don't know why she had large metal sheets—it was probably a project Zane was going to occupy himself with after returning. Penny was not interested in the garden enough to start building projects.

The shadow at one of the top corners of the kitchen shifted. The light could not quite reach that part of the room, the cupboards got in the way. There was nothing that could move on top of the cupboard, no unboxed gadgets, and Penny made sure there was nothing larger than a stray housefly in the kitchen.

The patch of darkness pulsed, as though something at its centre had been pressed until hard. It lost what shape there was and floated onto the cupboard, slithered down the door like a patch of noxious smoke. As it drifted towards the floor, it extended, became more diffuse. The swirls and motes within it moved with purpose, mind. At my head height, it pulsed again. Instead of diminishing, it became a larger mass. It was barely more than a wisp, but the vortices within it sometimes looked like fingers. They pointed at me.

Without a word, I stood and left the kitchen. Penny worked outside, complaining and shifting heavy items. I had to get out. I clamped my hand to the back of my neck, memory, a learned habit.

I didn't stop when I was in the street and I slammed the front door shut. I walked to my car and got in. Despite the unchecked fear, I managed to open the car door and insert the key. I even managed to drive away without speeding.

It thought it was a dream that woke me from the nap. I was surprised that my hands were empty. My book had tumbled onto the floor when I could not fight the tiredness anymore. It had been a stealthy takeover, I did notice I was asleep until I was awake again.

I was slumped in my chair, head resting on my shoulder, an ache forming in the bones of my neck. A band of stiffness had already formed along the middle of my back that reached along my ribs, making breathing uncomfortable.

The voice still lingered, clinging in my mind like a tatter from a filthy shirt. I didn't like it, even though I don't know what the words were. I could understand the intent, the desire to hurt me, make me feel unsafe.

In the rare times I get to sleep, my dreams are filled with unpleasant things, shades eager to do me harm. The images my mind conjures linger with me for longer than I have even admitted to George. Some days they would still be with me by the time I went back to bed. I was as used to it as I could be, while still hating it.

Somehow this was different. I looked around the room, the daylight was weak. I swallowed, tried to get rid of the sour, dry taste in my mouth. I felt as though the words had not come from my dreams. That was something new. For all the times I felt afraid and discomfited by things in my dreams, I always knew they were just that: dreams. I was well aware that my subconscious had conjured the situations, the phantoms, and the sounds, even through the dread.

I tried to convince myself this was the case again, even though I felt afraid and vulnerable, exposed to something I couldn't describe.

A shadow moved. The sinuous grace of a diffuse cloud of black smoke brought it to my attention and into the middle of the room. For a moment I was terrified something had caught fire, a lamp, the television or the radio. There was no acrid smell and no alien, flickering source of light.

The dark filaments pulsed, and I saw recognisable shapes. A hand. A nose. Half a face. The realisation of how cold the room had become shocked me.

I wanted to run again, as I had from Penny's kitchen. I was rooted to the chair, the cloud twisted and whirled, driven by a desperation I can feel as much as the cold.

The words were incomprehensible and almost inaudible at first. As they got louder, they didn't form any discernible words. The meaning and intent were strong though, hate and anger. Threats without true words. Familiarity drove me to my feet at last and I ran from the room, alternately pressing my hands to my ears and to the back of my neck. The vapour did not follow, but the feelings would not go away.

George was on his way out again when Penny came to the door. He looked surprised to see her. They exchanged a few pleasantries, and he left the moment he let her in. He gave me a worried look over Penny's shoulder before he went out of sight.

She stood in the living room doorway and stared at me in the same way she had a few days before. This time there was a hint of anger on her face, a shimmer of annoyance.

I had been avoiding my phone entirely since leaving her house. George hadn't noticed because work had kept him busy. There was no way he wouldn't have said something if he had noticed.

'You're not sleeping,' she said.

Involuntarily, I touched my cheek, close to the eye. The flesh was soft and spongy.

'I noticed it when you came to visit. You look like you've been put through a cement mixer,' she said.

I put my book down, weary. It was a minor relief, as I had been staring at the same three sentences for the last fifteen minutes, recognising the words, yet unable to absorb them.

She sat across from me, in George's chair, without breaking eye contact. It struck me how familiar she was with my house and how familiar I was with hers. How I had spent so much more time in her house than my parents' home and moved in when I was old enough. It was a temporary arrangement, as I had never felt comfortable sharing Penny's home, though I'm sure she would have let me stay for any length of time.

'They can't get to you anymore, Marn,' she said after a long time.

Tears rolled over my eyes, blurring her face, and my bottom lip fidgeted. I blotted the tears with the tattered cuff of my jumper. Swirling smoky darkness appeared behind her, a large mass of ebbing images, hands, eyes, whole faces, and open mouths. I didn't want to look at it, had not wanted to look at it, but it demanded my attention, pulled my gaze with all the pain of a fishing hook buried in my eyeball.

I wanted to tell Penny about it. I had tried to tell George about it, but he had stared at it and looked at me with the worst pity I had ever faced. That look had hurt coming from George and it would be devastating from Penny. The constant sympathetic looks were bad enough.

'Are you listening to me?' she said.

My gaze snapped back to her face. Her eyes were red and drowned by tears, too. Her jaw held firm. Somehow her gaze remained direct despite the barrier of tears.

The black mass shifted like a terrified flock of birds, imploding and expanding within a few heartbeats. Large, thick-fingered hands surrounded her head. Hands that I knew too well. When my back stiffened the fingers dissipated, merged into the snaking substance.

'George phoned me, you know,' she said. 'From work, so that you wouldn't know. He's terrified for you, Marn. He doesn't understand what's happening. You won't talk to him. He thinks you'll talk to me.'

'I want to sleep, Penny. I do.'

'Have you been to see a doctor?'

I laughed. I still don't know why. It didn't sound like me. I clamped my hand over my mouth. Penny was disturbed by the sound too. I wondered if she was upset for the same reason I was. The laugh sounded like my mother's.

The dark cloud had grown so that it covered most of the wall behind Penny. Eyes that had formerly appeared in random places in the misty, shifting vapour were appearing more noticeably close to the top of the column. Four eyes, two sets, twitching with malice and venomous humour.

'Marn! I'm serious. Have you considered making an appointment?' Penny said.

'I'll see her again in a couple of weeks.'

'You need to see her sooner than that.' The tension in Penny's voice was palpable and I thought that perhaps she could sense the cloud looming behind her.

'I have pills.'

'You need stronger ones.'

'I can cope.'

The cloud pulsed again, and I could see outlines. The random body parts were no longer visible, the wisps now looked like silhouettes. I clenched my fist, resisted the urge to gasp. I couldn't stop my breathing from getting faster, becoming shallower.

'No. You can't. You aren't,' Penny said, and her words, like those in the book, barely entered my brain.

She stood, a figure of certainty, of positive action, and walked to me. The cloud grew and moved with her and I couldn't stand it anymore. I screamed and rushed past her. Words spilled from me, unfamiliar, coarse, unfettered, blasting the air and ringing in the confined space. Penny jumped and held her hand up to defend herself.

I rushed past her into the outstretched arms of the thin black cloud. My body struck it and stopped. Vile, stinking cold sheered into my skull. I could still hear my words, screamed incoherently at something that was not in a position to respond. The blade of tearing hate split my brain, I fought and I struggled, even as I felt Penny's hands on me, her soothing words lost as I screeched my monologue.

The last thing I saw as my consciousness failed was the grinning black faces of my parents, younger than I ever saw them. Their eyes glittered, knowing what they were capable of doing to me. Feeding on the fact that I knew what they could do too.

I stare at the doll. It doesn't mean anything. I took it for reasons I will never be able to explain.

George has come into the room and stands close. I can't hear what he is saying to me. I don't hear much over their voices anymore.

DIABOLUS ET PROPHETIIS
by David Philips

In the first and second centuries after the crucifixion of Jesus Christ, priests and sages began to write a book based on the texts of those who followed His teachings. They also included works of other contemporary writers of the time. This book would come to be known as the New Testament. Those who collaborated on this work were scrupulous in what they notated. Those who compiled this Book omitted some writings because they were similar or identical to other accounts of the period. More tractates were disregarded for different reasons, and others still were not included as they were considered too dangerous, heretical, and even blasphemous. Some of these forbidden works were burnt, but others were kept hidden in secret vaults whose existence was known only to a select group of biblical scholars and people of the highest learning. Throughout the centuries, the knowledge of these papers was handed down to a secret cadre of similarly minded individuals, known as The Group Of Twelve. Each member swore on the most sacred of oaths never to reveal their contents. Discussion of these sealed documents was confined to specific times, and only those bound by these vows were permitted to attend such gatherings. With each generation, more understanding was gained of these works until the time would come when it was believed that the portents they contained were finally about to be fulfilled. These writings were known as *Diabolus Et Prophetiis* or The Satanic Prophecies.

Neville Buchanan had spent more years than he cared to remember in the service of the state. In fact, he could not recall any life he had before joining the Directorate. His past had been erased from his memory. They had seen to that. Better he did not know how he had come to work for them. It might cloud his judgment, skew his reasoning when reasoning was all-important to the job at hand. He might remember he once had a conscience, a moral compass which, however flawed, was still an integral part of his being. They had turned him from a man of peace, with a quiet, insightful intellect, into a murderer. Neville was an assassin, a dedicated killer, trained to eliminate those his government said were their adversaries, enemies of his country. They taught him how to use all kinds of firearms. From rifles with telescopic sights which fired projectiles that could kill someone over a mile away, to more personal sidearms, revolvers, automatic and semi-automatic, machine pistols, all of it. They showed him how to use a knife and, if a knife wasn't available, how to improvise with whatever sharp object was on hand. They instructed him in all sorts of hand-to-hand combat techniques and the quickest, quietest, and most effective way to take out his opponents. They even showed him how to use a garrotte, how to strangle manually, how to take a life with a rolled-up newspaper, and how to stop someone breathing with the use of only one finger. They explained the times it might be better to use poisons and taught him how to administer them so no trace of the lethal cocktail could ever be traced. They schooled him in all the arts of killing, and he employed each of them during his long and non-illustrious career.

Early on in his time with them, they told Neville that it was not his place to ask questions about the moral, ethical, or even legal imperatives. His role was a simple one; best not to over-complicate it. So he dispatched his country's foes without question, without demurring, without remorse. It was his job; it was what he did.

But now, he had had enough. He wanted out. He was starting to experience dreams, something he had never done. Or if he did, they had vanished on his awakening, like an early morning summer mist. But these dreams did not disappear when he opened his eyes. He could remember them all too vividly. Visions of those he had killed in the service of his country, now coming back to sit in judgment on him. Pointing accusing fingers, showing the scars or holes he had made on them. At first, he ignored these mental images, shaking his head as if to excise them from his mind. For a while, this tactic had worked. But then they became more persistent. They encroached on his thought patterns and eventually made him doubt what he was doing and why he was doing what he did. He even asked himself the most heretical of questions: who exactly were the good guys? Were they the people he worked for or those they had tasked him with killing? He did not know anymore.

So he had tendered his resignation. They accepted his decision with equanimity. It was not as if they could do much about his intentions. His was not a nine-to-five job with a manager always standing over him, overseeing his work. They had invested much in his training, but he had repaid them time after time until the debit was definitely on their side of the balance sheet. And he had been good. He had been the best they had ever used, had never failed an assignment. His performance had always been exemplary, so they had no reason to refuse him his retiral with a pension.

But they had one last job for him to do. Just one more, then he was out. Out for good. But he had heard that one before. There would always be 'just one more.' Neville knew how they worked, but not this time. He was too smart for them. Neville wanted this in writing, signed, sealed, and delivered; in triplicate. There was always the fine print, of course, but he would make damn sure he read and re-read every word of every line of every sentence of every paragraph of the whole document. There would be no loopholes, no subtle clauses for them to hide behind, to use against him. When he said he wanted out, he meant out.

He would accommodate their request and carry out this final assignment. Then it would be over for good. When they gave him the identity of his target, he thought this was their idea of a going-away prank. Or it would have been if they had had a sense of humour. It couldn't be him; it just couldn't be! For the first, last, and only time in his career, he queried the hit. Was this right? Surely there had to be a mistake. Not this individual, never him! But he was told there was no mistake. The mark had been identified and verified. This was a code five mission. He had only ever had to handle one other such directive before. Code five—you must, if necessary, forfeit your own life to achieve your objective. Not that they thought it would be essential in this case, but the target was so important, they had to consider all eventualities. And this edict had come from the Head of The Directorate himself. No one had ever seen or spoken to this figure. It might even be a woman. No-one knew. All communications to and from this person were conducted through email, SMS, and other untraceable means of correspondence. But not by him. Even his immediate superior had no direct access. He might walk past them in the street or be in the same well-lit room. He would still be in the dark.

And as for his final target. There was no doubt that this was who he had to eliminate. But this man was a man of the highest integrity, the most exceptional calibre. Someone who had done so much to bring people together. Those of diametrically opposite political views, both domestically and internationally. Politicians and others who would barely agree to be in the same room as their counterparts. Somehow he had managed it. He had made the impossible possible. Countries who sought to conquer their neighbours by force, governments who mistrusted the motives of other administrations, all suddenly found that, in his presence, they had more in common than that which divided them. This individual was a person who was beyond reproach, above condemnation. It did not make any sense. This man, Doctor Walter Aitchison, was the world's best hope for survival, for salvation.

But then the Directorate told him. This figure was not all he seemed to be. There was a dark side to his nature that he had kept hidden. It would be no good to expose it, even if they had had the evidence to do so. No one would believe it. But this man was a danger, the greatest threat the world had ever known. He was just biding his time, awaiting the opportunity to put his evil plans into operation. Then everyone would see him for who he truly was, what he truly was. But by then, it would be too late. This situation could not be allowed to happen. He had to be stopped, and The Directorate was given the mission. This order had not just come from his government. It had come from many. All united in concern regarding Aitchison's secret agenda. And there was one final condition to this contract. He was not to carry out the execution remotely. Neville had to execute this kill face to face. Aitchison had to see, he had to know in his final moments alive, that all his schemes, his years of planning, his patient manoeuvring, had been for nothing. He had to know that at the last, he had failed.

Before his recruitment to this ultra-clandestine organization, Neville had been a priest. He had worked, had volunteered to work in the poorest parts of the community, doing what he could to help those less fortunate, those whom society had ceased to see as human beings. Wives and children who were beaten and abused by their menfolk and fathers; men and women who did not know how to say 'no,' when to stop, either drinking or gambling or doing drugs. He tended the homeless and the dispossessed, those who once had everything but now had nothing. Sometimes all he could give them was God's benediction, His pity, His love. But he could provide them with something more, something greater even than those; he could give them hope.

Until that day. It started like any other day, with no reason to think it should end any differently, but it did. He was in his local store, purchasing some groceries for an old couple who had fallen on hard times. They had lost all their money on bad investments, investments their broker assured them were 'solid gold.' They were anything but. Not even tin, and as for the broker? He was long gone, with their money. So there they both were, this elderly, loving, naïve couple having to decide day by day whether they should eat or keep warm. They could not do both. And into all this, there came a young woman with a baby in her arms. She was buying formula for her infant when out of nowhere, two masked gunmen burst into the grocery store, demanding all the money in the till. It all happened at the same moment when the young mother was reaching into her coat pocket for her purse. Mistaking her actions, the gunmen fired off countless shots at her, killing both her and her infant daughter. It all happened within a few seconds, and the men fled without waiting for the money that the storekeeper was about to hand over. Rooted to the spot in helplessness and impotence, something changed within Neville. Something snapped. He had put himself among these people to help them, yet others valued human life so cheaply. Well, those who thought such things would only have themselves to blame from now on. He would still be a priest and carry out his parochial duties, but now he would become someone else, something else, too.

He continued to believe in God, but he found it harder to maintain his faith, especially after what had occurred in front of him. Where was God then? Even if the mother had somehow sinned in her past and deserved what happened to her, how could an infant be punished in such a cruel and final way? A child who had probably not yet even reached her first birthday. It seemed that the Almighty was indiscriminate as to whom He chose to punish and those He elected to save. Well, he, Neville Buchanan, would not be so arbitrary. The good, the pious, and the Godfearing would have nothing to fear from him. Only those who walked the path of evil would suffer his wrath, and yes, they would suffer. He would see to it.

In his day garb, Neville was the last person anyone suspected when local villains started disappearing or turning up beaten, knifed, or shot. Whoever it was who was doing it, well, they could keep on doing it, as far as the law-abiding folks were concerned. The more scum who ended up dead, the fewer there would be to terrorize them. But Neville was not a professional killer. Not then. He made mistakes, and eventually, they caught him. The Church managed to use its influence to keep their priest's name out of the media, and some of the detectives who finally arrested Neville only did so reluctantly. He was doing what they would have liked to do but could not.

The Church had arranged for one of their lawyers, an attorney named Graham Chalmers, to defend Neville. He was still being held in the precinct cell. Chalmers had read the brief with astonishment. It was almost unbelievable that anyone, especially a priest, could have performed so many slayings. The fact that all his victims were low-life hoods made no difference. What had surprised the attorney more than anything was the natural proficiency at which Neville had carried out his 'work.' It was almost as if the priest had been born into the role. Chalmers had the merest germ of an idea, one which might save the young priest from a lifetime in prison. He had heard of a group of people, part of a secret organization dedicated to preserving the country's security. This group was not accountable to its government, was above regular scrutiny, and answerable only to its own code of conduct. The lawyer's brother was involved with the Secret Service, those whose remit was to guard the life of the country's leader. It was through him that he had become familiar with the rumours. That was all they were—rumours. But what if there were any substance to these 'myths'? There was only one way to find out. He would ask his brother to investigate discreetly.

As it happened, the Directorate was already aware of the avenging priest and saw the potential of having someone like him within their ranks. It did not take much to convince Neville that he could do far more good outside prison than within its walls, a position with which the young priest agreed. And so it was arranged that he was secretly removed from where he was imprisoned. They took him to the Directorate's training facility, where they honed his innate abilities, sharpened his skills, moulded him into what they wanted—a capable killing machine. But they also did something else. They destroyed his soul.

It had not been difficult to arrange a meeting between Neville and Aitchison. He was, or had been, a priest, after all. Very few people knew he was no longer a man of the cloth. The Directorate had suppressed his criminal activities, and even the Bishop had no idea what had happened to him. He had just simply vanished. Better that way. The Directorate had used its considerable influence to manage the interview. Aitchison seemed more than happy to give the young 'priest' a few minutes of his valuable time. It might be constructive for both parties.

With his weapon safely concealed under his robes, Neville approached his target. The man appeared eager to meet with him and motioned him to sit down on the opposite armchair in his hotel room. Aitchison was so busy these days he barely remembered the last time he had been home. Sometimes, he found it hard to recall where his home actually was. The doctor waved away his security team. If he couldn't trust a priest, who could he trust? It would be fine; everything would be just fine.

Neville engaged in some small talk and spoke of religious matters concerning his church. Aitchison turned away to relight his Meerschaum pipe, the pipe he carried everywhere. When he looked up, he saw Neville, Neville the Priest, standing before him with the knife. It was not so much a knife, more a stiletto, with a long slim blade. Neville did not know what to expect, but Aitchison's reaction was certainly not what he imagined it would be. It was not one of terror. His expression was a mixture of calmness, pity, and sadness. A smile of serene, almost beatific, acceptance played around his lips. It was almost as if Aitchison had been expecting this to happen. Aitchison, one of The Group Of Twelve, who, as Neville's blade was entering his heart, recalled the words of *Diabolus Et Prophetiis*. 'And it is foretold that in the final days when men have waged war upon men, and brother has fought with brother, that one will come to heal. He will be the bearer of peace and shall speak with a voice of great fellowship, so man will no longer have grievance with each other and shall turn from the ways of conflict. His words shall flow like sweet wine, and many will see the truth in his goodness. But others shall arise who will plot against this man of goodwill and confound his teachings. They shall call themselves the Righteous Ones but will speak with false oaths and will cause the truly righteous one to be quietened. He who once walked with the Almighty shall turn away his ear from His teachings, and no more shall sanctify the Name. He will be filled with the rage of the false prophets and smite the one who would bring peace. And these false prophets shall sow the seeds of discord and chaos in the hearts and minds of men until the truth shall not be known. Then they will know the ways of war once more and take up arms against their fellow man. And destruction shall rain down from the heavens, bringing death in its wake, and the skies will be rent asunder until a great cloud of smoke consumes all the nations. And when all the spears of fire have been extinguished, and the world shall be in darkness and ruin, then man shall say unto man, "What have we done to bring this calamity upon ourselves?" From out of this devastation, the One shall arise to take dominion over all the men of the earth and the beasts of the field and the fishes of the sea. To Him alone shall praises be sung and worship be offered. The One True God shall turn His face away from the hearts of men, and The Lord Of Darkness shall reign. To the Antichrist alone shall all men's souls belong. And His kingdom shall be everlasting, and man will know peace no more.'

Neville did not yet see that outside, the skies had begun to darken, a symbolic metaphor, perhaps, for what was to come. He had completed his final mission, as it had been written, as it had been foretold.

SONS OF THE SPIDER-GOD

CELYN THE EXILE

A SWORD AND SORCERY NOVELLA

LORENZO D. LOPEZ

CAITLYN'S KITTY
by Stephen Faulkner

Shady was a black cat. The extreme dark colour of her fur was a clear indication of the personality of the animal. She was exceptionally ill tempered and given to fits of hissing rages at less than a moment's notice. She also enjoyed lying hidden in wait for an unsuspecting victim—human or animal, it did not matter—so as to pounce as soon as the innocent passer-by came within range. Many of the neighbour children bore the painful marks of Shady's claws and fangs on their ankles and calves as evidence of such surreptitious attacks by the marauding kitty.

The black cat's owner was the only person on the block who did not incite Shady's hair trigger wrath. In Caitlyin Drether's arms Shady did nothing more threatening than flex her paws in feline bliss while at the same time purring loud enough to vie with a tuba for the volume and thrumming depth of its pitch. Caitlyn, a sweet natured though facially plain child, would hum tunelessly as she rocked her contented pet like a babe in her pale arms for long stretches of time. The end of such pleasurable interludes would never happen at either Caitlyn's or Shady's instigation; they usually only quit their mutual enjoyment of one another when the girl was called into the house either for her to eat her supper or finish her homework for school. Since the two were never left to themselves without being bothered by obligations, the question of how long they would have remained so lovingly entwined with one another without parental intervention was never answered. It was something that Jeffy, Caitlyn's kid brother, continuously wondered about from the time he first spied his sister so sweetly cuddling with her cat when he was only five years old and Caitlyn was seven.

At the time this story takes place Jeffy had celebrated his twelfth birthday only a few days prior. He was still wondering, even after so long, about the apparent love his sister shared with her evil natured feline friend.

His friends in the neighbourhood shared his wonder. "How come the cat doesn't tear her to shreds?" Billy Delton once asked seriously. "Is your sister a witch or something?"

The idea caught Jeffy by surprise. "I don't think so," he said. "I think she would have shown some kind of sign about that if she was, don't you think?"

"Not really," Shelly from next door said. She was Jeffy's and Billy's one real girlfriend in their gang of cronies from school. "Not if she means to keep it a secret. Witches can be real sneaky about stuff like that when they feel they have to."

"If she is a witch," Billy added, not wanting to be bested by a girl, "then the cat liking her makes sense. It's something called a familiar is what it is. It acts as her agent in getting things done magically. Maybe that humming she does that the cat likes so much is her way of communicating with it, letting it know what she wants to have done."

"Yeah?" Jeff said derisively. "Get done, like what?"

"Like getting you sick last year when you had to miss a week's worth of schoolwork," suggested Shelly. "Or your Dad coming home early from work that one time so he caught Billy and me in the bushes behind your house where we were peeking in the window to the downstairs bathroom while Caitlyn was getting ready to go somewhere."

"We didn't see anything," said Billy in their defence. "She got the room all steamed up from her shower. But your Dad yelled at us like we'd just robbed a bank or something just as bad."

"We were both scared sick and silly that he'd go and tell our parents," said Shelly. "Mine never said anything to me about it, so I guess he didn't let on to them about what we did. I'm still worried, though, that he just might take it into his head to blab about it later on. Then I'll be grounded 'til I get married or go to college."

"Don't worry about stuff like that," said Jeffy. "If my Dad was going to let the cat out of the bag about that—so to speak—he would have done it right after he caught you, maybe even with you right there when he made the phone call to your folks. If this happened a while ago..." Jeffy shook his head knowingly. "He's probably forgotten all about it already."

"You really think so?" Shelly asked hopefully.

Jeff assured her that there was nothing to worry about from his old man.

"But what about the witch thing?" Billy asked. "Are you sure your sister isn't part of a coven or something like that?"

"Coven?" Jeffy said. He stopped to think for a long minute before shaking his head. "I don't think so. I mean I don't know many of her friends but the ones I do sure don't seem anything like the witches you hear about in stories."

"Maybe today's modern witches are different," Shelly offered. "And if so, how can we be sure of anything? I mean be certain whether she is or isn't."

Jeffy shrugged. "Caity and I get along really well and she's pretty easy to talk to," he said. "Best I can think to do is ask her. I'm sure she'll tell me the truth."

Neither Billy nor Shelly was quite convinced. However they both assured their friend that what he had proposed seemed to be the best plan under the circumstances. Each of them hid their right hands behind their backs so Jeffy wouldn't see their crossed fingers.

Shelly still couldn't get the idea out of her mind that Jeffy's sister might be a witch or something equally as bizarre. As she walked the few blocks with Billy to his house before heading on home herself, they talked things over until Billy felt it was all totally futile. There was no way they would come to an agreement about the subject just by talking about it. What they needed was definite proof about the girl.

"Did you say girl?" Shelly asked accusingly. "Caitlyn turned fourteen two months ago. She's a woman, my friend. A full-fledged, menstruating wom..." Right then in the middle of a word in the middle of a sentence, Shelly had an epiphany, a leap not of faith but to a sudden understanding of what might be the crux of the matter. It concerned Caitlyn's starting having her period, her menses, puberty, the beginning of sexual maturity. She told Billy that she recalled reading somewhere that some ancient wisdom ascribed magical properties to the time in a girl's life. "That's when she's most open to spiritual manipulation by the powers of good and evil," she said as if it was a truth that she had intensely studied until she was due accolades for her research.

"Like being open to a spiritual awakening," said Billy uncertainly, "through her cat?"

"Well," Shelly said, quickly coming to a stop since she and Billy were now directly in front of his house. "Maybe I make it sound a lot simpler than it actually is. But, yes, I guess that's the main gist of it."

"And you think Caitlyn has been in communication with Shady from who she gets the power to do.... Well, stuff I guess is all that we can call it. Is that what you're telling me?"

"That's it in a nutshell," said Shelly. "But it's only a big maybe right now. I can't be really sure that's what this is all about."

Billy stood silent for a moment, thinking. "Are you old enough to have had your first period?" he finally asked.

"About the same time that Caitlyn did, and I'm a year younger than she is," she said proudly. Then, after a moment her demeanour changed from pride to something worrisome as the memory of that event washed over her. "Freaked me out like nothing else I've ever gone through ever did. Scary as hell."

"And did your becoming a woman give you any special powers like we're saying that Caity might have? You know—witch powers?"

Shelly laughed as if Billy had just told her the funniest joke. "First of all," she said, "I don't have a cat. And secondly, when the freakiness of it wore off I got too busy checking myself out naked in the mirror to see what other changes my body might have in store for me."

Shelly's very personal admission made Billy's whole body redden and go hot in embarrassment. He stuttered that he thought he heard his Mom calling even though Shelly hadn't heard anything of the sort. Hoping that that excuse was sufficient he turned and rushed up the path to his house and slammed the front door behind him. It was only when he caught his breath that he realized his friend had given him an opportunity to ask what she saw when she studied her naked body in the mirror. He figured that no matter what answer she gave him it would surely have been enough to fuel his fervid imagination for days to come.

"Witch, witch, witch," Jeffy said aloud to himself behind the closed door of his bedroom. And then: "But which witch is which?" That little piece of wordplay made him laugh for about a second, then his mind got serious again. *Caity, a witch?* he thought. *Yeah, that should make me laugh, right?*

The answer to his own question should unquestionably have been in the positive. Still, there was at least some evidence to bear out the idea that she maybe possibly could be a practitioner of the dark arts, using Shady as her familiar to help whatever spells she wanted to cast. But what kind of magical mayhem would his sweet and gentle natured sister need to perform?

At that moment there was the subtle sound of someone or something scratching at his door. When he was only five years old or so he and Caitlyn used just such scratching at the other's door as a code for who was there and to please be let in. Assuming it was his sister playing some kind of childish game he went and opened the door, ready to hear what she had to say.

There was no one there, at least not at eye level. A low rumble emanating from near floor level drew his gaze downward. There was Shady and she was looking at her mistress's brother, right in the eye, giving him a chill of something akin to fear but less intense. The cat vocalized a three note muttered yowl that Jeffy took as a warning.

Shady then squatted and peed on the floor in the hall in front of the boy's bedroom door. She then hissed loudly as if for effect and then sauntered away towards the stairs leading to the living room on the first floor.

Later that day Jeffy and Caitlyn sat on the couch in the living room, reminiscing on how Shady had come to live with the Drether family. He knew that Shady had appeared on the deck attached to the back of their house one rainy afternoon. He also knew that Caity had opened the sliding glass door only to be surprised by the cat coming in and affectionately rubbing her whole body against the girl's legs. That was when Jeffy came on the scene. The cat purred loud enough to be heard by the boy, several rooms away in the kitchen. He tried to stroke the animal as it cozied up to his sister's leg. All he got for this friendly action was a nasty scratch on the back of his hand. The line had been drawn; the cat had showed its preference for Caitlyn over Jeffy without any doubt about it whatsoever. Later the black feline made its choice of humans even more apparent when it swatted at both Mr. and Mrs. Drether. She coupled this with a deep throated warning growl and a snarl that one would assume to have come from a much larger member of the family *Felidae* of which Shady was definitely a significant though much smaller example. There was no doubt about it; Shady belonged to Caitlyn and to no one else.

Jeffy usually loved to hear his sister laugh, her pure alto voice rising in an inimitable trill of sheer delight. This time, though, he shuddered at the note of derision her laughter held. "A witch?" she asked, still tittering happily. "Are you serious?" She then checked the mirth in her voice and looked her younger brother in the eye. "And if you are, then tell me this: Are you out of your flipping mind?"

Jeffy blamed the notion on Billy and whose mere possibility was seconded by Shelly. He had promised his friends he would look into the matter and get back to them with what he found out. "I knew from the start that it sounded stupid," he said sheepishly. "But a promise is a promise and, well..." He let the words hang there, a subject and verb devoid of an object to make the sentence whole and actually say something.

Even so, Caitlyn caught on to what her brother was trying to say.

"Only a novice," she admitted with a sigh. "Not a real witch in any sense of the word, even though my familiar has found and claimed me."

"Shady," Jeffy whispered and his sister nodded.

"Anyway, whatever I am I really don't know what to do with it. With Shady's help I turned one of the lab frogs at school into a turtle but it died before I came home. So, if I'm a witch, I'm not a very good one."

"I guess it takes a lot of practice," Jeffy said, trying to sound like he understood more than he did. "You'll get better at it the more you try."

"That's just it," she said with a tinge of sadness informing her tone of voice. "I don't even know if I want to be better at it. Or even if I really want to do whatever it is that witches do at all."

"Well," said her brother, still feeling like he had something profound to tell. "Then you've got a lot of thinking to do before you say yes or no to whatever it is you're trying to decide about. To magic or not to magic—that is the question."

The melodramatic way that he made his silly proclamation caused his sister to laugh the way he loved to hear; her being honest, happy and fun loving and letting the laughter just pour out of her like a sonic fountain of delight. Just hearing it made Jeffy shudder with an unrelenting tide of glee cascading through him

"I'll leave you to your decision making," he said as he left the room. As he walked through the door he passed Shady coming in from the hall. The door to his sister's bedroom remained open. He slowed down and then stopped in the middle of the hall as he heard her talking to the cat. "What do you think I should do, Shady?" she asked seriously. Shady rattled off a series of vocalizations that sounded like an alien language. He was surprised when, after Shady stopped "talking," Caitlyn said, "Oh, you really think so?"

The cat then spoke one quick, elongated meow which elicited the reply from the boy's sister, "Well, I guess there's only one thing to do, then." As he resumed his sauntering way down the hall to his own room his mind raced in several directions at once. Nothing he thought, assumed or seemed to understand made any sense to him now. His mind was a ship without a tiller or a sail. He was foundering in a sea of thoughts that seemed to be created within whose only purpose was to drive him crazy if he would only let them. Before they could do their worst to him, though, he heard a loud crash come from his sister's room accompanied by the terrified and anguished shriek of a cat in great pain and peril.

When he raced back to Caitlyn's room he found his sister with a bloody pair of scissors in one hand and a dead, disembowelled Shady dangling by its tail in the other.

"No more familiar," she said breathlessly and shook her head. "Not a witch. No, no, not a witch and never will be."

Luckily Caity and Jeffy had been left alone. Their father was at work and their mother had to do some last minute grocery shopping for a few missing ingredients for a recipe she was intent on trying out. Had either of them been home when, as Jeffy later thought of the incident, Caity temporarily lost her mind and offed the cat, then there would have been an immense degree of drama punctuated by much screaming, yelling, crying and the slamming of doors as both the Drether children were relegated to their rooms for much of the foreseeable future.

As it was they spent their free time in the productive pursuit of a much less negative existence once their parents got home. This pursuit consisted of them digging a four foot deep hole beneath the ancient maple tree whose thickly leaved branches shaded a good two thirds of the backyard. It was the shade underneath the canopy provided by this tree that had given Caitlyn the inspiration for the name for the black cat whose grave they were presently digging.

The job took less time than either of them thought it would. As they went back into the house they talked about what they would say to their folks about the absence of Shady. It was quickly decided that they had discovered Shady missing when they Caitlyn got home from school. They would also make sure that they were both present when the initial lie was told so that both of them would later know what was said and thereby avoiding the possibility of their individual stories about what happened to Shady not agreeing. Jeffy recalled such a disastrous thing happening in a novel he read that was geared toward middle schoolers and he was determined that such circumstances would not happen in this very scary instance in his and his sister's lives.

Jeffy's fears never came true. His and Caitlyn's folks bought their story at face value. Jeffy was sure that this was partly due to Caitlyn's pitiful crying jag as she recounted coming home from school to a silent and empty house. Her tears flowed even more freely as she described the shock at not being greeted by Shady's calming presence and mewling insistence that she be picked up and cuddled.

"I looked everywhere," she blubbered. "Everywhere! I ran up and down the street calling her name. That's when Jeffy came home and I told him what happened and we both looked high and low, each of calling Shady! Shady! Shady!"

The melodrama continued for some time thereafter as their parents did their best to comfort the girl and calm her down. Caitlyn allowed them to be parentally concerned and caring as her apparent distress lessened to a point where they could cajole her into having something to eat, seeing that it was dinner time, and perhaps go to bed a little earlier than usual, maybe with the help of an over-the-counter sleep aid to minimize the sting of loss.

Yes, Caitlyn played her part very well, indeed.

Both Drether siblings were very circumspect in how they spoke to their parents when the subject of Shady came up. To the relief of both of them such nervous conversations only happened twice, both times happened individually with their mother. Their precaution of being sure that their individual versions gelled to such an extent that there would be no question that they were telling the truth turned out to be a stroke of adolescent genius. Their mother's questions about the loss of the family (or, at least Caitlyn's) cat were the same for the both of them and their answers were so close that, in essence, their mother really had only one conversation on the matter—times two.

The feeling that they had gotten away scot-free with a horrific secret was a heady experience for Caitlyn but a nerve wracking one for Jeffy. "You know we'll have to play up our not knowing what happened to Shady to the hilt for the rest of our lives," he said to her with a bit of a tremor in his voice. "Like, we'll be living a lie until mom and dad both pass away. Doesn't that bother you in the least?"

Caitlyn didn't even bother to think about how to answer that question. She immediately shook her head and said, cavalierly, "Nope. Not in the least bit."

Her brother was floored by the admission. Pragmatically he understood the attitude behind what she said. He just couldn't fathom her being so cynical about the whole thing that something so horrifyingly gory didn't seem to bother his sister at all. *She killed her own pet kitty, for God's sake,* he thought. Something like that has to have some kind of adverse effect on a person. Doesn't it?

In his sister's case the tacit answer to that question was apparently not.

The incidents and decisions and gestures of life all moved smoothly along as such things often do in the course of the passage of time. Such was the case with summer inexorably leading into autumn that year for the Drether family. Caitlyn had already graduated from middle school and, in collusion with her parents, the decision as well as the arrangements had long since been made that she would attend a boarding prep school some seventy miles away for her high school work. She would return home for all major holidays as well as her and her brother's birthdays. As was traditional in the Drether family, neither parent expected gifts on either Mothers' or Fathers' Day; such tangible expressions of love and affection would only be presented on each parent's birthday and neither to exceed ten dollars in expense.

The weekend before Caity's exodus from the homeplace her folks threw a sort of a bon voyage party for her in the form of a meal of barbecued meats and grilled vegetables served around the picnic table that was the centrepiece of the back deck. Decoratively balled watermelon waited in the refrigerator in the kitchen to be served as the dessert course. All the food was simple and unadulterated by much in the way of seasoning or added flavours. That, however, was the way that each of the Drethers liked their food, so everyone was satisfied and pleasantly stuffed when the meal was over.

As he was scrubbing out the charcoal pan of the grill before covering it for later use, Mister Drether's attention was drawn by an unusual feature of the backyard that he hadn't previously noticed. "Jeffy," he said. "Why is there a big patch of grass under that tree that's so much lighter in colour than the rest of the lawn?"

Jeffy was nervous as he answered this question with a statement he had long ago prepared for just such a contingency. "It was a bare patch that I noticed a while ago," he said. "I reseeded and watered it, made sure the seeds took and so now..." He purposefully let the final sentence lapse to silence, hoping that his father would understand the implication of what he had just told him.

There was no further discussion. The explanation was accepted and the reason for its being given quickly forgotten.

That, though, was hardly the end of the matter. Several weeks after Caitlyn had left for school Jeffy was mowing the lawn one last time before the chill of autumn swept in to claim its right of being. As he approached the patch of lawn that was now evenly coloured with the rest of the grass an increasingly unnerving feeling of doom rose in him. The air around him seemed to buzz as if with ill heard voices until he was at the periphery of the grave itself when what had seemed to be many voices suddenly coalesced into one angrily whispering susurrant tone hanging at the farthest edge of his hearing. The first word he thought he heard was either "betrayer" or "betrayal." The second one was the one that really frightened him. Though it was still whispered, it came through loud and clear, accompanied by the vision of the bloody face of Shady, spitting blood as she hissed the word, "Revenge!"

Later, when he called Caitlyn at school and told her of this unsettling experience, she laughed. "You're letting it get to you," she said in a placating tone one might use to comfort a child who has been frightened by thunder. "It's your nerves getting the better of you," she rationalized. Then, after a heartbeat of a pause, her voice lowered as she asked, "Are you feeling guilty about what happened to Shady?"

When he muttered a non-answer she told that she was the one who shouldered the blame for how Shady died and that Jeffy had nothing to concern himself in the matter. His sister's acceptance of the truth of what had really happened, of what she had done, comforted Jeffy to some extent. As he hung up the phone, though, he could not help but come to the conclusion that he had at least some degree of culpability in the cat's unnecessary demise.

Caitlyn was nearly in tears as she stood dead centre of Shady's now invisible grave.

She was home for Thanksgiving break. Her brother had waylaid her at the front door before their parents were even aware of her arrival and led her out to the backyard. He chattered nervously all the way about how he was so glad to see her, was her trip back home easy and uneventful and there was something he just had to show her right away.

"I guess so," she said semi-sarcastically as she felt his tight grip on her hand in order to lead her to the place she was sure he was aiming for. "But couldn't it wait until I said hello to Mom and Dad?"

Jeffy shook his head as soon as he stopped her at the exact point in the backyard lawn where he had placed her. She did not recognize the spot since she was expecting a bare or, at least, a spot sparsely covered in grass. She looked down and could not see her feet; the grass was so dense and overgrown at this spot as it was throughout the entire lawn. "This is it?" she asked. "I would have never known."

"You will soon enough," he said, not meaning to sound mysterious even though the way he couched his remark had a rather enigmatic ring to it. "Just wait."

It did not take long. Caitlyn's and Jeffy's parents came out into the backyard to welcome their daughter back home after being away so long at school. The young woman they found, slumped forward into their son's arms, was a teary eyed, blubbering mess.

Caitlyn later explained away her little breakdown at Thanksgiving dinner as a result of her talk with Jeffy about the boy at school who she thought was interested in her but who instead had said some really nasty things about her behind her back. The story was true but it wasn't something she had confided to her brother. It was only an excuse so she wouldn't have to tell her folks why she was crying so piteously when they came out to greet her. Her mother commiserated shamelessly as she recalled having gone through something similar with a boy when she was in college. Her husband eyed her suspiciously since this wasn't a story she had ever confided to him in all their years of courtship and marriage.

Later, when she and Jeffy were alone she told him that she couldn't talk about what had really happened in the yard. It was too gruesome and heart-breaking. The only real clue he had to what she was talking about was when she sighed deeply and muttered something about "That poor, poor kitty."

It was deep in the night-time and the rest of the house, as far as Jeffy was aware, was all asleep. He, however, could not seem to find that familiar solitude in his own unconsciousness, no matter how intently he stared at the gloom shrouded ceiling of his bedroom. He tossed and turned, went to the bathroom even though he didn't really need to, punched his pillow as if it was the bed's fault for his frustrating bout of insomnia. His last idea to help himself into the land of sleepy rest was to open his window in the hopes that fresh air would help him slumber. It was the least helpful idea he had all night.

Not only was the air too chilly to be conducive to lulling the mind down into its own dreaming depths, there was also the high pitched murmur of a female voice out there in a one sided conversation with an unseen someone. Of course it was Caitlyn, talking to the air. As soon as he saw that it was her and there was no one in the yard to join her in her chatting, he knew right away who she was talking to.

Shady. Or at least the supposed ghost of the deceased kitty with love only for his sister and the wrath of the devil for everyone else. That, however, was when the cat was alive. Now Caitlyn's fluttering voice told a much different story.

"You see, don't you?" she said to her unseen audience of one. "I simply had to do it. You were the one thing that stood in my way of being a normal girl. Everyone pegged me as being a witch and..."

There came a short burst of hisses, growls and the tuh-tuh-tuh sound of feline expectoration all jumbled in a seemingly random pattern. It was a pattern, it became clear, that Caitlyn understood without any trouble at all. "Well, yes," she said, "You were my familiar and you were a very good one, too. You did everything that I asked of you. But don't you see? I was done with all that and you wouldn't let go... You wouldn't let me go or let me let go of what I once was and didn't want or need to be anymore..."

Jeffy was tired. He lowered the window sash so that it remained open only a few inches to let in some fresh air with a minimum of cold. When he got into the bed this time he slipped away from reality and fell asleep in only a few minutes.

He was awakened not long after that by a rapidly frantic knocking at his door. In a sleep-muffled voice he told who was there to come in. Jeffy was had only just come out of an unsettling dream about Shady approaching him with hatred in her ghostly eyes, ready to envelop him with her ectoplasmic corpus and so have him become an intrinsic part of her. With those images still instilled in his mind he was quite unprepared to see his sister come through the door holding out her badly scratched, bitten and bleeding arms to him. "See what she did to me," she said fearfully. Seeing her thus and hearing the terror fully implicit in her voice, he was jarred to the sharpest attention to his surroundings he had ever experienced.

"Shady?" he said, finally finding his voice, though it was barely a whisper.

"It was terrible, Jeffy," she said, near to tears. "She came at me again and again, each time either biting or scratching, all the while her thoughts accused me of murder and black magic and being the main inspiration for the evil she'd become."

It was then that Caitlyn broke down into a prolonged fit of sobs and stifled wails as her beleaguered spirit let loose its anguish.

As he embraced and comforted his sister, Jeffy also worried at the fact that all the physical torture Caitlyn had endured had been caused by a ghost, a wisp of what had once been the essence of the personality not of a human being but a mere cat. A cat of a particularly evil mien, it was true, but just a cat nonetheless. A cat's ghost had done all this, he thought, trembling as he murmured consoling words into his sister's ear. My God, what do we do now?

He did the only thing, at that very moment, that he could think to do. He slathered triple antibiotic ointment on Caitlyn's pinhole bite marks and the shallow as well as the deep scratches on her arms, chest and face. He understood that his dear sister had been so freaked out by her experience in the backyard that she was now almost totally incapable of making the simplest decision. It was up to him, then, to lead her, zombie-like, to her bedroom and help her strip down to her bra and panties before turning to leave her to, hopefully, a good night's rest.

"Jeffy, no!" she said. "Please, I can't be alone."

Jeffy started to protest with the lame rationalization that he had his own bed to go to. Seeing the look of abject terror on his sister's face changed his mind and so he said nothing. The compromise was that he would guard her door so that no ghostly kitties would come in to do her any harm that night.

Needless to say neither Drether sibling was able to get a restful sleep that night.

Almost all of the clothing that Caitlyn had brought home with her from school was in three drawers of the dresser in her old bedroom. To pack her stuff in order to be ready to go back, all she had to do was pile that three drawers' worth of stuff into her suitcase and the task would be mostly done. As simple as that tidy little chore was, she never had a chance to start. She didn't even begin the first step of the process by getting her suitcase out from under the bed.

Her mother's terrified shriek coming from the backyard changed all the girl's carefully laid out plans in a single split second.

She met Jeffy in the hall and they nearly knocked one another over in their rush to get downstairs and out into the backyard to be of whatever help that they could. What they saw as they came through the back door onto the deck stopped them dead in their tracks. Jeffy ran into his sister, nearly knocking her over as he braked to a skidding halt right behind her.

Their mother stood transfixed before the hovering, smudgy visage of what looked like the hissing face of a black cat. She held her left forearm with blood oozing from between her fingers. Both Jeffy and Caitlyn looked from their mother's wounded arm to the thick tendril of blood dripping from the mouth of the ghoulish kitty. "Leave our mother alone!" Jeffy shouted at the thing, trying vainly to draw its attention to himself.

Caitlyn then shouted something that her brother couldn't make out; as if it were in some language he had never heard used before. It was thick and guttural, sounding as if it was meant to express concepts no longer understood by the philosophies of humanity. It was this, then, that made the apparition turn away from Mrs. Drether and direct its maleficent glare at Caitlyn. It only studied her for a moment before letting out a terrifying yowl that hurt Jeffy's ears.

Then, just as suddenly, it pounced, its smokelike body enveloping the girl until she disappeared in a swirl of thick, putrid dust, still chanting imprecations in the ancient language that she only knew and but which, it was evident, the ghost of Shady understood all too well.

From Jeffy's point of view it seemed that the spirit of Caitlyn's erstwhile familiar was devouring its former mistress. Soon, though, Caitlyn pulled free of the dark maelstrom and landed with a wind stealing thud on the hard ground, unconscious and unmoving.

The apparition, then, quickly disappeared as if a wind had come along and dissipated the darkness and rage in a single blow even though no one in that yard felt any gust of air at all. Jeffy and his mother ran to Caitlyn. Mrs. Drether, whose arm was still coated in a patina of blood, prattled on about her own experience at the mercy of the devilish thing and how she thought that she was losing her mind.

Jeffy was left to deal with both females of his family. He did his best to console his mother while at the same time trying to revive his sister with the skills learned in a poorly recalled course in CPR. "Please, Mom," he said, annoyed at her constant jabber and inability to be of any assistance. "Let me... Let me do this..."

Caitlyn coughed and moaned, then blew a long sigh in her brother's face. She looked at him for a moment in confusion, then smiled brightly and coughed again as she tried to get up.

"Be careful," he told her, noting in his mind that their mother's running commentary had ceased. "You took a pretty heavy hit when you fell."

Caitlyn nodded and moved more carefully as she got to her feet.

Jeffy rose and hugged her, asking, "What the hell was that?"

His sister shook her head.

"I mean, does this mean it's over?"

She looked at him enquiringly. "Over?" she said in a raspy voice that sounded to Jeffy as if it had a weird undertone of a purr in it. A light came into the girl's eyes as if she suddenly understood what this boy meant by his words. "Oh yes, it's over," she said earnestly.

Then, after a moment's pause, she said something that made Jeffy shudder in realization of what had just happened. "And now it's really just beginning, too," is what she said.

THE BELIEVERS
by Christopher T Dabrowski
Translated by: Julia Mraczny

I look down on them.

They're kneeling. Praying. Begging for a better tomorrow. For peace. For health.

They look with fear at the image I encoded in their minds. Their image of God.

It makes me laugh when I recall who they worship—a creature called Pokémon. I told them to call him Dick.

And so they worship the great Dick, pray to the ancient cartoon character.

They are unaware that I created them a few days ago, and are convinced that they lived for decades. They don't know that they are biobots to whom I have uploaded memory and faith.

Printed in Great Britain
by Amazon